D0119403

90710 000 430 581

Praise for Tommy Wieringa's previous books

The Death of Murat Idrissi

'A taut, intense contemporary thriller of multiple exploitations … The full mercilessness of the migrant dilemma is confronted here to devastating effect.'
Eileen Battersby, *The Observer*

'Has the grip of a nightmare that is all too plausible.'
The Sunday Times

'A savagely effective little novel … A nasty masterpiece of narrative tension; it's brutally spare.'
Evening Standard

'The sentences are concise, propelling the action along and keeping readers on the edge of their seats … a vital must-read.'
Asymptote

'A lucidly written reflection on the migrant crisis, by a Dutch master storyteller.'
Saga Magazine

'As scintillating as it is unforgiving, this tiny diamond of a novel from Dutch author Tommy Wieringa is such a masterpiece of compression it could stand as an object lesson for students of creative writing … A deceptively simple, yet intricately layered, tale of complicity and exploitation.'
The Age

A Beautiful Young Wife

'You don't so much read this novel as take it in intravenously. It goes straight to the blood — brief, brutal, and beautiful.'
Samantha Harvey, author of *Dear Thief*

'While the narrative focuses on the collapse of one man's world, it still raises huge moral questions … Haunting.'
The Sunday Times

'Fiction at its most precise and potent.'
The Observer

'A painful, razor-sharp portrait of what it is to be an ageing man … Beautiful, concise, taut.'
Mariella Frostrup, BBC Radio 4 'Open Book'

'Brilliant … Merciless in the gentle accuracy with which it asks, very simply and persistently: "What did you think was going to happen?" *A Beautiful Young Wife* is a book that could derail someone.'
Cynan Jones, author of *The Dig*

'Perfectly dosed prose (translated with elegance by Sam Garrett) and unfaltering narrative control.'
The Spectator

'With this luminous study of a life in slow crisis, Wieringa seems on fertile new ground. He forgoes the motions of cause and effect to give something as profound and puzzling as life itself.'
Sheena Joughin, *TLS*

'Wieringa is a writer with range and skill … Mesmerising.'
Sunday Herald

These Are the Names

'An important and profoundly felt book about displacement and migration.'
Patrick McGuinness, author of *The Last Hundred Days*

'Poetic, ambitious … The pricelessness of our common humanity is one of numerous heavyweight ideas Wieringa balances carefully on his novel's laden back.'
Phoebe Taplin, *The Guardian*

'A bewitching delight … I can't recommend this profound, thoughtful, truthful book enough.'
Jane Graham, *The Big Issue*

'Superb … Within pages it becomes clear that this is a rare novel possessed with a sense of place and a purpose … This is a bravura performance. Far closer to Joseph Conrad than one might expect, it makes a case for the saving power of small continuities.'
Eileen Battersby, *The Irish Times*

Little Caesar

'Captivating — a modern day odyssey that leads us via porn stars and artists and houses falling off cliffs into the heart of a singular character.'
Kamila Shamsie

'A brilliant exploration of the uneasy transition from adolescence into adulthood — the restlessness, yearning for stability, irrational decisions and erotic obsessions.'
The Independent

Joe Speedboat

'A rewarding journey into the unfamiliar … Witty, thoughtful, and surprisingly tender.'
The Independent

THE BLESSED RITA

Tommy Wieringa was born in 1967 and grew up partly in the Netherlands, and partly in the tropics. He began his writing career with travel stories and journalism, and is the author of several internationally bestselling novels. His fiction has been longlisted for the Booker International Prize, shortlisted for the International IMPAC Dublin Literary Award and the Oxford/Weidenfeld Prize, and has won Holland's Libris Literature Prize.

Sam Garrett has translated some fifty novels and works of nonfiction. He has won prizes and appeared on shortlists for some of the world's most prestigious literary awards, and is the only translator to have twice won the British Society of Authors' Vondel Prize for Dutch–English translation.

TOMMY WIERINGA

THE BLESSED RITA

Translated from the Dutch
by Sam Garrett

SCRIBE
Melbourne • London

Scribe Publications
2 John St, Clerkenwell, London, WC1N 2ES, United Kingdom
18–20 Edward St, Brunswick, Victoria 3056, Australia

Originally published in Dutch by De Bezige Bij as *De heilige Rita* in 2017
First published in English by Scribe in 2020

Nederlands letterenfonds dutch foundation for literature

This publication has been made possible with financial support from the Dutch Foundation for Literature.

Typeset in Adobe Garamond Pro by the publishers

Printed and bound in the UK by CPI Group (UK) Ltd, Croydon CR0 4YY

Scribe Publications is committed to the sustainable use of natural resources and the use of paper products made responsibly from those resources.

9781911344902 (UK edition)
9781925713268 (Australian edition)
9781925693737 (ebook)

Catalogue records for this book are available from the National Library of Australia and the British Library.

scribepublications.co.uk
scribepublications.com.au

For my father, mushy eater
And for Marinus

First

Paul Krüzen spat on his hands, seized the handle, and swung the axe over his head. The log on the chopping block burst open, but didn't cleave. Birds seeking evening shelter in the trees fled into the dusk. Furiously twittering blackbirds burst through the undergrowth. Paul Krüzen brought the axe down, again and again, until the chunk of oak parted. Then it got easier. The pieces flew. Woodchips everywhere, spots of light on the forest soil. Let the axe do the work, his father had taught him long ago, but what he liked was to put some power behind it.

A few pale stars appeared in the sky. Deep below that, in the clearing in the woods, the demon swung his axe. He made it crack like a whip. Blocks tumbled through the air. The beeches all around, strong and smooth as a young man's arms, shivered with each blow.

This was his life: he put wood on the block and he split it. His shirt stuck to his body. Jabs of pain in his lower back. Each blow found its mark. He had been doing this for so long, all with measured, controlled haste. He had to sweat; it had to hurt.

He swiped his armpits with roll-on and put on a clean check shirt. 'I'm off,' he told his father, who was reading in his chair beneath the lamp.

The evening air was chilly, with a whiff of celery above the grass. With the car window open, he drove to the village. Three jarring speedbumps. Speed ramps and roundabouts were a mark of progress, of a jacked-up pace of living that had to be slowed down, even in Mariënveen, where the clodhoppers tended to get themselves killed at the weekend. Once every couple of years, Paul Krüzen would sit straight up in bed, awakened by the impact, the sirens, and the whine of chainsaws a little later, the play of phantom light on the oaks along the curve. The next morning, he would see that yet another wedge had been ripped from the bark. In recent years, the bereaved sometimes placed flowers and photographs beside the tree.

Paul pulled up in front of Hedwig Geerdink's place. He rang the bell and went back to wait in the car, the door open. He had no thoughts at all. Early June, the last light on the western horizon. A little later, Hedwig slid in beside him. 'Good evening, one and all,' his friend said in his high voice. Hedwig had two voices: the high squeaky voice, or his low, hoarse, chesty one. Anyone hearing him for the first time immediately saw him split in two: the high Hedwig and the low Hedwig. Horseradish Hedwig, as they called him in the village.

Paul pulled his legs into the car, closed the door, and drove into the village.

At Shu Dynasty, formerly the Kottink Bar & Party Centre, Laurens Steggink and a stranger were at the billiard table.

'Gents,' Steggink greeted them.

Paul took a seat at the end of the bar, in the pine-panelled niche. He liked to have his back covered, like a cowboy, where he could see whoever came in. Hedwig slid onto the barstool beside him. The radio was stuck halfway between channels; waves of static brought them *Die Sonne geht unter in Texas*.

Mama Shu said 'Hai Paul' and 'Hai Hedwig', and put down a bottle of Grolsch in front of Paul and a glass of cola for Hedwig. The pirate station thanked cafeterias, contractors, sawmills, and wrecking yards for their support. Paul knew where the studio was, in a shed off the Tien Ellenweg; the booming bass could sometimes be heard for kilometres around.

Steggink bent down and eyed along the cue. He took his time. He was good. Learned to play billiards in the army, during the long, empty hours in the tactical unit bar at Seedorf.

Paul Krüzen, Hedwig Geerdink, and Laurens Steggink had all been in the same class at school.

One day, Paul and Steggink had built an underground hut in the woods. They were going to sleep there. They roasted frozen hot dogs over a smoky fire and rolled out their sleeping bags, but when it got dark Paul baulked at spending a night in the burrow, amid the spiders and woodlice, and cycled home. Steggink remained in the woods alone. He wasn't afraid of the dark.

The friendship faded; Paul had developed a growing distaste for Steggink's pranks and stories, as well as for the greasy plait that hung over his collar. At Theo Abbink's twenty-third birthday party, Steggink had taken three kittens that belong to Abbink's girlfriend, wrung their necks, and tossed them into the field. His defence: he was drunk, and he hated cats.

The silence between them had lasted about twenty years.

The day Paul heard that Steggink had been convicted for maintaining a weed plantation in the barn belonging to his fiancée's parents, and of fraudulent practices on a classified advertising site, it came as no surprise. Not to Paul, not to anyone else, really. They had all seen it coming. Laurens Steggink didn't have a biography, he had a charge sheet. His ex was still scared shitless of him.

When they let him out, he moved his business activities across the border. In what used to be a printing plant at a pathetic industrial estate outside Stattau, he ran a brothel with girls from all over the world. His long frame perched on a bar stool, he watched over Club Pacha with a soft drink in front of him and his phone glued to his ear. Nothing escaped him. But today was Monday, and on Monday the club was closed.

Paul sometimes crossed the border in the hope of finding one of his favourites, profligate Thong from Bangkok or, even better, motherly

Rita from Quezon. Anyone who didn't believe in the existence of love that could be bought knew nothing of their fervent hearts.

The ball thumped dully against the cushion of the long rail, nicked the yellow ball, and smacked straight into the red. A fine sound, Paul thought, the tick of a skilful shot delivered with power and confidence.

Steggink took two more before missing. The other man moved into position; his face appeared under the lamp. Pale eyes, a Pole no doubt, the stooped torso heavy from lard and pig's trotters. They showed up on Paul's driveway on occasion, the Mareks and Witeks, they were never much of a good deal. But you had to be ready for the exceptions. Like the dealer from Wrocław, who had showed him a wonder: a trunk full of Russian summer uniforms from the Great War, the medals still pinned to them.

The Pole took his shot. The balls skipped across the felt.

Skittishly, the Hennies entered and sat beside each other at the bar. They bent over their new phone, the light from the screen casting a blue glow over their faces. After a few minutes, the female Hennie looked up and asked, 'And your father, Paul?'

Paul Krüzen held up his hand and made a so-so gesture. What use was there in telling them about how every day he had to disinfect the wound on his father's shin that simply wouldn't heal? Before long he would have to take him back to the hospital to have it checked.

They had been in each other's lives for forty-nine years now, his father and he. One day, not long from now, he would remain behind, alone in the Saxon farmhouse at Muldershoek, where he would retreat into strangeness and conversations with himself.

The billiards clock buzzed. Steggink took a fifty-cent piece from the pile on top and dropped it in the slot.

The Hennies went back to their new Sony Xperia. The myriad ways one could spend one's benefits. At home, their kiddies were already in bed. You could ask yourself whether people like them should be allowed to reproduce, but the calamity had already taken place; beyond the watchful eye of some government agency or other, they had multiplied their misfortune twice over.

Soon, with the arrival of Theo Abbink and Alfons Oliemuller, the band of loners was complete. Ashtrays were laid out. The smoking ban had not yet made it to this part of the country; before reaching Mariënveen, the law had lost much of its force and lustre.

When the little mountain of coins atop the billiard clock had dwindled to nothing, Steggink and the stranger dismantled their cues like hitmen and slid the halves back into their soft cases.

The bar was now full, down to the very last stool. Alfons Oliemuller looked over the shoulder of the male Hennie and said: 'You need 4G for that. In Kloosterzand they've got 4G, here there isn't any.' And on the conversation rolled, about the flexibility of the new iPhone and the factory defect in the housing of the Galaxy Note. Talk died, however, when Steggink jammed his sinewy arm like a sword into the group. They all fell silent, dumbfounded, as though he had laid a handful of winning cards on the table.

'What's that supposed to be?' Oliemuller asked.

'What do you think?' Steggink said.

Oliemuller took the smartphone from his hand and turned it over. 'Gresso,' he read out loud.

'Made in Russki,' Steggink stated. He grinned at the unknown Pole.

The object glistened obscenely in Oliemuller's hand. They all stared at it, the same way they had all stared at Steggink's Ferrari the first time he pulled up in front of the bar. Like serfs along a sandy road, seeing an automobile go chuffing by for the first time. If he had honked the horn they would have fallen to their knees and genuflected.

Steggink's blood-red Ferrari Testarossa, his sun chariot — no one should have it so good. And especially not an equal, a boy from Zouavenstraat who they had seen fall and get back onto his feet, fall and get back onto his feet, all the way to where he was now.

'Bit of a wee screen, if you're asking me,' said Oliemuller at last.

'Sapphire,' Steggink said. 'And the case, that's gold and African ebony, the case is.'

'Shi-it,' Abbink breathed.

At the far end of the bar, Paul Krüzen raised the bottle of Grolsch to his lips without taking his eyes off the group. His index finger smelled of rotting onion.

'Only one like it in the world,' Steggink said smugly.

'But what 'bout that screen?' said Oliemuller.

Steggink stuck out his chin. 'What about it?'

'Well,' Oliemuller said hesitantly, 'it's not that big or nothing.'

'That's what they call *design*,' Steggink scowled. 'By an Italian fellow you've never even heard of.'

No one spoke for a bit. On the radio, the pirate dealt out greetings.

'That there Italian fellow's into wee screens like that,' the male Hennie sniggered amazedly. And Theo Abbink chirped: 'Does it come with a magnifying glass, Laurens?'

The group burst out laughing, and recovered their damaged self-esteem.

In the nineteenth century, their forefathers had become small property holders. A patch of land, a cow, and a farmhouse. Back when the prices were still good, the last two generations had sold everything their ancestors had culled so painstakingly, and went off to live in the new housing tracts. And so they had become dispossessed farmers once more, peering into each other's livings with greedy little eyes, closely comparing their own prosperity with that of their neighbours.

Ming, the Shus' grown-up daughter, shuffled around behind the bar on flip-flops and spoke openhearted, broken English with the stranger. From snatches of their conversation, Paul Krüzen made out that the man was Russian and not a Pole. He grunted in disapproval. Russians, he had no use for them, not here and not at the all-inclusive resorts in Thailand or the Philippines where he and Hedwig spent a few weeks each year.

Mama Shu swiped at the screen of her phone. A thousand filaments attached her to a distant land. Her body was here, but her thoughts were in a sooty megalopolis in southwestern China. She knew about an attack in Chengdu sooner than a car accident down the street.

The Russian, who had started off keeping his mouth shut, now began shouting 'Hey-ya Mutti!' ever-louder, every time he wanted a beer. When he smacked the male Hennie on the shoulder and yelled: '*Za hollandskyo-russkyo druzbu*!' everyone knew they were in for a case of Slavic drunk and disorderly in Shu Dynasty that evening, and that it would end with the entire Shu family coming out from behind the swinging kitchen door to wrestle the big Russian out onto the street.

Paul Krüzen braced himself. You didn't want to miss anything, but at the same time you wanted to stay out of it. Beside him at the bar, Hedwig was whining about the RTV East broadcast from which he had gleaned the term 'shrinkage region'. A good term, Hedwig thought, a perfect description of the pace at which the clientele of his little grocery shop was declining. 'They're all dying on me,' he said. 'Last week it was Ullie.'

'Ullie?' Paul said, in spite of himself.

'Tonnie's Ullie. Burial's on Wednesday. The way things are going, there won't be anyone left.'

'But you've made your millions already, Hedwig!' the female Hennie said suddenly, in a louder voice.

Hedwig blinked as though someone had snatched his glasses. Did he actually ever shave, Paul wondered suddenly? He couldn't recall him doing that during their holidays. Maybe he had no beard growth at all. His cheeks, at least, were as smooth and pale as wax.

'What's that, Hedwig,' said Laurens Steggink, elbows on the bar and his beer bottle clenched in his big hands, 'are you a millionaire?'

Hedwig's chin jutted in a rare fit of stubbornness; he straightened his back. He crowed: 'You bet I am!' He nodded, sniffed loudly, and said in his high voice: 'Easy. And what about it?'

The barely perceptible blip in time. With nervous chuckling, life began again. It could be true, Horseradish Hedwig being a millionaire. They all knew the stories about tight-fisted farmers who turned out to be filthy rich after they were dead. Hedwig Geerdink fit the profile. Always a tight hand on his purse, come to think of it — he would spend three euros when Paul spent thirty. He always ordered half a portion of babi pangang or nasi goreng, then stole the chicken from Paul's plate.

Steggink raised his shoulders. 'Well, that's fine, isn't it?' He looked around. 'Good old Hedwig, or am I wrong?'

'Dumb,' Paul said quietly.

'But if it's true, I'm not going to lie about it, now am I?' Hedwig said shrilly.

Paul shook his head. Stay small, he'd told him that often enough before, always look smaller and dumber than the others. To have nothing and be capable of nothing, that's what they know, they can live with that. But it wasn't that kind of evening for Hedwig Johannes Geerdink, who felt like sloughing off his puny, pale hide and enjoying the doubt he had sown. Hedwig the *mill-ion-aire*, oh yeah!

Paul could tell from the way Hedwig raised his glass to his lips and tried to drink like a man. Somewhere inside him lay a hidden reserve of testosterone, and he had tapped into it now. Of course, Hedwig had plenty of money, but he lived like a church mouse, always afraid he would lose it all and die in penury. That was why he already acted like he had nothing, not a single penny.

He had bought land, Paul knew, a little here and there, and back behind De Steenkoele even a few hectares for the new housing estate. Land was worth a fortune, and Hedwig had an unknown quantity of it, scraped together by his family cent-by-cent, ever since 1911, selling bushels of buckwheat and beans in the grocery shop on Bunderweg.

And now everyone knew.

Second

Paul Krüzen's mother was a daughter of the last blacksmith in the village. His smithy had been across from the church, at the start of Bunderweg, where later, during the construction goldrush, a white-stone insurance office would arise. The smith's name was Mans Klein Haarhuis and he was tawny as a Sicilian fisherman, but his two daughters were creamy-white children of Mariënveen. His son Gerard, the youngest, looked like him though: stocky, and with a head of dark, wavy hair.

It was the Klein Haarhuis sisters who were biking along Bunderweg to Kloosterzand on that cloudy day in 1955. Marion and Alice crossed the little bridge over the Molenbeek and did not notice the boy sitting beside the stream, listening to their cheerful twittering. Once they were past the bridge, he climbed onto the road and watched until they disappeared from sight. From along the banks he quickly picked all the flowers he could find — irises, cowslips, and a few final spikes of seeding elderflower — and placed the bouquet on the road when he saw them coming back in the distance. Then he hid behind a tree, his heart pounding. Just as they reached the bridge, a fire-engine red McCormick roared past — the girls could barely maintain their balance and hissed indignantly at the machine.

Aloïs Krüzen was twenty-six when he married Alice Klein Haarhuis. Round, blushing, and in the blossom of late youth, she stepped across the grey paving stones to the altar, arm-in-arm with the smith in his Sunday best, his greying curls held in sway at the last moment with Brylcreem. Square and grim, he was on the verge of giving away the loveliest thing he possessed. Her clearly audible, sing-songy 'I do' a few minutes later broke, with equal clarity, a few of the hearts present in the church. The *fait accompli* — she had vanished through the door ironclad by the sacrament, and all they had left to hope for was the breach.

It was a miracle that Alice Klein Haarhuis had fallen for Aloïs Krüzen, and only because, as people said, she refused to marry a farmer. Aloïs had gone to teacher's college in town and returned a schoolmaster. A man with an indoor job and a fixed income, how much better could it get? That was how Aloïs Krüzen got his bride, and no one could help but feel that it was cheating.

They went on honeymoon in his father-in-law's car, the first automatic in the village, a brand-spanking-new, 2.6-litre Opel Kapitän; Mans Klein Haarhuis had walked around Aloïs' Lloyd Alexander TS a few weeks earlier and said: 'You can't take your lassie away in that ...'

They skimmed down the road like a canoe through water, six cylinders working in silence. Her hand lay on his thigh, as still as though she'd forgotten it. The low sky was of graphite, green as the first day on earth.

After they had crossed the IJssel at Zutphen, the landscape changed. Dark rises on the horizon, where the old ice had left moraines. Rivers of lead snaked across the low land. The further south they ventured, the heavier the stone on Aloïs' chest became. The horror that awaited them — the frontal collision that would crush them, their blood mixed with oil on the asphalt ...

Him counting his blessings — a magnificent girl beside him, a bag full of money, and an automatic at his fingertips — didn't help in the slightest: the feeling was under his skin.

'Still, it's further than I thought,' Alice said absently. She stared out the window.

'Always is,' he said. The stone pressed down. Keep the wheel straight, drive defensively, know that you can never escape from yourself.

That day was the first time he ate in a roadside restaurant. When the waitress asked whether he would perhaps like a glass of wine with his schnitzel and potato salad, he fell prey to indecision. Only when he remembered that this was his honeymoon did he nod.

'And what kind of wine will it be?' the waitress asked.

'Do whatever's open,' he said with a grimace.

And so it also became the day on which he first drank a glass of white wine.

Because they took a second glass as well and then got lost around Nijmegen, the sun had already set by the time they reached Mook, where to their amazement they found the hotel dark and locked.

Further down the main road they found another hotel, a country cottage on a pond, where the only available room had two single beds. The bar was already closed.

Aloïs lay waiting from her to come out of the bathroom. It took a long time. The proceedings on the other side of the door were a mystery to him; he knew nothing of women's lives. The beds could not be slid together, for the nightstands were bolted to the wall.

She unlocked the door, appeared with a flood of light behind her. Stretched across her breasts and hips, the silk nightgown made her glisten like a fish. Walking to the bed beside the window, she threw back the blanket and crawled in. The box spring creaked.

He lay on his back, waiting for his envisagement of this night to reveal itself. He longed for a sign, something that would set him in motion, but Alice lay quietly in the one bed and he, his body heavy and useless, in the other. Footsteps in the hall, a door that opened and closed.

What was she thinking about? What did she expect from him?

Suddenly, quietly, her voice. 'Come.'

He slid in beside her and switched off the nightlight.

'Hey, hello,' she said.

Their kiss on lips hard, numb with the weight of events. The people, the good father, the element of duty.

Fifteen minutes later she reached over him, turned the nightlight back on and said: 'I can't breathe like this …'

Back in his own bed, he folded his arms behind his head and became immobile again.

'G'night,' she said.

'Yeah, sleep tight,' he said.

The next morning, they went walking on the Mooker heath. The cloud cover hung in place without moving. He told her about how Ludwig and Hendrik van Nassau had been defeated by the Spaniards, here along the valley of the Meuse. The deaths of thousands of soldiers, the ragged retreat, how countless men had drowned in the swamps and how their restless souls since then had wandered as lights above the heathlands.

She nodded at him encouragingly, and a bit distractedly.

'History is my subject,' he said in apology.

After lunch, they retired to their room for a nap. He was already dozing off when she came and lay beside him. Their clothing rustled. They mated in the grey afternoon light, their eyes wide open.

The second stop on their honeymoon trip was Amsterdam. They had a room at Hotel Neutraal on Damrak. Plastic curtains at the windows, the wallpaper flaking. The shabbiness of it all left them weak with laughter.

The weather had turned warm and sunny, so they left the hotel room for a walk. They tried to saunter as though the city was theirs by rights, it was their capital too after all, but they were intimidated by the young men with long hair and the girls who smoked on the street; the atmosphere of giddy provocation they breathed. These things showed them their place. Provincials is what they were, staring wide-eyed at everything they had heard and read about in their far corner of the country. A small country that, measured by the differences between the centre and the periphery, still seemed of continental proportions.

Had they really left home only four days ago?

The strangest thing of all were the black men they saw on the street. Aloïs would turn and watch them go by. Where he and Alice came from there were no blacks, none had ever even been there. Sure, these were people, just like him, but he had to do his best to realise that. A person like that might have been born in the jungle, in a village with palm-frond roofs on the banks of the Marowijne or the Corantijn. And now there he walked, the black man, down the streets of the capital of the realm, a stranger like Aloïs himself, although his dark skin made it so much easier to see.

They toured the canals in a sightseeing boat. Aloïs looked in breathless admiration at the canalside houses and seventeenth-century *entrepôts*. Grand were the houses, grander still the glory of the Golden Age. Intrepid the seamen, crafty the merchants and bankers. They had piled up stones to make a city, and in the shadows of their mansions now walked the Provos and the rockers, or whatever it was they called themselves. History did not exist for them — they were the beginning and the end all in one, the time before them needed annihilating, and after them the deluge. Aloïs Krüzen admired and feared them. In the newspapers they were referred to as a tumour to be excised, cauterised — the pillory would be too kind a punishment. That is the way the papers wrote about them, and although Aloïs had an instinctive distaste for the new-fashioned, he knew that words like that were written by fearful old boys at the end of their reign.

Their boat pulled out onto the IJ waterway. He looked at his brand-new bride and tried to imagine a life in this city, among these people. He could teach at a school where the students would have a good laugh at the dialect he spoke. He could change the way he dressed and the things he was used to doing, but it would always be a disguise. And what about Alice? She would be admired silently by poets and be a mistress to painters — a muse is what she'd be, a muse with an eastern Dutch accent they would think was exotic, rather than countrified.

Central Station glided by, they passed the eastern docks, the islands and storehouses named after remote parts of the world. Ships loaded with riches from around the globe had sailed up this same waterway. Maybe things hadn't always been done properly, Aloïs thought, but they'd pulled it off anyway, from this little fly-speck of a country. They had made a name for themselves that resounded in the ends of the earth. Genesis warned against pride, but the Dutchman had been both proud and God-fearing, and he had been rewarded with all the world's riches.

And so, squinting against the flicker of light off the water, Aloïs Krüzen dreamed, and longed for a day that was not his.

On their second night in Amsterdam, in a bout of overconfidence, they entered a gambling house on Halvemaansteeg. When he came back from the bar, she was standing at a roulette table. She took the glass of sweet white wine from him without even looking up. 'I think I get it,' she said. The ball rolled round, the wheel turned slower and slower until the ball landed in a red pocket. A Chinese man across the table sucked in air through the corner of his mouth. Once again, the croupier launched the ball onto the wheel, and an old lady and the Chinaman slid piles of chips onto the squares of the layout.

'Mrs Krüzen ...' he said admonishingly when she came back from the cash window. She placed her bet, her eyes tried to bend the ball to her will during its journey past the red and black pockets. She lost, won, lost again and then again. 'This is really fun,' she sighed. 'If only we would win every once in a while.'

'Unlucky at games, lucky at love,' Aloïs said, but she was no longer listening.

An hour later they were back outside. The water of the Amstel had lost its gleam, flowed darkly beneath the bridges. They didn't speak. As though they had tossed money to the wind, ten- and twenty-five-guilder notes from the envelopes of the wedding guests. A hundred and fifty guilders they had blown. It didn't matter, they told each other, there was still plenty left, but it was a bit of a pity.

'Tomorrow my luck will change,' she said. She saw his shocked expression and said: 'Sorry, that wasn't funny.'

In the cafe on Leidseplein, when he came back from the bar with two glasses in his hands, she said, 'What are you doing, trying to get me drunk?'

'Depends,' he said.

'Maybe I'd get up and dance on the table, how do you know?'

He grinned. 'All right, show us.'

There, in that cafe, was the first time he told her about the mashed flowers on Bunderweg, back when it had still been a cobblestone road where the Marshall-Plan tractors raced back and forth.

'But if I actually had seen them,' Alice said in amazement, 'how would I have known who they were for?'

'You would have known.'

'That they were for Marion?'

'Oh, get out of here.'

This was how it was meant to be, he thought, this is the way he wanted to be and the way he wanted her to be, and he was proud and happy later when he danced with her in a club down one of the side streets off the big square, where all the black men they had seen earlier seemed to have gathered.

The band played kaseko and Latin, everyone was drinking and laughing. The band leader nodded at Alice and said: 'This one's specially for a very lovely lady.' He gave a little bow. The band launched into a fast, happy number and the audience cheered. Nimbly, the band leader sang: 'If you want to be happy for the rest of your life, never make a pretty woman your wife. As soon as he marries her then she starts, to do the things that will break his heart.'

The audience clapped and sang along at the top of their voices, they knew the whole thing. Alice smiled embarrassedly, Aloïs moved woodenly to the beat. Dozens of men were looking at his wife, they'd been drinking and God only knows what else; he cursed the moment that he and Alice had gone in there.

They were, with the exception of the pianist and the bass player and two other couples, the only white people in the club. He saw hands reaching out at her from the shadows, grabbing her, closing over her mouth and around her breasts, disappearing under her skirt and pulling her along, and he, who had vowed to care for her and protect her, stood rooted to the ground. He shrugged off his stupor, leaned forward a bit to hide his erection. He shuffled backwards until he was standing against a wall. Alice danced in a cheerful tizzy amid that ecstatic Negro tribe.

And he longed for home.

That night, the city behind the curtains. He was not one man, he was all of them. Her eyes in the darkness gleamed like a calf's. He leaned with his fists on the mattress and took her as his. Her open mouth, the wine on her breath. It had never been like this before. The blissful tension at the base of his dick. Her body tautening like a bow.

Five minutes, six, that was how long his dominion lasted.

Was she thinking about it? he wondered at breakfast. Her breath at his ear, the glistening between her legs? They both had so little experience, and marriage seemed such a bad place to gain any of that. Their looks bounced off each other. The future seemed dreary, hopeless.

He lowered his gaze to his plate.

She watched him, the meticulous way he spread the butter. The knife scraping slowly across the toast. After a while, she asked: 'Do you think you can go faster than that?'

He shook his head.

'You're not going to take fruit too, are you?' she said jokingly.

Then he came out with it: 'I want to go home.'

She looked. Was he kidding?

He shook his head. 'I've always had this. I can't stay away from home too long.'

'Come on, Aloïs,' she said. 'Are you telling me you're *homesick*?'

The knife's long trajectory to the butter dish and back again.

'Even in Amsterdam?' she asked.

'I've been counting the days.'

'So how many days left?'

'Three,' he said without pausing.

It remained silent for a long time. Then she said: 'This is our honeymoon, you know.'

'True.'

'One time,' she said. 'Once in your life.'

He nodded. The knife broke the toast, didn't cut it.

He heard the way she tried to stifle the sneer in her voice when she said: 'Then we would have been better off going to Bad Bentheim, or something.'

Again, he nodded. 'Yeah, that's closer to home, yeah.'

They said nothing.

'That's the way things go,' he said after a while.

'Couldn't you have said that a little earlier — I mean, we could have ...'

'I didn't know,' he said, 'not really.' He took a deep breath. 'I really want to go home.'

She nodded. 'Of course, we're going home. It's just that I would have liked to know about it beforehand.'

Third

Three-thirty in the morning. The child breathed, it howled, they named it Paul Thomas Krüzen. Throughout his adult life he would look for the horoscope in newspapers and magazines with the sign of the crab above it, also often represented as a *69*; the solicitous sign, the astrologers said, a soft heart beneath heavy armour. Regularly, he read that the love of his life was on its way, or that he should count on an addition to the family, but it seemed that his branch of the Krüzen family tree would wither and die out along with him.

His father had wanted more children, albeit more as a precautionary measure than out of paternal love: ''Cause we live on a busy road.'

His mother's answer was, 'Well then how about bearing them yourself?!'

The child waddled after its mother all around the house. Sometimes she tripped over him.

'Jesus … Paul!'

In the morning she did the housekeeping with him in her wake. He had only learned to walk, Aloïs said, in order to pursue her more closely.

'Mama,' Paul said one day, and pointed at the floor. 'The sun.'

In the clear morning light, she saw a little pile of dust on the floor with the strokes of the broom around it like rays. Poetic, she thought. The promise of special talent.

In preschool he'd had a hard time keeping up. Anaemia, his mother said, but he himself believed, in the rare moments in later life when he thought back on his childhood, that he had spent the first years of his life in a wavering transition of phase. Fluid plasma, still without form. Only later in life had he entered a state of fixed matter.

Wherever his mother was, there he popped up beside her; sometimes it drove her so crazy that she would smack him against the side of the head. He would tremble with gratitude when the hand that had struck caressed him again only minutes later. Like a puppy, he submitted to the consuming sense of guilt in her embraces.

One afternoon she talked to her sister about it. 'The way he sticks to me the whole livelong day. I don't have room to breathe.'

'You spoil him too much,' Marion said.

A wrinkle appeared between Alice's eyes. 'I don't do a thing, that's what. Yeah, ignore him. I don't want him going into the toilet with me anymore.'

'The *toilet*?'

Alice nodded. 'It's getting to be a bit too much.'

'The toilet …' her sister repeated again.

Alice changed her tone. Glossing it over this time: 'It's not all that bad.'

'Have you got any more sweeteners?'

'He plays alone nicely, too, now and then.'

'This one's empty.'

'You have to shake it a bit. Moisture. This house …'

Marion rattled the shaker of sweeteners fiercely and said, 'Seems tough to me, all in all.'

Alice brushed a few hairs from her face. Paul took the box of gingersnaps off the table.

'No, sweetheart, you've already had some.'

In the garden, dark molehills had emerged from beneath the melting snow. Marion looked absently at her little nephew.

'It's not really all that bad, you know,' Alice said. She had dealt wrongly with the whole subject, she realised. Her sister had three children, three little angels, but now she'd made it seem as though she were stuck with a bargain-basement remainder. She started praising her three-year-old son lavishly — how he was so good at helping her sweep the floor and peel potatoes, and that there would never be another man who loved her as much as he did. 'Isn't that right, little prince?' She leaned over and pinched him on the nose.

Paul beamed. 'Happened to my nose?' he crowed.

She smiled resignedly. The tip of her thumb stuck between index and middle finger, she tapped him on the nose. 'There's your nose back, you little rascal.'

The last of the paper festoons from his third birthday party were blowing in the wind in the barbary hedge. January, four-thirty in the afternoon. Actually, she never drank coffee this late in the day.

Her son came back with the box of animal dominos and put it on the table. He flipped the dominos over one by one and slid five of them to her. She shook her head. 'I'm talking to Aunt Marion, sweetie. And I have to make dinner in a few minutes.'

He walked away from the table again and came back from the dark hallway to the attached stable, carrying the wicker potato basket.

Marion stood up, her lips twisted in a smile. 'A pain, you're right,' she said. 'I see what you mean.'

The tile roof rested heavily on the house, the windows peeked out beneath the low eaves. When it was dusk outside, it was already dark inside; on grey days, the shadows never dispersed. Once, it had been a proud, three-roofed Saxon farmhouse, but an ancestor who fell upon hard times had had the wings on either side torn down, leaving only the middle section. At the front, beside the drive, was the attached stable with big, rounded doors; the animals had once been kept there, the people lived at the back. The stable no longer served as such, filling gradually with machinery that had passed into disuse. Flat-worn Bentheim millstones, a hay tedder, a portable drinking trough; the archive of Krüzen family failures.

When Paul was eight, he walked through the dark corridor that connected the house with the pantry. He took the key off a nail on the doorpost there and entered the former stables. They smelled of old straw. He walked around carefully, as though afraid of waking someone from their slumber. The manure gutters had been covered with paving stones. He thought about the warm bovine bodies that had once stood here, the rattling at the feeders and slobbering from the cast-iron watering troughs fixed to the uprights, and he felt a vague longing for a time long before he was born. The moist heat beneath the cobweb-covered beams, the sourish smell of fermented hay. He wandered amid piles of car tyres and junked machines whose functions he did not know. His temple brushed the rusty tooth of the tedder; blood on his hand when he wiped at it. The cracks beneath the dirty stall windows were sealed with wads of paper; the air in the stables stood still.

He climbed the wooden ladder to the front loft. When his eyes grew accustomed to the darkness, he saw piles of half-decayed hay against a dividing wall. A sharp odour of mould rose from them. The loft was divided in two; the largest part extended the full length of the house and was behind the dividing wall, which had been equipped with an old stall door. The door was closed tight, it was impossible for him to lift the latch. The space he was trying to enter must be huge, and suddenly he was afraid of what was waiting behind that door; his excitement faded into icy fear. His rattling with the latch — he had awakened it rudely and now it was coming towards him behind the door. He turned and as he did so fell, then scrambled to his feet and fled down the ladder.

'What's that?' his mother said a little later. She pulled him towards her to examine the scratch beside his eye. 'What were you doing there anyway? He should have cleaned up all that junk a long time ago …'

The house belonged to the two of them, to him and his mother. In late afternoon there was added to that a third resident, who seemed satisfied with his role as silent extra. The bit player was not inclined to assert influence, everything went smoothly enough without him. He acted the perfect boarder, saw to the fixed costs, handed over the rest of his salary for shopping, and, one afternoon, tried to teach his little boy the instep kick.

For almost fifty years now they had been living at Muldershoek, Paul and his father Alöis, but for the first eight of those Paul had barely any memories of the man. Had he existed before that? Of that prehistory there remained at most a few impressions, nothing you could call a memory. Neither name nor shape. The web of varicose veins beneath the thin skin of his feet, the smell of tobacco smoke in the toilet, mingled with that of his shit. From further back the sound of his trouser legs brushing together when he walked — and so there was image, sound, and even smell, but it all refused to coalesce into one man in particular. His father floated through his earliest years like smoke.

Only when Paul saw him emerge from the corn one day, ranting and raving, dragging a stranger behind him by the legs, did the first, clear-cut memory of his father arise — midsummer, overexposed, everything in plain sight.

Fourth

The late afternoon on which his father came stumbling into his life — the foliage at the forest's edge swelling expectantly, the green maize on the bottom ten standing high. To start with, there had been a resounding crash, somewhere outside, and Paul had run out in the hope that a meteorite had struck. A huge din was coming from down in the hollow, amid the maize that bordered their land, a heavy casting about of some thing: the spasms of a monster, the stomping of a horse — yes, a horse was going to come breaking out of that wall of green, a wild horse, slavering and gleaming with sweat, it heralded itself with the cracking of cornstalks beneath the force of its heavy body, it would show itself to him, tall as a wall, snorting and with bulging eyes — but it was not a horse that came out of the maize, it was a body made of two men: his father was dragging another man by his ankles, a dead man with streaks of blood on his cheeks, who he was now hoisting over the earthen dam that separated Voorthuis' land from their own. His father let go of the man's ankles and wrapped his arms around his chest, lifted him like that over the property line. When he saw Paul standing there looking, he yelled: '*Get your mother, call Montizaan!*'

Paul gaped at him.

'Now!' barked his father, who he had never heard raise his voice before.

The boy raced across the lawn and into the house, but instead of calling the family doctor right away his mother ran outside, where her husband was dragging a man through the grass and shouting in desperation: 'Call Montizaan now, goddamnit.'

This was what Paul Krüzen was able to say about it later: that, right before all this, his father had been in the truck garden with his watering can, pinching green beans off the stalk. In the distance he had heard a sputtering aeroplane engine. The engine cut out, then coughed and kicked in again. His father searched the sky above the poplars and was just turning back to the beanstalks when he heard a loud bang. A shudder ran through the trees and grass. His father dropped his watering can and ran towards the house. *The hole in the roof, his wife and child crushed by a plane fallen from the sky …* But the house was whole, everything was peaceful and quiet. He ran then through the stand of trees to the stream, and then along the path through the woods behind his house, parallel to the water. He sprang over old roots growing over the ground and ducked under low-hanging branches. All the way to the back he ran, to the edge of his own property, and there he climbed into an oak, using the thick branches of the hazelnut beside it for a leg up. Higher and higher he climbed, until he could see the orange tile roof of his house sticking out above the rampant elders. He looked out over the sea of maize. Then he saw the tip of a wing, sticking up in the middle of the field. It poked out above the brown plumes, the final salute of a sinking ship.

In a flash he was down again and wading through the maize. The sharp leaves crackled and scratched his skin, crushing stalks as he ran. *A plane*, the thought raced through his mind, *a goddamned aeroplane has crashed behind my house …* Presentiment of great change. He felt slightly nauseous.

At the edge of the open spot he stopped, panting like a dog. A havoc of churned earth, broken maize stalks, the biplane that had ploughed the soil in its glide. The nose had drilled its way into the earth, the propeller and left wings were broken off. The proximity of death made his skin shiver.

He walked round the tail. The plane seemed to have been made from everything someone had been able to find in their shed. The torn canvas of the fuselage was the colour of weathered army tents and had been patched here and there like an old pair of overalls. Blood was smeared across the side window of the cockpit; moving closer, he saw the backward angle of the pilot's head.

Aloïs climbed onto the strut and looked into the cockpit. The broad, immobile face of a man, encased in a leather aviator's cap. His dead eyes, pale blue as ribbons in a girl's hair. Then Aloïs saw the bloody tendrils of mucus between the man's lips move. The shock — *he's breathing, he's alive.*

The strands between his dehydrated lips burst as his mouth formed words Aloïs did not understand.

'What's that,' Aloïs shouted, 'did the thing crash on you?'

The feeble words from behind the Plexiglas, his eyes that slowly opened and shut again. Aloïs yanked fruitlessly on the bottom of the canopy's metal frame. 'Open it!' he shouted to the man. 'Ya gotta open the damn thing!' He pointed to the handle on the inside of the canopy. The pilot moved his right arm across his chest. His other arm hung limply beside him. He twisted his torso to the left, gritting his teeth, and placed his hand on the handle.

'Harder!' Aloïs shouted. 'Damn it, man, push the damn thing!'

Stepping down off the wing, he found a rock in the turned earth. He used it to smash the window. He stuck his hand into the clammy warmth inside the cockpit, pulled on the handle and opened the canopy above the aviator's head. 'Come on, climb out,' he said.

The pilot whispered something in a foreign language.

It was clear that he could not get out of the plane on his own. Aloïs leaned over and tried to pick him up, but the man groaned so terribly that he quickly let go.

Aloïs looked at the sky and inhaled deeply. A cloud, flat and grey as a river rock, had drifted above their heads. On the road down below, a car drove by. Had the driver looked up, he would have seen a man sticking up above the maize, on a rise in the field, and waving to get his attention, but the driver kept his eyes riveted on the asphalt and disappeared beneath the stand of oaks in the next curve.

'This isn't going to work,' Aloïs mumbled. A flock of crows above his head fused into a ribbon of black. He bent down over the man again, threw his arms around his chest, and pulled him out of his seat. The pilot bellowed in pain and fright and passed out when Aloïs dragged him from the plane with all his might.

Lying on the churned earth now was a stranger, a man from far away, that much was clear by now. The aviator cap, his worn, old-fashioned clothing — as though he hadn't so much come flying in from a different country as from a different age. The blockish leather boots he wore — a farmer? A flying farmer? A Pole, Aloïs thought, Poles had pale eyes like that. He pulled off the man's boots, grabbed him by the ankles, and began, in the furrow between two rows of maize, the long journey home.

Fifth

The pale-yellow fields around Muldershoek lay drowsing in the sun. The hired hands had left; the haying was finished for the day. Young fellows still, didn't care about a thing. Yes, about Saturday night, about getting wrecked at De Lindeboom, but how impossibly distant was Saturday night … High atop their machines they crossed the boundless valley of obligation, and long before reaching that hot-blooded, come-hither Saturday night they were sure to have died of boredom.

At the field's periphery, in the shadow of the forest's edge, stood Paul Krüzen. He looked out over the land that belonged to Harry Voorthuizen and his son, bordering their own. Myriad insects buzzed amid the trees, a slow and deep droning generated by the warm days of June.

Long ago, his father had shown him the spot where the aviator had crashed. When Paul went back there with his metal detector, it was at that very spot in the field that he picked up a strong iron signal. Winter, mud caked to his soles in layers. He dug up an old boot with hobnails in the heel, and a little further along a muddy, badly rusted object that he did not recognise. Down on his knees in the ploughed field, he used his pocket knife to scrape the glutinous earth from the metal object. The search coil went on signalling disturbances beneath the surface. At a little over eighteen inches he found a sort of wheelbarrow rim with a half-decayed rubber tyre around it. His heart raced. The past — it existed, it had existed, and even if it was done and gone, he had dug it up again. So it was true — the Russian, his plane, the things that had played out in the twilight of his early childhood and that he remembered as a dream — the contours grew sharper now. With his discovery he felt he had now, finally, claimed his place in the course of events.

It was more than thirty years ago that he had gone into that field with his metal detector — he was sixteen or seventeen at the time, and after that he had never found anything as important as the boot, the compass, and the aeroplane wheel.

Down from the sky a crow descended now, a big healthy crow with a big healthy appetite. It landed in the open field, close to a young orphaned hare that had lost its mother in the storm of harvesters. The crow took a few rocking steps, stood still, and ruffled its feathers. Its head cocked to one side, it sized up its prey. The young hare ran a ways, away from the crow, and pressed itself against the ground. Earlier in the day, the grass had still been lying in rows to dry, it could have hidden there or crawled beneath a pile of hay, but now the ground was stripped bare. The crow hopped along after it. It was in no hurry. The hare was small and the field was endless; ah, if only it was always this easy.

The little animal made a courageous *sortie*. Just as it seemed about to crash into the crow, it did a buttonhook — a hare's old, favourite trick. The crow flapped and hopped backwards, then reversed right away and rowed its way forward again. The bird was not much of a hunter, but time was on its side.

Paul Krüzen watched the unfair fight from a distance. He repressed the urge to go running into the field, waving his arms. He had thoughts of his own about hunting and being hunted. In the shade of the trees he kept out of sight and minded his own business. Everything had to run its course. In the lives of animals, in his own life, that of Paul Krüzen — more hare than crow. Solitary prey. Rabbit-hearted.

Far away, on the far side of the high, rolling field, a car passed.

Then a tractor. You heard them for a while, then it was still. Only the yellow field and he, in the shadow. The whispering brook back behind there. Unusually low for the time of year. The stream dragged itself quietly along through the semi-darkness beneath the trees. The bottom was red with ore.

The hare, the size of a little girl's hand, was giving up. It pressed itself trembling against the ground. The time had come, and time took the form of a sharp-billed bird in widow's weeds. It picked at you. You felt everything, every sabre-cut, Paul thought, but you had to steel yourself. It took a strong suit of armour to be neutral. The bird lashed out at him with its dagger-bill. Paul didn't blink. You had to know your place in the food chain, he thought. Know your place in the food chain, and arm yourself.

A flight of jackdaws flew over. The crow crouched and turned one piercing eye upwards, to see if it needed to brace itself for competition. Then he got back to work. The hare's resistance was broken. Maybe the little animal was actually dead already. With its prey in its beak, the crow took off a little later. It flew low over the newly mown field, pale as the shorn scalps of the neo-Nazis Paul sometimes saw at the gun fairs where they, like him, searched for paraphernalia from the latest of the great wars to plough the continent and alter its complexion. Outcasts, these kids were. The sea-green Odal rune tattoo on the back of the neck or forearm destined them to a life in the margins. A job driving forklift or sorting packages, that's all that lay in store for them. He avoided them, those boys with their eyes ablaze, who dreamed of a different world than he did.

'You're awfully late, aren't you?' said his father when he came in.

'Nuh, you just sat down too early,' Paul said.

He made him a pot of tea, and a slice of bread with liverwurst. His father folded his hands and was quiet for a moment. That's the way it went: once his father had taken care of him, now he was taking care of his father. In the course of time, he had become not only his chief clerk, but also his nurse, cook, and food-taster. Sometimes in his daydreams he tossed a handful of sand on the old man's coffin and felt relieved.

Aloïs chewed diligently. Thirty-seven times for each mouthful, Paul knew, because that was good for your digestion, but every time he tried to catch him at it he lost count.

The bread his father could handle had grown paler and paler, easier to grind, right up to the moist, snowy-white tin-loaf he bought for him these days. Paul read his father's digestion the way augurs did the flight of birds. 'You need to drink more liquids,' he said when his bowel movements were too hard. 'And eat more fibre. I'll buy some of those San Francisco whole-wheat cookies for you next time. You've been liking those.'

Anyone seeing them, he thought, couldn't imagine what it had once been like. He himself barely could anymore. In a certain sense, nothing had changed — two men in a house and a half-century passing without a ripple — but seen with the light from a different angle, none of it had remained the same.

'Get in late tonight again, hm?' his father asked.

'Didn't look.'

'Anything special?'

Paul thought of the Russian, but said nothing. In the way the legendary cyclist Luis Ocaña used to rile himself before the race by letting himself be stung by bees, his father could be raised from the dead by starting in about Russians. Or, better yet, that one, particular Russian. If you asked Aloïs about it these days, he would still say: 'I ought to've let him rot away where he hit the ground.'

'Ullie's dead,' Paul said then. 'Tonnie's Ullie. Hedwig told me.'

His father shook his head. Now that he had stopped going into the village on his mobility scooter, after having spent an hour and a half once on a bike path with an empty battery, he heard very little in the way of news. 'Ullie,' he said, and nodded. 'What did he have?'

'Doctor, lawyer, Indian chief, the Big C brings 'em all to grief.'

'Knock on wood,' said his father, and rapped his knuckles on the tabletop.

Paul's thoughts wandered outside, to the animals in the field and the heat hovering over the soil. Once he had been a friend to the hares. He'd spied on the hunters from his hiding place high in the oak at the far back of the woods, the same one from which his father had picked out the aeroplane in the maize, and sent them his powerless hatred. They slung hares and wood pigeons from their belts, but let crows and jackdaws lie. *There!* A hare appeared from where it had been lying low. *Run, hare, run* ... The hunters aimed and fired. Two, three crisp reports and yonder the hare stumbling, somersaulting and lying dead in the field. Killed in the same field where it had first seen the light of day, for the hare is no traveller. 'A hare,' the hunters said, 'wants shooting there where he was born,' and each year they thinned their ranks even further. They shot hares, pheasants, jaybirds, wood pigeons, ducks, crows, and the occasional fox. Fingers tightened on the triggers, they fired and fired, smoke curled up from the hot barrels, birds tumbled from the sky and the shotgun shells remained lying in the field. The dogs yelped with doggy pleasure, their masters wiped their bloody hands on the seat of their pants, and the sun and Paul Krüzen saw it all.

Sixth

His name was Anton Rubin and he had escaped from the Evil Empire in a crop-duster. Beneath pale ribbons of stars, he flew over sleeping barracks and recumbent artillery. He flew at four or five hundred feet, low enough to stay under the radar. Grazing deer may have looked up for a moment, foxes ceased their snuffling and listened to the droning in the sky. A border guard may have raised an eyebrow, but the sirens remained silent.

Even more than MiGs that might suddenly appear on his wing, Anton Rubin feared the black silhouettes of hills. When they rose up before him in the moonlight, he would escape to eight or nine hundred feet, as much as was needed to avoid them. When there were no hills, he strained his eyes to pick out nuclear plants and power pylons in the darkness. At all costs, he had to avoid appearing as an unidentified object on a radar screen, something a MiG could playfully pick out of the air.

Rubin flew almost blind through the night, with only a few flight instruments at his disposal. By a weak glow he could read the speedometer, the altimeter, and rate-of-turn indicator. Because the compass on the console was out — the glass was broken and the needle had disappeared — he read his northwesterly course from the army compass in his hand. Oh, how he wished he had an artificial horizon in front of him, but instruments like that were expensive and hard to come by. With an artificial horizon he could have seen what was up and what was down; the sporadic lights on the ground had a way of merging seamlessly with the starry sky, so he could just as easily have been flying upside-down. That was why he had waited for a clear night, in order to have the moon as his beacon. It was a calm flight in the absence of thermals, and the plane cut through the smooth air, yet still Rubin was one huge, overstrained sensory apparatus, tensed for the slightest cough or sputter of the engine. A cylinder missing a beat or a blip in the fuel supply — indicators of possible disaster. From the smell of the oil he could tell if he was pushing the engine too hard; he could pick out the odour of burned oil at a thousand paces.

Whenever a light went on in a window below, his heart rose. There was life there, a fellow human being — what a beacon, what a light on earth for someone floating alone through the boundless heavens!

His eyes stung from peering into the darkness; he struggled against sleep and slapped himself across the face to stay awake. He dictated letters to his mother, his sisters, and his friends, a hopeful chain of words in the darkness that enclosed him like the ocean's depths. Hour after hour he flew over forests, hills, and rivers, his body surrounded by fuel tanks containing enough gas to get him from his village of Zagubieni all the way to Denmark. In Denmark, he'd been told, you had human rights, and the women were creatures of butter and honey. But human rights you can't see, they're written invisibly above the gates of the institutions; the women, on the other hand, marched leggily through his mind and chased away sleep for a time. Across the screen of the night they paraded before him, with broad hips and rounded thighs, tapering off to petite ankles that wanted Anton Rubin to kiss them. 'Anton!' the women shouted. 'Anton? Where are you? We've been waiting so long! What's keeping you?'

Luck had been with him thus far. Like a feather, he'd been blown across the clear, cloudless sky, just as the weather charts had predicted before his departure.

Relieved, he greeted the faint glow of morning, fast growing brighter. The darkness faded to a Prussian blue, the stars paled. The shadows lengthened and everything turned to liquid gold — the forests, fields, and villages below him, a sensation he remembered from the times he had taken off at the crack of dawn. The watercourses, too, glistened golden in the depth; the light at his back seemed to push him along through the cold sky.

A bath, how he longed for a bath to rinse away the night's fearful sweat and loosen his cold, stiff muscles.

According to his calculations, he was now somewhere above the DDR; not out of danger yet. Fleeing was treason, punishable by the firing squad or the gulag, where you rotted away at the world's end.

He could have taken a shortcut across the Baltic, but he wanted to stay above land; engine trouble or meteorological problems at sea would be the death of him. He would fly over northern Germany to Denmark, with the sun at his back; around nine in the morning, however, the compass fell from his stiff fingers. It rolled under his seat or somewhere behind him, beyond reach of his desperate groping. He cursed and twisted back and forth but could not find it. He would have to land the plane first, but he didn't want to take that risk. He flew on, hoping for the best, and tried to hold his northwesterly course by the sun's position.

As the morning wore on, the buildings beneath him crowded closer together and the network of roads grew more complex; the sun glanced off the roofs of cars. Long plumes of smoke blew from factory chimneys. Had he passed the Iron Curtain without even noticing it, was it that easy? It could only be West Germany there below him now, so many roads, cars, and industry — no doubt about it, he was flying over the free world!

But he wasn't in Denmark, not yet, and he wasn't about to stay in Germany. He had been born two years before Hitler's march on Moscow, and had grown up with stories about the German atrocities. His father and mother, like most of their generation, had served in the Great Patriotic War and spoke of the fascists with fear and contempt.

The knowledge that he was flying over NATO territory disturbed him. They, too, had jetfighters to deal with small planes without a transponder, planes that gave no reply when asked who they were and where they came from. He was flying so low that he could see the cattle on the ground. Rolling pastureland, full of cows. Those cows gave more than five thousand litres of milk each year, he knew, the quantities prompted by the geneticists' work was staggering.

The sun struck the cockpit at an angle, he began warming up slowly. Rivers here flowed north; before sunset, he had to set the plane down somewhere. He happened to catch sight of an airstrip down below, but he had no desire to be interrogated by the Germans, who might think he was a spy from the East. Fritz still knew how to break Ivan.

He ate bread and drank *kvass*. At times, he dozed with his eyes open, in the wake of images of this, that, and the other, luring him into the domain of dreams — slowly, his eyes fell shut. He awoke with a start each time. A quick glance at the altimeter — he had barely lost altitude. He slid open the window and let cold air blow in his face. One more hour, he told himself, one more hour and that's enough. Denmark can't be that far away, the sea should show up on his right at any moment now, misty and vague. He would bank round it and make his approach to Denmark from the southeast. But all he saw were cities, roads, fields, and forests. No sea. Where was he, for holy Christ's sake?

His eyes on the landscape below, he ascertained that he was, in any case, flying over a different world. A world full of colour. A web of roads brought everyone wherever they wanted to go. There was no way he could still be airborne over the Soviet empire which, however immense it might be, still had borders to mark its end.

He scoured the ground for an airfield. He still had time. He was heading into the sun now, and he craned his neck to look into the future. Five o'clock in the afternoon, and he was flying over a world without landing strips.

Seventh

Once, Hedwig Geerdink's shop had smelled of potatoes, apples, and leeks, but with the arrival of the village's first supermarket he had got rid of the fresh produce. There was no competing with the green stamps from the Plus. Soap powder, dried sausage, and tobacco had remained. North State, Mantano, brands you looked for to no avail in other parts of the country. Hedwig was the last shopkeeper in the country who still sold instant pudding. Paul scanned the shelves. *O hand soap, o canned vegetables* ... The plastic roses in the vases on the top shelves were still there, from the days of Hedwig's mother. Paul would rather have done his shopping at the Plus, but loyalty was sometimes its own reward. Horseradish Hedwig ... If you could choose your friends, you'd hardly choose him, but some things are just the way they are.

The shop hadn't changed much since Great-Grandpa Geerdink had started it in 1911, although it had been a donkey's age since Hedwig had last scooped the dried beans and peas from the wooden troughs behind him. These days, the legumes had been manipulated into exemplary crops, grown in Uganda or Vietnam, but they still ended up on the shelf at Hedwig's; now in one of those Hak jars with a lid that makes that wonderful, dry click when you open it.

Paul placed a roll of San Francisco whole-wheat cookies on the counter. In the narrow corridor between house and store, he heard Hedwig's shuffling tread. 'Heey, Paulie,' he said in that high voice of his, and stepped into the dusty light of late afternoon.

'Well, well, Mr Millionaire.'

'They'll forget all about that.'

'I hope so, for your sake.' Paul took a jar of tomato sauce down off the shelf. Elbow macaroni, a packet of parmesan powder. He looked at the dates on the packaging. Everything at Hedwig's, people said, was way past its due date. There was no harm in checking.

Hedwig had emerged from behind the counter and was standing at the window now, his arms crossed, looking outside. Was it out of habit or professional pride that he still always wore that grey grocer's apron?

His mother had stood at the window like that, too, his grandmother probably had as well, waiting for his grandfather to bring the wagon back from his grocery rounds to the local farmers. Bunderweg was only freshly paved in 1911 when Hedwig's great-grandfather bought the plot of ground just outside the village and started his dry goods store there. Now, more than a hundred years later, an end would come to that at last; his great-grandson Hedwig, like Paul, didn't have a soul in the world.

'So what's the damage?' Paul asked.

Hedwig slid behind the counter and rang up the groceries. Paul fished the money out of his pocket, the change loose, the bills in his silver money clip. 'Swing by around eight?' he asked.

'Fine by me,' said Hedwig.

You never really got used to that weird voice of his. Folks were startled by it. At the weekend, the local bumpkins tore the drainpipes off the front of his house. Ambiguity is never a good sign.

There were girls working at the Plus who Paul once would never have given a second look, but who were now consecrated by virtue of their youth. The quality of their skin. Fresh and healthy, just like the produce department promised. Some of them were hefty, others not; Paul had enough experience by now to know that each variety had its advantages. An unattractive fatso could sometimes make a believer out of you.

Back in the late 1980s, he had still known the cashiers, they were girls he had gone to school with. In due time, however, they disappeared one by one, claimed by family life. Their places were taken by new girls, often the daughters of his former classmates; sometimes he recognised their surnames from the tags on their chest.

He dropped his milk, bread, and ground beef on the checkout conveyor. Did he save green stamps? The cashier gave him a friendly look.

'Sure, why not,' he said.

She tore two of them off the roll. He stuffed the stamps in his back pocket, paid, and left. Outside, when he looked back in through the window, he saw that she was already re-immersed in the wonders of her Samsung Galaxy S5.

At home, he fried an onion, stirred the ground beef around in it, and added the tomato sauce. While the sauce was simmering, he saw to his father's leg. He pulled on a pair of latex gloves, dabbed at the wound on the old man's shin, and rubbed silver sulfadiazine on it. Paul breathed through his mouth, the necrotic stench made him gag. His father submitted to the treatment without complaint. They knew what they were in for, if the mortification couldn't be stopped. The doctor had not yet spoken the word 'amputation', yet it hung already in the gravitational field around their lives.

His father was reading the *Tubantia*. A cascade of elbow macaroni slid into the steaming water. Paul had added both pasta and rice to the menu long ago, as his revolt against the regimen of potatoes. He himself favoured potatoes, too, but you couldn't just give in to the rut. It made a zombie out of you.

When it was done, he put the pans on the table and sat down across from his father. The old man folded his hands. Paul had an early childhood memory of those hands, lit by the dining-room lamp, still wearing the wedding ring. Large hands. Big enough to easily clasp both his son's wrists in one. Paul wanted to have hands like that too.

'And bless it to its intended use, amen,' Aloïs concluded.

'Yep,' Paul said.

His father opened the plastic box beside his plate, counted out his pills, and rinsed them down with water. Paul sprinkled parmesan powder over the sauce and spooned his plate clean. Across the table each bite was finely ground, as though the old man had a mouth full of dry leaves.

The ceiling creaked. Paul looked up. It sounded like someone climbing a set of wooden stairs. The oldest beams in the attic, encroached upon by woodworm and fire, dated from around 1650, when the first farmhouse was built on this spot. The trees for it, Paul reckoned, had been seedlings around the time Columbus set sail for the West, and were lumbered when Abel Tasman dropped anchor off the coast of the island that came to bear his name. Ever since, the beams had borne the weight of this house's roof, and of the farmers who'd hanged themselves from them throughout the centuries. Paul reached for the newspaper, to kill time by skimming the articles that hadn't interested him that morning. How much time had he wasted, waiting for his father to finish eating? A year? Two years? He could have learned a language in the time he'd spent waiting. Russian, so he could have understood that fellow's ranting in Shu Dynasty last night. Spanish, so he could whisper sweet nothings in Rita's sweet little ears.

He was halfway through a chronological reconstruction of the currency-rate fraud at the good old Cooperative Farmers' Credit Union when his father took his last bite, put down his spoon, and looked out the window. The lavish blossoming, the exhaustion. It was about time to mow the grass again. Aloïs exhaled loudly through the spaces in his dentures. Then he raised a finger to his mouth and poked around between his front teeth. The pasta had been perhaps just a bit too *al dente*. 'Way too hot it is,' he said, 'for May.'

'This is June,' Paul said, folding the newspaper. While clearing the table, he asked, as casually as he could, 'What I was wondering, you know — that Russian, that Rubin, what actually made him crash? I never heard about that.'

His father placed his hands on the table in front of him and looked at them.

'Pa?' Paul asked after a while.

His father glanced up briefly. 'About twenty hours he'd been sittin' in that thing, without sleeping.'

'But you said the engine was sputtering, right? Was his gas all done, or what?'

'Possible. But the air base is that away.' His father pointed out the window. 'He had no business being here. Got a toothpick?'

'You never asked him?'

'I couldn't make head nor tails of it all. Your mother, okay. Not me.'

Your mother, okay. The story of their life.

'So a fellow knows a plane like the back of his hand,' Paul said, 'and flies two thousand kilometres in it, and then crashes. I don't get it. You'd expect … that somebody like that would know how to land a plane, right? In a field or on a road, something like that?'

'Couldn't say,' his father said in a tone that put an end to the conversation as far as he was concerned.

Paul stuck his forearms into the hot suds and brought up a dish. The Russian had been the first foreigner in Mariënveen. After him came the Chinese. The Russian went away again, the Chinese stayed.

The first Chinese had come along with Baptist Weening. Three in total. 'My wife and children,' Baptist said.

It had all started with a question someone asked Baptist at his previous cafeteria, the one in Vennenoord. A question that sounded as simple as can be. You wouldn't have gone looking for anything behind it when you heard it, and that's precisely the way it went with Baptist, standing there at the display case full of deep-frozen gravy rolls and chow mein patties.

There were two slot machines in the dining area; almost every day around noon, a Chinese man came in and tossed money into them — first guilders, later euros. 'Baptist,' that Chinaman had asked him one day, 'don't you wish you had a woman?'

Baptist thought about it. Not about whether he wanted a woman, but about what he should say in reply. Then he laughed a little crookedly and said: 'Yeah, sure.'

A week later, the Chinese man jammed a cardboard coaster between the buttons on the machine and asked: 'Baptist, do you still really want a woman?'

Baptist watched as combinations of apples, bells, bananas, and four-leaf clovers formed behind the Chinaman's back. The machines had been on the point of paying out for a while, like a cow in calf, but it could just as easily happen tomorrow. He thought about women, about a woman. The world was full of them, but the one for him was never in there among them. He laughed again mildly and nodded. Then the Chinese man said that he had a sister in Guangzhou. A good woman; she worked like a horse. He had already told her about him, she was packed and ready to come.

Baptist looked at the gold bars and dollar signs spinning at a dizzying pace behind the Chinaman's back, and thought: in the slot machine of love, you have to toss in a euro now and then. 'Tell her to come,' he said.

And that was how, one day, he found three Chinese people standing on his doorstep: two more than he'd counted on. The woman had brought her son and daughter along, too, the small print, as it were, that her brother had neglected to mention.

He had a big heart, Baptist did, but no heart is big enough to house a family of four. And so he went looking for a new cafeteria, with living quarters to billet his Chinese invasion. He found it on Dorpstraat in Mariënveen, where Alferink's fish store had been standing empty for a while. Along one of the outside walls was still written in huge letters alferink's fish, so you're sure it's what it is, which had been one of the great conundrums of Paul's youth. How often, in impotent rage, had he asked himself: *Then you're sure* what *is what it is?*

And if you asked Baptist how that had gone, with him and all his Chinese folks, he would say pensively: 'In for a penny, in for a pound.'

They were the first Chinese in Mariënveen. They learned to deep-fry potatoes and swirl soft-serve ice cream, and they were dedicated and modest and nothing ever went wrong with the petty cash. Not long afterwards, the second wave rolled in and took over the Kottink Bar & Party Centre, across the street from Happytaria Weening, where they opened a cafe-restaurant with 'live cooking' as their specialty. The lettering on the window now said shu dynasty, and underneath that the same thing in Chinese. Suddenly now there were seven of them, not counting the ones sleeping in the attic.

Seven-some Chinese people, a restaurant with two gold lions out in front and inside a whopper of a party hall where a hundred people could all dine at the same time. Paul remembered the first time he'd tasted babi pangang. The revolution in his mouth. Three hundred years of meat, potatoes, and gravy, and now this.

'Tha's dog,' Theo Abbink said.

Dog, was he really eating dog?

But after a while, almost no one ever went into the party hall anymore. There were a few wedding receptions, but the place was so big you drowned in it. The cafe section was the place to be. Sitting at the bar, working on a bottle of Grolsch and a plate of chicken with bird's nest noodles. As long as 'our own recipe' was written after the entree, it didn't matter much what you ordered; you always got more.

'Mama,' was all you had to say when your bottle was empty, and Mama Shu would put a new one down in front of you. If you wanted to drink from a glass, though, you had to ask.

Eighth

At Club Pacha, life began all over again every night. You never had to apologise for what went wrong the last time. Yesterday's score had been erased.

It started with three or four beers. Sometimes after that he would dance with one of the girls beneath the disco lights. Up on the little stage was a metal pole; some of the ladies performed miracles up there. Her warm back beneath the palm of his hand, the arched rise on the way to her buttocks. *Good-bye, oh, please don't cry, 'cause we both know that I'm not what you need ...* The Asian girls' petite voices shot sky-high when they got to the refrain. *I will always love you ... You-ou-ou-ou ...*

Hedwig gobbled down a whole plate of peanuts. Sometimes one of the girls would talk to him, in a friendly, sisterly way. They teased him, made bets about him. Then the girl on his lap would pull out all the stops, but Hedwig was immune to coaxing.

Paul came and sat beside him. One of the new girls was standing at their table, making a drinking gesture. 'Beer,' Paul said in English. 'Cola for my friend. For you, too.' He pointed at her.

'Blue Lady!' the girl laughed.

Paul gave her the thumbs up. He couldn't quite tell her age, but after a certain point in his life they had all suddenly become just young.

She came back with a little serving tray. The cocktail glass with some kind of blue liqueur in it. The colour of a dream. The music played, Paul leaned back and exhaled deeply. The pressure in his chest decreased, his worries blew away along with his breath. The girl chattered with Hedwig. A white laundry tag was sticking out the back of her tanga. Her youthfulness bothered him. Somewhere in Thailand or Burma, people were thinking about her. Photos on the wall, a missing that fanned out without direction, without destination. And here she sat in her tanga with the label sticking out, in Stattau, sipping at her magic potion. She could have been his daughter. The same went for most of the girls here. He was the father of Teresita, Luana, and Ludmilla, of Sunny, Lola, and Susanna. But he couldn't tell them that when they led him by the hand to one of the back rooms. That his hard-on had developed a conscience. Instead, he said, 'I'm here for Thong' or 'I'm here for Rita'. The grandmothers of the family, as it were, even though both of them were still under forty. But they didn't let themselves be shooed away that easily, those hussies. They were there as a body, and the body needed to work, just like the bodies on the farm or in the factory. *Let's play, Paul, let's play.*

Laurens Steggink would then say: 'Fireworks, Paulie, the little kit-kat, I swear to God.'

Steggink hit them if they didn't listen to him. Paul wished they wouldn't tell him. If Steggink found out that they talked to customers about it, he hit them even harder. When that happened, Paul despised himself, even more than he despised Steggink. Sometimes he would stay away for a while.

One time, after Rita had complained, Paul broached the subject with him.

'You don't get it, Paulie,' Steggink said. 'They're wild, they head in all directions except the right one. I have to break them in a little, otherwise this place would go to hell.'

The simulation of their former friendship, that was the hardest thing to take.

He drove home down the windy border road, the earth-dark pastures and wooded banks on both sides, and thought: *If that son of a bitch says 'break them in' one more time, I'll blow his brains out.*

After that one time, Rita disappeared for a while, then came back with a shroud across her eyes, her soul. They lay beside each other silently, the washed-out sheet pulled up around them. Paul ran his fingers down her cheek to feel if she was crying. She was not crying. When he left, he slipped her an extra hundred euros. 'For your birthday,' he said.

'It's not my birthday,' she said.

'Pretend it is.'

Rita and Thong weren't in this evening. He didn't see Steggink either. He stood up to go for a smoke, and the Russian walked in. Paul watched him as he climbed the stairs to the office without even looking around.

Paul smoked his cigarette outside, under the night sky. The Russian's presence disturbed him. His involvement in the club was something new; Paul had no idea what it meant.

In the courtyard jacuzzi, Luana was lying in the arms of a greying fifty-something. His hands were wrapped around her little breasts. They lay back in the bubbling water, not speaking a word, looking at the stars. Paul stubbed out his cigarette in an ashtray full of soaking butts and went inside.

Could he borrow a pair of scissors, he asked the Polish girl behind the bar. It was a quiet evening, only the music and the high voices of Hedwig and the girl. Paul slid in on the couch beside her and, leaning over, took the tag of her tanga between thumb and forefinger and cut it off. When she jumped to her feet, she almost knocked over the table. She twisted her head round and pulled hard on the elastic band of her underwear, to see what he had done. 'You crazy!' she shouted, followed by expletives he did not understand.

Paul held up the tag for her to see. 'Okay, whoa,' he said, 'it's only this little, eh ...'

She snatched it out of his hand. 'You crazy!' Wobbling on her pumps, she disappeared into the back. The Russian appeared on the little landing at the top of the office stairs. He scanned the floor with his cold, caprine eyes, and stood there like that for a while.

'That was a weird move,' Hedwig said quietly, once the Russian had disappeared.

'Not my night, I guess,' Paul said. 'Come on, let's go.'

Steggink's Ferrari was in the lot behind the club. Paul placed his hand on the hood. Warm. A fast, rhythmic ticking sound was coming from underneath it, the engine had been running hard. Did Steggink let the Russian drive it? Were they that chummy?

They climbed into Paul's car and pulled out onto the road. The club's windows were shuttered, the letters on the roof glowed in flesh-tinted neon.

He remembered better times at Club Pacha, nights without duration or duty. Drinking, drinking, and the *amore* that seemed to fall like manna from heaven. You forgot that they were going to present you with a bill at the end of it all.

Hedwig rolled down his window a bit to let in the cool night air. A deep-blue haze had risen above the treetops. Thin mist lay across the fields. They drove through the desolate borderlands, the light from a farmhouse window stuttering through the trees sometimes like Morse code. Paul thought about the Russian. What was his part in it, what was his connection with Steggink? There was something deep and impenetrable about him, something that to Paul seemed typical of a people hardened by centuries of hardship and repression.

He had seen more and more folks from the East in recent years. Mostly gypsies, people said. Bulgarians, Romanians — you could tell by the plates on the vans and the car trailers. The Poles had been around for some time already. Burglaries, thefts. The blessings of the new Europe. The empty, lawless borderlands were fruitful hunting grounds for them. You loaded a car onto the trailer and you were across the border. They poached roe deer and wild swine in the forests.

Someone at Shu once told him that a hiker had stepped on a steel trap. Gangs. They obeyed the orders of men, far away to the East, who lived in marble palaces and drove fancy cars. At Theo Abbink's, they had cut the fence and taken two Audis. One of the cars didn't even have an engine in it.

'Why don't you go on holiday to Romania, Theo,' Alfons Oliemuller had said to Abbink that night, 'your car already did.'

Abbink and Oliemuller, the car dealer and the salvager, neighbours on the industrial estate between Mariënveen and Kloosterzand. There wasn't much those two hadn't seen.

Back in March, in Deurlo, a man had come running into a garage, bleeding like a stuck pig, his hands lashed behind his back with cable-ties. They had kidnapped him at gunpoint and tortured him in the back of a van. When they took off driving again, he was able to open the back doors and roll out onto the street. No one knew all the details, only that it had to do with seven hundred kilos of cocaine smuggled from Willemstad to Hamburg in a container full of scrap metal. Later that afternoon, two men were arrested on suspicion of kidnapping at the industrial park in Mariënveen.

The abolition of Europe's internal frontiers had not only resulted in free trade, but also in that kind of business. Willemstad, Hamburg, Mariënveen, the mind boggled.

Paul had upgraded the security equipment around his shed full of militaria. There were cameras in the trees along the drive and above the entrance. The images were sent to the database of Safety4U and stored there for six months.

Starting as a junk collector who combed the former DDR in search of antiques, he had gone on to become a major dealer in militaria. Uniforms, weapons, helmets, medals, radio equipment, mortar shells — everything, all of it. He'd even had a Sherman tank for a while, but then he had stopped doing rolling stock, except for one Daimler Dingo; too much mass, too little in the way of margins.

Sooner or later, scrap turns to money, that's what was said about Krüzen Militaria. Most of the traffic went by the Internet, his working days largely consisted of preparing packages for shipment. Direct sales weren't that attractive anymore. He had even thought about stopping with that completely, but hesitated; that would make it awfully quiet around the farm.

Still, he preferred the anonymity of Internet commerce. Ten orders and his day was made. Every time the email tone sounded, it was jackpot. He was a reliable address for German militaria. He could tell original from replica at a glance. In China they made ten times the amount of Nazi uniforms, daggers, busts of the Führer, and insignia than the entire Third Reich ever had. He'd heard about a printer's where all that rolled from the press were new copies of *Mein Kampf*, in every language you could think of. They even buried the stuff to make it look worn. Imitation had ruined the market, but it made him a good living; an expert eye was in greater demand than ever before.

The sign Hedwig had painted for him twenty-five years ago, with the steady hand of a grocer's son, was still standing along the road:

KRÜZEN
CUROSIA
&
MILITARIA

The first half of the text was fairly weathered, the much more legible & MILITARIA had been added later.

Paul clearly remembered the day they'd installed the sign along the road. They'd stood looking at it for a while; a few cars had driven past.

'What have you done now, dipstick?' Paul said at last.

'What do you mean?' Hedwig asked.

'Curosia …'

'So what's wrong with that?'

'It's wrong, that's what's wrong with that.'

'What do you mean?' Hedwig asked again.

'It's curiosa, not curosia.'

'Aw, damn it,' Hedwig said, nodding as though he'd known it all along.

'Want me to do it over?' he asked at last.

Paul shook his head. 'Let 'em think we're dumb around here. Good for a little negotiating room.'

A gust of wind shook the oaks along the bend in the road, acorns rattled on the asphalt. They stayed a while, looking at the white ornamental letters against the dark green background.

'But otherwise it's okay?' Hedwig asked.

'The first half's just brilliant.'

They walked up the drive towards the house, the gravel crunching beneath their feet. Paul slapped him on the shoulder and said: 'I'm just glad I didn't ask you to write "paraphernalia".'

Ninth

Henry Montizaan, general practitioner to the villages of Mariënveen, Kloosterzand, and Deurlo, got there before the ambulance. While Aloïs Krüzen was providing him with a detailed account of his adventure in the maize field, he percussed the abdomen of the man on the couch. 'You need to tell me this story again later on, Aloïs,' Montizaan said distractedly. The foreigner was conscious now, he groaned quietly at the doctor's probing. Montizaan immobilised the pilot's left arm and cut open his sleeve to give him an injection in the upper arm. Paul watched from a distance. The pilot's eyes lost their grip and rolled up into his head. He was a mass of blood and mud, like he'd been dug up out of the earth with great violence. Slowly, his eyes grew fixed, his jaw slack. Paul came one step closer. It looked almost like his eyes were slanted, but there was nothing Asian about his build or the colour of his skin. An old soldier, surfacing from an old war. Bloodless lips behind a dark growth of whiskers.

Montizaan straightened up. He took the cup of coffee Alice held out to him, and set it aside immediately. Once again, he bent his old knees and knelt beside the man, running his long, bony fingers along the inside of the man's collar. He pulled out a chain necklace with a punched metal identification tag. 'But that's …' he said, holding up the tag and trying to read what was on it. He sat, shaking his head and mumbling. 'Unless I'm mistaken,' he said, holding up the piece of metal for the others to see, 'you folks have got a Russian on your hands here.'

At the hospital, the Russian was given further treatment and interrogation, while outside the press crowded in search of snippets of news about the pilot who had fled Brezhnev's empire. In Mariënveen, camera crews trampled the maize to get footage of the plane. Aloïs Krüzen was interviewed about the chain of events at various spots on his property. He spoke formally — 'that gentleman was unknown to me' — and modestly about his actions: 'I had no other recourse but to drag the gentleman back to the house.'

The Internal Security Service kept the Russian hermetically sealed off from the outside world. When they were finished debriefing him, a popular weekly news report dedicated a broadcast to 'the intrepid hero who defied a superpower'. The reporter stared gravely into the camera. 'Anton Rubin risked his life in a crop-duster and accepted the risk of crashing or being banished to Siberia.'

He was interviewed from his hospital bed, his left arm in a sling. In addition to a fractured vertebra, he also had broken four ribs, so for a time he had been on artificial respiration and a morphine drip. His ruptured spleen had been removed: all things considered, it was a miracle that he had survived the plunge.

The subtitles told viewers that he had grown up in a village two hundred kilometres east of Kiev, that he had served in the Red Army and then went on to work as a truck mechanic. In spring and summer, he flew the superannuated Polikarpov over the black fields and sprayed the crops with artificial fertilizer and pesticides. Endless was the rolling countryside that had once yielded the world's richest harvests of grain. High above it all, the reckless musing had begun, thoughts that would not be dismissed with objections and arguments. The advantage of the Po-2, a lightweight biplane with a range of only four hundred kilometres and a cruising speed of one hundred and ten kilometres an hour, was that it was built of plywood and canvas and not easily detectable by radar. And because the plane was so slow, you could fly quite low with it; you had all the time in the world to avoid obstacles. The plane — which owed its nickname 'Kukuruznik' to the Russian word for maize, *kukuruza* — was old but reliable; he had done all the maintenance on it himself.

Assuming a sixteen-hour flight, he calculated, he would need three hundred and twenty litres of gasoline — plus another eighty as backup. That should be enough to get him to Denmark, some sixteen hundred kilometres northwest of Zagubieni. The engine was strong enough to make it; during the Great Patriotic War, the Polikarpov had been used to carry a pilot and a co-pilot and a couple of hundred kilos of bombs, and as a crop-duster the biplane had no trouble accommodating extra ballast either. Rubin would fill the pesticide tanks with fuel. During the flight, because the loss of weight had to be distributed equally, he would switch back and forth between tanks Again and again, he pilfered tiny amounts of fuel from the tanks at the *kolkhoz*; in the end, the jerrycans were piled up in his hiding place in the hangar.

Because the plane had only a simple windscreen, he built a canopy on the sly that could be placed over the entire cockpit. He installed new fuel lines and extra switches on the control panel. It was, he thought, like equipping an old camel for a long trip through the desert. He spoke to no one about his plans, not even his friends and family. That way he could always change his mind: there would be no one to remind him of his reckless plan. He was thirty-six years old. Thirty-six, he felt, was a good age to start anew.

August of 1975 came, and Anton Rubin flew over bright yellow fields of colza and sunflower, over pale blue chicory flower and fields of grain as far as the eye could see. Tall, straight plumes of smoke rose to the sky here and there, storks drifted on the thermals. Field after field he sprayed with a fine chemical mist. He was fond of the vast land below, but greater even than his love for his native soil was his longing for freedom, the kind of freedom that makes you flare your nostrils and want to run like a horse in the open field. The moon would be full on the twenty-first of the month. The forecasts predicted high cirrus clouds without much turbulence. The jerrycans were ready, he had checked and double-checked the Kukuruznik's engine and other moving parts, but he was still hashing it over.

Late in the afternoon of 21 August, he sat on a chair in front of the hangar, smoking a cigarette and drinking his way to courage. A light breeze rustled through the poplars. Anyone seeing him sitting there, the pilot in his filthy trousers and vest, with smudges of oil on his neck, would have seen a man relaxing after a hard day's work; cup in hand, he was leaning back in his chair on two legs, against the outside wall of the hangar. All day, the sun had been shining full-force on the cracked earth. He smelled the gas and the flowers, the slender trace of waste oil from the hangar, and he wept soundlessly.

Now the sun was gradually losing its strength. The last plane drifted in, the An-2, the 'badger', back from its route past the eastern fields. The Antonov's wheels bounced off the broken concrete and touched again. The pilot parked the plane beside the landing strip, chocked the wheels, and went home. He raised his hand to Rubin in greeting and shouted something unintelligible. With the hand holding the cup, Rubin waved back.

He set the chair back down on all fours and lit another cigarette. A pale moon, transparent still, had appeared in the sky; later, he would have a weak southeasterly wind at his back. He went into the hangar, dragged the jerrycans from their hiding place, and filled the pesticide tanks with fuel. The canopy he attached with nuts and bolts, and hung a bag containing bread and a few bottles of kvass beside the pilot's seat. Behind it he laid the heavy Manchester jacket that would help him through the cold night. One last time, he checked the oil, looked under the cowling, and checked the cylinders. He gave the landing gear and brakes a once-over, then ran his hand over the propeller to make sure it was not damaged. Lastly, he pushed the flaps up and down, squeezed the rear wheel, and then rolled the plane out of the hangar.

The sun went down, the twilight darkly bruised as a beaten boxer. Rubin locked up the hangar and walked to the office, a cigarette between his lips. He laid the key on the desk that belonged to the chief of planning; his absence would not be noticed until Monday morning. By then he would already be somewhere far away, dead or alive, in freedom or imprisonment; he didn't dare to imagine it. Slowly, he walked back. Sweat itched on his scalp, at his temples. His decision, it seemed, had become irreversible. He pushed the world he knew further away with every action he undertook. Grinding out the cigarette with his shoe, he climbed into the plane. The landing strip lay before him pale as bones. He lowered the canopy, opened the fuel valve, and turned the key in the ignition — consecrated acts. A deep shudder shook the Kukuruznik. He let the engine warm up for a few minutes, until the oil temperature was what it should be, then revved it all the way with the safety brake on, to reach the maximum rpms. His gaze slid over the oil indicator, he reset the altimeter to zero and checked to be sure there was nothing blocking the rudders.

Then he breathed in deeply and popped the brake. The Kukuruznik shot forward; the wheels thundered across the concrete. It was only just before the end of the strip that the plane, with its burden of extra fuel, left the ground and took off. He climbed slowly above the treetops. Anton made one final pass over his village, poor old Zagubieni with its little white houses and its blue doors and shutters, a final salute, his eyes filled with tears. Then he set course for the northwest. That is how his long journey began, the chalk-white moon his only companion.

Tenth

The ambulance pulled up into the garden for the second time in late November. The Russian had been released from hospital and was being brought back to the address where they'd picked him up three months before. The driver pointed to the piece of paper, holding it up like a packing list for Alice to see: 'But this *is* Bunderweg 120, isn't it?' Alice nodded suspiciously. The attendant folded up the paper, stuck it in his pocket, and said contentedly: 'Well, so I was right about that.' His partner opened the back doors of the vehicle; the Russian was sitting on a stretcher.

It would have taken a heart of stone and a heap of bad manners to send a fallen Soviet hero packing, so Alice agreed to let them roll him into the house. While installing him on the couch, she called her husband's school. He was fetched from the history classroom and listened to his wife on the phone in the little office used by the receptionist. 'You don't say?' he said, and, 'Is that what they said?', then was silent for so long that his wife shouted, 'Aloïs, come on, say something!'

But the receptionist was looking at him, he didn't dare to show his confusion, and so he said: 'I'll be back at five.' He hung up and went back to the classroom, where his pupils were waiting for him. He taught two more periods, and only then did he return home.

There, he found the Russian on the couch and his wife on a stool in front of the fireplace, beside his eight-year-old son who was viewing the stranger in silent astonishment. Aloïs stood outside the circle of light and viewed the scene. Alice poked at the feeble flames. The Russian, who hadn't been shaved during his stay at the hospital, had a beard like a polar explorer's.

'Aloïs,' his wife said worriedly, and got up to greet him. A fleeting embrace, low on reassurance.

Aloïs put down his schoolbag and walked up to his guest. 'Hello,' he said.

The Russian narrowed his eyes — slanty eyes, Paul thought again — and nodded. Their hands fumbled at each other.

'His name is Anton,' Alice said.

'Yeah, I read about that, um-hum,' Aloïs replied.

'He doesn't speak Dutch,' said Alice. 'Russian. And a few words of English.'

Aloïs nodded, took another step towards the Russian, and said with solemn emphasis: '*Dobryden.*'

No reaction. Aloïs turned to his wife and said: 'Altena says that means "hello" in Russian. He used to belong to the communist young folks' organisation.'

'Try it again,' Alice said.

'*Dobryden*,' Aloïs said again, using a different stress this time. The man looked at him sympathetically, but showed no sign of understanding. Aloïs shrugged. 'That's the way I wrote it down,' he said, looking at the back of his hand. '*Dobryden*, that's the way he said it.'

'*Dobry den*!' the Russian on the couch said then. '*Vy govorite po-russki*!'

'Now *I* don't understand *him*,' Aloïs said.

'Zanks ferry much,' the Russian went on, for that was a phrase he'd learned in the hospital. He pointed around the room and gave Aloïs the thumbs-up. '*Kakoy u vas krasivy dom.*'

'A nice house, I think that's what he's saying,' Alice said. 'He started talking about that a while ago, too.'

She disappeared into the kitchen with Paul in her wake. Aloïs followed. At the counter, she rounded and faced him. 'We can't, Aloïs, this is ridiculous.'

'What am I supposed to do about it?' he asked in a muted tone. 'You're the one who let him in.'

'What was I supposed to do? Where else could he go?'

She turned her back and began fixing dinner.

'I'll call tomorrow,' he said. 'There's been some mistake. An administrative mix-up. They'll straighten it out.'

She peeled potatoes in silence, her back was a wall.

'Tomorrow we'll know more,' Aloïs said. 'It will be okay, don't worry. I'll call and then they'll just come and pick him up.'

Her hands remained poised above the basket of potatoes. 'And exactly who,' she said slowly, without turning round, 'are you going to call, if you don't mind my asking?'

The Russian, unable to get off the couch, ate with his plate on his lap. 'Zanks ferry much,' he said again.

'Well at least he's a polite Russian,' Aloïs said.

Alice granted him a faint smile.

They prayed silently, heads bowed beneath the lamp. From the couch came the sound of knife and fork scraping across the plate. Paul peeked at the visitor over his folded hands, the man was partly hidden by the back of the couch. His fractured vertebra made it hard for him to eat. His beard bounced up and down as he chewed. As slowly as his father ate, that's how voracious the Russian was.

'And bless it to its intended use, amen,' he heard his father say.

The Russian had already finished everything on his plate. He put down his knife and fork and wiped his mouth with the back of his hand.

What it all boiled down to, Aloïs said the next afternoon, was that no one had ever dealt with something like this before. The Russian didn't fall under any government agency, he was simply no one's responsibility. Then, at the hospital, they had thought of him, the man who had saved the pilot's life. That's what the medical superintendent at the Saksonia hospital told him when he'd called that afternoon. 'I don't know if I'm quoting the poet correctly,' the superintendent went on to say, 'but according to me it was something like: where you fall, there you lie … Have I got that right?' The GP, he said, would see to the patient from here on out. Had the ambulance people left behind enough painkillers? With sufficient rest and physical therapy, he should be able to do everything by himself by the time spring rolled around.

'But by the way,' the medical superintendent said then with renewed enthusiasm, 'it was really quite an adventure, wasn't it? What an amazing guy, a real hero, I wouldn't know what else to call it.'

Alice interrupted Aloïs' story: 'If he was so impressed by him, why didn't he keep him for himself?'

'That's what I said, but …'

'You didn't say that at all.'

'The rehab ward didn't have enough beds. And since he didn't need acute medical attention anymore, they figured … So …'

'So we're left holding the bag.'

Aloïs smiled a little and shrugged.

'So now what?'

'Yeah, that's the question, yeah.'

'He can't stay here.'

Aloïs took a deep breath and then, with the courage born of desperation, he asked: 'But why not, actually?' It would only be until March. They could already put him on the waiting list at the housing association. Three, three and a half months, no more than that. Less. It would be a crime to just kick him out the door, wouldn't it, someone who had risked his life for the sake of freedom?

Alice fixed up the ironing room for the Russian, beside the attached stables, the place where she kept her canned goods and bottles of elderflower syrup, as well as the emergency packages she'd brought in, the way the civil defense authorities recommended, in case there was a nuclear attack or an invasion by the Red Army. She cleared the shelves, feather-mopped the dust traps and cobwebs, and dragged in a single bed. There was a transistor radio from the shed, and she put a pile of Aloïs' illustrated history books on the side table. Her father loaned them a wheelchair, to roll their guest from the bed to the couch and back again.

The Russian was a legend. People came from all around to see him, the man who had tied on a pair of wings and flown away from the Red Empire; its western frontier was so close that people claimed that only eight kilometres away, in Deurlo, there were Pershing missiles pointed East. They tapped on the little window beside the side door, shouted 'Anybody home?' in the hallway, and entered the house on stockinged feet. They warmed their hands at the fire, said 'thank you kindly' when Alice offered them coffee, said there was frost on its way, you could smell it in the air. Meanwhile, they stared unabashedly at the Russian, who sat by the desk lamp reading *Dutch for Foreigners*, with Russian wordlists at the back. He seemed content. He may not have made it to Denmark, but fate had still directed him to a fireplace and a pretty woman who diagrammed sentences with him patiently and repeated the correct pronunciation. She brought him his meals and didn't think twice about sliding a bedpan under him.

'Anton,' she asked, 'would you like some coffee, too?'

He raised his head from the book. 'Noi. Zanks ferry much. Missus.'

'*Thank* you very much,' she corrected him.

'*Thank* you ferry much,' he said.

'Goodness,' the visitor said.

Her vague smile. 'He's a good student.'

The general conclusion was that Aloïs Krüzen, who could only have ensnared his wife with the prospect of a civil servant's income and stability, had with the Russian admitted his own, personal Trojan Horse. No one warned him about it. They all watched and waited. With some things, the conclusion is clear from the very start, but you go on watching anyway, simply because you want to know *how* it's going to happen.

The maize had been cut and Harry Voorthuis had dragged the plane from the field and placed it on Krüzen's drive. Muddied and battered, it stood there, the landing gear, propeller, and left wing in a messy pile beside it. There was a sickening buckle in the fuselage, there where Rubin had been seated. Everyone who entered the yard drummed their fingers against the tightly stretched canvas. The Kukuruznik was a relic, the Russian a saint who had slain the Red Dragon.

The sky turned dark and stayed dark, Jan Oude Booijink said that his bees had sealed the entrance to their hives up tight, and they readied themselves for a long and brutal winter. The house was filled with the sound of declensions and rudimentary sentences, and the grammar of fate ran according to its own, ironclad rules. And what about Aloïs? Doesn't he see it? Her flushed cheeks when he comes home, the sparkle in her eyes? Has he forgotten that she once looked at him that way, too? It slipped out of her gaze too slowly for him to notice in the course of time. And now it's gone and he doesn't think about it anymore.

And he doesn't understand her outburst in the bedroom either, on Christmas Eve, when she announces with a rage she can barely contain that she wants Rubin out of the house immediately. The Russian disrupts everything, she says, hasn't he noticed? Her arms are crossed beneath her breasts, her big, warm breasts — he regrets that they're heading for an argument.

But all he does is sit there, he objects, he's not causing anyone harm, is he? And right before Christmas like this, that's no time to send someone away, is it? He asks her to be patient, their guest is already able to walk with crutches, before long he'll be completely mobile again and then everything will be the way it was.

Her outburst that evening is the final warning he fails to understand, and only later, once it's too late, will it resound in his ears like the blast of trumpets. Poor Aloïs Krüzen, who will try for the rest of his life to size up the loss, a man measuring the distance to vanished stars.

Eleventh

Mightn't it be an idea, Gerard Meinders said during the neighbourhood meeting, for them to build a float for Carnival with a replica of that plane on it? Then they could set the Russian in it, flanked by a battery of Scud missiles, and the carnival crew members could dress up as Red Army soldiers. The plane would be flying, as it were, above the soldiers and the missiles, because it would be up on a pillar with a ladder to it, so the Russian could climb in and out. Gerard had already made a few drawings.

They had, in fact, already started on a float with the theme 'Smurfs', but the crew members from Muldershoek and surroundings welcomed this plan so enthusiastically that they gave that one up. Now all they had to do was ask the Russian himself. Aloïs took the drawings home and showed them to Anton Rubin. What did he think of it?

'He doesn't know what Carnival is,' Alice said testily. She tried to explain it to the Russian, half in Dutch and half in Russian, for just as he was learning her language, she was learning his.

Rubin began laughing loudly and said: '*Otlichny plan! Moy kukuruznik otlichno godicha dlia karnavalnogo shestvia.*'

'In Dutch, Anton,' Alice said.

He sighed deeply and said: 'Coot …' He looked at her in desperation, then tapped his index finger against his temple. 'Plan!' he shouted. 'Coot. Plan!'

In the big cowshed in Krüzen's yard, they started on the float that would represent Muldershoek in the parade. They met a few evenings a week, and transformed an old flatbed cart into their representation of Rubin's flight. All around the cart, about eighteen inches off the ground, they added a battery of plywood ballistic missiles that hid the wheels from sight and also served as a balustrade, to keep the crew members from falling off. In the middle of the cart there arose a superstructure of wood and metal, strong enough to support the plane. The shed smelled of sawdust and paint; everyone agreed that this was the best idea in the history of Carnival in Mariënveen. This would give them something to think about, the other crews with their floats full of Barbapapas and creatures from *The Daily Fable*. Rubin sat in a chair and smoked, handing out the occasional instruction for building the replica of his plane. At regular intervals they put down their hammers, saws, and paintbrushes, drank a glass of Dutch gin, and said '*Nazdarovya!*'

The plane's frame was fabricated by Gerard Meinders, who owned a joinery firm, and his brother Berthold, who had started a sawmill halfway between the village proper and Muldershoek.

Never before had Mariënveen been in the news, not once since its name first appeared in a title deed from 1013, and now they had actually been front-page news for days. And the Russian was a fine fellow, too; he was always in for a snorter and he was good with his hands. He had made the propeller for the plane himself, in that faraway shed in Zagubieni. Making a propeller was a wondrous feat of equilibration: even the lacquer you used could ruin the balance. For reasons understood to no one, Rubin actually had a propeller tattooed over the entire length of his upper arm.

The broken propeller was repaired passably well and attached to the nose of the replica. Theo Lesscher messed around with an electromotor and a car battery until he was able to make the thing spin.

When the plane was finished, they used a beam to hoist up the behemoth and roll the cart underneath it. It had become a sinister Soviet monument. The silvery-grey missiles gleamed coldly, the plane lifted itself heroically above that bristling thicket. Rubin wept and drank to these new friends who had told his story in wood, metal, and paint. Paul climbed into the cockpit, which contained a comfortable chair that Rubin would have to make do with for a few hours. Down below, Frans Huzink went around with the bottle again. 'To NATO then, right?' said Gerard Meinders, and again they raised the shot glasses once bought as a souvenir of the Teutoburgerwald.

On the day itself, they gathered at the shed, wearing the old army fatigues they had dug out of the duffels left from their time in military service. The wives had sewed on emblems with the hammer and sickle, with a red star as field. They helped Rubin up onto the cart and then, with might and main, into his chair. His legs dangled through the hole below him, he looked around contentedly. 'Gerard!' he shouted. 'You make good plane! *Seijas shadu y poletshu*. I go home!' He pointed to himself.

Voorthuis backed the tractor carefully into the shed and used an iron pin to connect the drawbar to the ring on the cart. 'Well, fellas,' he said happily, and rubbed together his work-worn farmer's hands.

At twelve o'clock the floats lined up in the village. The day started with drizzle but would gradually clear up; it was cold and clammy. Rubin sat smoking in his crow's nest, the leather aviator cap on his head. The brass band in the distance was driving the clamour of the Radetzky March down the street in front of it. There they came, marching in their royal blue uniforms, from up towards Sint Jozefschool. The brass blared, the drums at the back rumbled dully. The lime trees stood bare and dark along Dorpstraat, light and the sound of festivities were at this hour already pouring from Cafe De Lindeboom. Waitresses in dirndls ran from table to table with trays of beer. The people sang along loudly with the schlager *Es gibt kein Bier auf Hawaii*. Clemens II, the prince of Carnival, was handed the keys to the town and, after a speech no one could understand, blew his horn, and the whole crowd whirled out onto the street and climbed aboard the floats. In the wake of *When the Saints Go Marching In*, they moved at a snail's pace past the church, the Rabobank, and the shops; every now and then, a shaft of cold sunlight making its way through the cloud cover. The fourth float in the row was the one from Muldershoek. 'Anton!' the people along the street shouted. He smiled and waved to them, and they felt a flush of pride at the fact that he had picked their village to crash in.

The Muldershoek crew members saluted and aimed their hunting rifles at the biplane above them. Sometimes they marched in place to the rhythm of deafening martial music from the speakers at the back of the float. They had a tower of crates of Grolsch on board, Anton helped himself from a bottle of Puschkin. You had to take it easy with vodka, the crew members knew, although that wasn't much of a problem for Anton, he was used to it — but it was a cold day, one little glass couldn't hurt much. Halfway through the second loop around the village, the Red Army was already plastered, and the pilot in his aviator's cap sat on his perch, grinning wetly, with droplets of vodka in his beard.

Harry Voorthuis, who was driving the tractor, looked back in concern now and then at his neighbours, who had taken out the cassette tape with marches in favour of 'Holland's Glory' and were now bawling along with *Tulpen uit Amsterdam*. Stowaways climbed on board, all wanting to shake the Russian's hand.

Paul, dressed as a little farmer, waved his red handkerchief when the float passed the church square, but his father stared glassily over the heads of the crowd and held himself upright by clutching at the warhead of a Scud. There on high, it looked as though Rubin were taking a nap with his head leaning on the edge of the cockpit. Paul and his mother shivered when a cloud passed over the sun. They went to De Lindeboom to wait for the line of floats to return.

They installed Anton Rubin in a chair on the podium of the party hall, where he could observe the goings-on. Crowds of revellers flocked around him and slapped him on the shoulders. Sometimes he roared something no one could understand.

'Hey, 'ton, are ya hungry?' the young bucks shouted as they fed him chunks of bratwurst and poured schnapps from flight bottles straight into his mouth. The strength to raise a glass to his own lips seemed to have left him. The brass band made a circuit around the room, the people formed a conga line behind it.

Paul, standing on a table off to one side, put his hands over his ears. From a distance, his mother saw how the Russian wolfed down sausage and alcohol with equal measures of indifference and regularity. Dutch brandy and curry sauce dripped from his beard. A husky young man took Rubin's head in his arms and held his mouth open so that his companion could pour liquor into it. Yet another sausage was brought in from the mobile snack bar outside; Rubin's jaws slowly ground the meat and schnapps to a homogenous pulp.

'Aloïs!' Alice screamed as her husband swept past in the conga line. 'Aloïs!'

But Aloïs, hands on the shoulders of the man in the peasant blouse in front of him, was deaf to her voice in the hubbub.

She pushed her way towards the podium. Hands slid over her body — they squeezed her rear and her breasts, bound up in the bodice of her dirndl. Anton Rubin, pivot of the bacchanalian frenzy, had gone under in the darkness at the back of his own eyes, his jaws grinding mechanically, no longer feeling the fire in his gullet. The young bucks were busy killing him with bratwurst and alcohol. Every time he fell over forward, they pulled him upright again and stuffed more sausage in his mouth. When he gagged, one of them clasped a hand firmly over his mouth.

'He's choking!' Alice screamed. 'Stop that, right now!'

Her voice went under in the mayhem. Rubin's upper body convulsed. Alice clambered onto the podium and pushed the yokel away with both hands. The Russian fell forward, the laughing people at the edge of the podium shrank back in disgust as he puked, and puked again.

Two men lifted him and carried him outside, in the car he pissed himself. 'Anton!' Alice screamed, and slapped the Russian across the face. At home they put him to bed. Alice pulled his clothes off and cleaned him.

During the days that he remained in bed, recovering from the alcoholic poisoning, she brought him his meals in silence. Standing in the doorway, Paul peeked into the room. Rubin tried to say something, but Alice shook her head sternly. She left the room and closed the door with a click behind her.

Silence, of all punishments, is the hardest to take. Wholehearted, sustained silence, the kind that even a hard-bitten Russian can't take for more than a few days; on the sixth of them, Paul came into the living room and said to his mother: 'He's walking up by the road.'

'Who?'

'Anton.'

She looked up. 'Say that again?'

'He's walking up by the road. There.' Paul pointed outside.

'That can't be,' his mother said. She threw on a coat and raced outside, where a steady, icy rain was falling. She hurried up the drive and across the road. 'Stay there!' she shouted back to Paul. Zipping up her coat, she went after Rubin, who was far up ahead on his crutches. Slung over his shoulder was the linen sack they had given him at the hospital, containing his meagre belongings: letters and postcards from all over the country, a few newspaper clippings, his painkillers. Paul heard his mother's voice: 'Anton! Anton!'

Under the grey oaks, Paul shivered. Not from the cold, but from her voice that was not calling him but the Russian hobbling along the road up there. She crossed the little bridge and caught up with him by the sawmill. Far off, unintelligibly, he heard their voices. That his mother was crying, he could hear that, and that they hugged each other, he saw that — and just as his father would spend the rest of his life regretting that he hadn't left the Russian to die in that field of maize, so Paul would never forgive himself for having warned her when Anton Rubin took off. What if he hadn't done that? What if he had silently let the Russian go? What if.

Twelfth

Mariënveen made the news for the second time in its history when Ronnie Steeghuis reached the finals of *The X Factor*. About a hundred people gathered in the big party room at Shu Dynasty to watch it on the screen that was usually lowered only for important football matches. Ronnie Steeghuis' glory reflected on everyone in the room — he gave them a position in the world, the world that had already long forgotten the adventure with the Russian and never thought twice about Mariënveen anymore. Steeghuis, who in daily life travelled the region as a bar-room crooner, had somehow succeeded each week in making it to the next episode; now, in the final, something was actually on the line. The song he had chosen for tonight was Queen's 'These Are the Days of Our Lives'.

'Homo!' Abbink shouted.

Before he actually went on stage, they saw Steeghuis in a rehearsal room with a piano, being interviewed by host Wendy van Dijk. 'Ronnie Steeghuis, all the way from Mariënveen,' she said maternally. 'Your preparation for the big performance. Your grand finale, it's now or never ...'

What followed was a retrospective of his singing career, how he had made the rounds of the local party centres and old folks' homes as a band singer, before one day deciding to try out for *The X Factor*. With his childishly frank answers in the local dialect, he had achieved a certain cult status as the weeks wore on.

'And what is it,' Wendy van Dijk asked, 'if you look way down deep inside yourself, Ronnie, your dearest, dearest wish?'

'Oh,' he said, 'stayin' healthy. That's the most important thing, innit?'

She broke out laughing at this, yet another disarming reply. 'That's true,' she said, still hiccupping in the aftermath of laughter, 'that's what we all want, of course. But you, Ronnie, if you look way down deep in your heart, what is your dearest wish?'

Ronnie was quiet for a moment. He looked so deeply in his heart that he forgot the most obvious answer — 'Winning *The X Factor*, of course' — shrugged, and spoke the immortal words, 'Movin' out West.'

'You don't fuckin' mean it, do you?' everyone heard Abbink say.

'What a prick,' Paul mumbled in the direction of the big screen.

People got up and left the room. A little later, there was a round of cynical applause when Steeghuis won over one measly jury member, and slunk off ignominiously.

Maybe, Paul thought, and not for the first time, they really were a different brand of people around here. A remarkable residue that the Saxons and Tubantes had left behind when they turned tail and made a run for it. O, such endearing pride: Ronnie Steeghuis, on national television, no less … compensation for a life in the shadows at the far end of the kingdom, far from the sea — but when they asked Ronnie what he truly longed for, the little shit actually went and spoke the truth: that there was nothing here and that everyone who got the chance left as soon as he could. Even the Chinese newcomers looked down on them. Oh sure, they smiled at you the livelong day and were compliant as could be, but no one doubted that, once they were alone behind the swinging kitchen door, they laughed heartily at the local yokels. Day in, day out, you heard the Chinese snorting with laughter at the clodhoppers on the other side of the bar.

Paul was amazed at the chauvinistic pride that had apparently lain hidden at the bottom of his soul, only to be ignited by the appearance of a fellow villager on national television. He stood grumbling to himself as Mama Shu and her daughter Ming went on opening beer bottles and lining them up on the bar. That idiot of a Steeghuis had disgraced them all. Cretins without the talent to succeed anywhere else. Anyone who could do anything got out. Herbert Kieftenbelt, with his transport firm across the border; Henny Löwik, whose name you saw everywhere on big signs beside construction sites; neither of those two had ever come back to Mariënveen. 'From right here in the village,' you said casually when one of them was mentioned. 'Too big for his britches,' you said when someone asked why they never showed up in Mariënveen. And why should they? They had more money than Kloosterzand and Deurlo put together. There was building going on; if at all possible they threw up Saxon houses, historicised fake to be sure, but fine, solid houses. They owned a textile mill and a few more half-timbered farmhouses a few centuries old. Around here, they'd even had to deal with international drug traffickers, everyone had seen that a few years back when they arrested a gang that operated from Cafe Halfweg along the provincial road to Kloosterzand. Cafe Halfweg with its playground where they sold soft ice cream and candy from inside a giant mushroom — when the mushroom opened its doors you knew that spring had come, how much more symbolic did the loss of innocence get? And only last March they had nabbed those men in Mariënveen, in connection with smuggling cocaine into the port of Hamburg. Good God, who would ever have expected that from such a little village!

The screen was rolled up again, the party room and cafe largely emptied out. 'Ming, my sweet thing,' Abbink said, 'give us another one, just like the other one.'

On one occasion, Ming, the eldest of the two Shu children, had made the mistake of saying she would rather spend her time watching TV and living off the dole than putting bottles of beer and plates of fried noodles down in front of them. On one occasion only. From then on, it was Ming Collect-ing.

Paul felt sorry for her. Life had done her no favours. She was skinny as a rail and her teeth were covered in a blue-black film. Her hair was dull and greasy, as though the cooking oil had crept into it at birth and never gone out again. But she possessed the capacity to endure. She smiled at the daisy-chain of rhyming words attached to her name and worked seven days a week without a complaint.

Paul went for Asian women, but not for Ming Shu. He had done his best to lust after her flat rear-end and tried to imagine that she might have nice little breasts or a delicate pussy, but it didn't work. She was actually, he felt, a woman with no clear front or back to her. In his daydreams at times, however, he imagined a life together with her. She was in her mid-30s, so they could still have children. He was almost fifty, but you couldn't tell by looking at him. Maybe he could settle for her, if she would settle for him. But at the end of his musings he always ran into the same old obstacles: he was too old, and Ming was too ugly. Day in, day out, she wore the same black trousers, tied high above her sharp hipbones, and a baggy black t-shirt that made her even more flat and formless.

She came out of the kitchen with a plate of chicken bami ketjap for Alfons Oliemuller.

'Didn't you have dinner yet, Alfons?' one of the Hennies asked.

He nodded, his head down right above the plate.

'What is this, Ming?' he said a little later. 'Was the chicken all finished?' He held his fork out to her across the bar.

Ming looked. 'That chicken, you know,' she said.

'Egg,' said Oliemuller.

'Chicken, sure,' said Ming.

'Taste it,' Oliemuller said. He stepped off his barstool and held the fork in front of her face.

Paul had heard the chicken–egg discussion a number of times before. It was one of the most stubborn suspicions concerning old Mr. Shu, that he fiddled with the chicken.

'I'm not going to take bite from your chicken,' Ming said indignantly.

'You people won't even eat what you put down in front of us,' Oliemuller said grimly. 'That garbage.'

Ming put on her dark-toothed smile. 'It good food, you know, Chinese food! Good for you!'

'So what do you people do with your garbage? You never throw anything away. It's all eaten up. By us.'

And there you had the second stubborn suspicion: that the Chinese used everything, all the food in the kitchen, from bruised right on through to overripe, mouldy, and rotten, everything. Everyone believed it, in the same way everyone went on ordering the fried rice, bami, and noodles as long as the words 'home made' were written after it. Maybe Ming knew her position in the food chain, too, Paul thought, and was realistic enough to expect no more from life than she had coming. In fact, they were both in one and the same boat. Neither of them had ever left their parental home and were, in that sense, still children. Prospects for her were that she would remain childless, too. Caring for her parents was all that lay in store for her. Her father probably wouldn't get very old, Paul thought. He barely had a tooth in his head and, when he was wasn't cooking, he shuffled on slide-on pool shoes with white socks to his table by the window, where he thought his Chinese thoughts and smoked one Marlboro after the other, clenched between ring and middle finger. Mama Shu, on the other hand, was sure to make it to a hundred. Even when Ming was walking to the baker's or taking the bus into the city, he bet she must have been able to hear her invalid mother's plaintive voice. That voice was everywhere, she wouldn't be able to escape it.

He himself sometimes heard his father's voice when he was far from home. *Paul? Paul, where be ya?* That voice carried for miles. What's more, the further away he was from his father, the clearer it sounded. Unremitting and plaintive, that voice resounded in his head, until he drove home and found his father already in bed or sitting at the table, reading a book about the East India Company or the history of Amsterdam, and then looking at his watch with an expression of amazement and the words: 'You'd be early enough t'night, wouldn't you?'

Looking out the window at the Happytaria across the street, Paul saw the light go out in the cooler display filled with chow mein patties, mexicanos, and frikandels. He thought about Baptist, who had married his Chinese woman because when you're in for a penny, you also have to be in for a pound. Lately he had occasionally started adding to that: 'The most expensive pound I ever spent.'

When Baptist came down with cancer, he had handed the Happytaria over to his stepchildren. Wen worked there the most, along with Xi, who she'd met at a Chinese celebration in Osnabrück. Baptist brought their little boy to school each day — hand in hand, they walked along the colonnade of trees past the library. The child was especially gifted. 'His piano lessons are paid for in fries,' Baptist said.

His hair had thinned and turned white. Within only a matter of months, the disease had turned him into an exhausted old man. He spent a lot of time sitting at the window and looking at the women who did their shopping along Dorpstraat, at the Aviko trucks driving by. 'It's amazing,' he said, 'how many people there are walking around a village like this who you've never seen before.'

He had started gardening again, in moderation. Last year, with the radiation therapy, he'd had to let it go. Rosacea brought the flush of blossom to his pale cheeks.

If you asked him 'How was that, having a Chinese wife?', he would lean back in his chair, fold his hands on his stomach, and say drily: 'Oh, you know, I'm as lonely as they get. I can't talk to her about anything. I still have to explain who Angela Merkel is. She follows the news, but only once it's been on Weibo a couple of days later.'

The start, that above all, had been very difficult: the dictionaries, the misunderstandings.

And if you asked Baptist what it was like to suddenly find yourself living among the Chinese, he would reply: 'Oh, it's like being on holiday all the time — I don't understand a word they say.'

But all things considered, he didn't regret the choice he'd made, he said calmly. During the radiotherapy, he couldn't have asked for a better nurse than his wife Lihua. She fixed herbal drinks for him and stuck acupuncture needles in his ears and forehead.

'And now let's just hope that the Big C keeps its head down,' he said.

Now, Xi was straightening the chairs in the Happytaria and turning off the lights. The only light in the place came from the streetlamps. He turned the sign saying closed to face the street, and disappeared into the shadows.

Thirteenth

Slowly they circled the blossoming woods' edge, he and his father. Elder bushes poked their profusion of white cymes towards the light. His father cut off the upper blossoms, Paul did the lower ones. 'Be nice and careful with that, boy,' his father said. 'The pollen's what gives it flavour.'

Behind the elder bushes lay the forest of beech and oak, which continued on the far side of the brook. There it found its limit again at a fallow stretch of high, sandy ground, where lapwings nested on the warm earth.

In the kitchen, his father filled a bucket until the clusters of flowers were under water. He put it in the pantry with a tea towel over it and mumbled, 'So that's that.' The next day, the blossoms floated drably in the bucket; the odour they spread was that of sourish piss. Alice's recipe book lay open on the counter. They brought the mixture to a boil in the biggest pan they had and stirred in citric acid and sugar. Then they ran it through a sieve and poured it into bottles. There weren't nearly enough of those.

In the pantry there were still full bottles from the year before, the white labels inscribed in his mother's precious handwriting:

Elder blossom syrup
Spring '75

Pale eddies of sediment rose from the bottoms of the bottles, transparent nebulae trapped under glass.

This year, the labels were written for the first time in his father's angular, teacher's hand. Everything needed to go on the way it always had.

This ritual would return each spring: he and his father making elder blossom syrup. It was one of the best things Paul had to say about him.

Within those first few months, his father taught himself to cook five different dishes, all of them with potatoes. Five basic meals, he called them, one for each weekday. The weekend was for leftovers. It was amazing, all the things you could do with potatoes. Boiled, mashed, pureed, fried, deep-fried. As sticks, cubes, wedges, and slices, and probably a whole lot more if you gave it some thought. But mashed was how Aloïs loved his potatoes best. They ate hodgepodge all year round. In the spring you could make it with turnip greens and purslane, and in summer with green beans and chard. That was enough to tide you over till the season for kale came around.

Paul peeled the potatoes. That was his task, had been from the word go. First with a peeler and then, when that was accidentally thrown away with the peels, with a knife. He washed the peeled potatoes and put them in a pan filled with water.

While his father cooked, he read *Fingerling Goes on a Trip*. The lid rattled. As the lump of Croma was melting in the pan, his father went into the garden with a colander to gather lettuce leaves. He mumbled approvingly to the vegetables. The kale was coming up, the beans had already wound their way to the ends of their poles. It wouldn't be long before they were eating green beans each and every day.

As soon as the ground-beef rolls began hissing in the fat, Paul set the table. His father made the gravy in accordance with what he claimed was an old family recipe. He slid the meat to one side of the pan and sautéed an onion. He added ketchup and mustard and mixed it all together. Then came his secret weapon: a dash of unsweetened coffee creamer. Add water, and bingo — there was his gravy, that faithful sidekick to the potato. That's the way he had learned to do it long ago, from his mother, he said, and that's the way he taught his son to do it, too.

'Did they have unsweetened coffee creamer back then?' Paul asked. 'And ketchup?' But his father insisted that the recipe was authentic.

A few minutes later, they folded their hands for a moment of silence. Paul examined the red haze behind his eyelids, a sunrise on Mars.

'And bless it to its intended use, amen,' said his father. He still wore his wedding ring. Because what if she came back someday?

'Amen,' Paul said as well. He mashed the steaming yellow potatoes with the back of his fork and arranged them in a landscape with a basin in the middle. For the gravy. Gradually, the lake swelled over its shores and washed down across the lowlands.

At Christmas, in a Van der Valk roadside restaurant, Paul had heard his father ask for an extra boat of gravy. He reacted to the waitress's amazement with the words: 'Because we're mushy eaters.'

Soup they never ate, for they had gravy.

A pillar of smoke rose up above the poplars, downstream along the brook. Masselink burning his rubbish.

No one ate slower than his father, that was humanly impossible. 'I still have to do some homework,' Paul said sometimes, but his father was like a donkey that takes two steps faster after receiving a smack to the haunches, then slows to the same pace as before. While Paul waited, he thought about school, his mother, the boys he hung around with. Everything, everyone. The past, the present, the things to come. Absurd prospects for the future.

The ceiling creaked again, like a galleon under full sail. It had been creaking up there for as long as anyone could remember. His father told him once about how, as a boy, he had lain awake all night in terror, staring at the ceiling, the floor of the big, empty attic where a gladiatorial battle was taking place. All hell had broken loose there, the beams groaned and the plank floor screeched as though the nails were being yanked out of it, and he lay riveted to his bed.

Aloïs immediately seemed to regret having told him about that.

Later, there were nights when Paul experienced the very same thing.

Now, he pricked up his ears, tried to pinpoint exactly where in the attic the noise was coming from. There was definitely life up there. No marten or rat. Bigger. Different. And not only there. Sometimes he saw things in the living room. A long chain of pilot flames, flickering blue and sliding energetically around the room. They went off in the direction of the back room, where they dissolved. He felt no fear of them; the blue flames were a familiar presence.

His ninth birthday — the new potatoes had been lifted from the fields. The machines slid growling over the earth. Summer, a sudden heightening of the heat just before the thunderstorm came. The wind dragged like a rake across the land. Huge clouds of dust rose heavenwards.

'Is she going to come today?' he asked his father.

'No idea,' Aloïs said. 'Don't count on anything. That's the best way.'

Paul peeled the potatoes doggedly. The wicker basket on his lap, he thought about the lives of the Bintjes slipping hard and dustily through his hands. They had been incubated in the warm earth, to fill their peels fine and firmly in the dry darkness. Having developed into sturdy tubers, they knew nothing of the dust and summer storms above their heads. How the greens were sprayed and the entire field lay wilted as though by a curse. The potato knew nothing, ignorant of all from start to finish.

Before they sat down at the table, his father gave him a model. A Panzer tank, manned by two Afrika Korps soldiers. 'I can still remember being nine,' his father said. For dessert, they had a cream slice.

Ever since she'd left, the house was draughty. Cold wafted from the kitchen cupboard when Paul opened it; when he kneeled beside his bed for prayers at night, a cold breath of air swirled around his legs.

She had come to pick up her clothing and household items in the spring, with a van.

The Russian stood smoking in the driveway, beside the wreckage of his plane. He raised a hand and waved to Paul, who was looking at him from a distance. Paul raised his hand, but let it fall again halfway through. The Russian felt at the canvas of the Kukuruznik, his fingers slid across the spots where the textile had been repaired. That, that was his skin, and he himself, he had been the flaming heart of that aeroplane-body.

Inside, his mother was rummaging through the cupboards. One moving crate after the other she filled with dresses, shoes, and underwear. She carried the boxes through the living room and hallway and handed them to the Russian at the door, who took them to the van. He still had a slight limp.

His father was sitting slumped at the kitchen table, reading the Saturday newspaper. Alice carried a box outside marked 'winter clothes'.

A little later, from the kitchen, she asked: 'This one, Aloïs?'

He looked up. She held up the frying pan. 'My mother's,' he said.

She nodded and put the pan back in the cupboard. When he heard the tinkling of cutlery, he looked up. 'Put that back,' he said.

She stuck out her chin. 'We got these from my parents,' she said.

'Back.'

'I'm not your dog.'

He rose to his feet. 'Put it back. And fast.'

'Damn it, Aloïs, this is my parents' wedding silver!'

Rounding the table, he was in the kitchen in a few steps. 'You goddamn leave that here.' He was panting.

'Who do you think you are,' she said, 'giving me orders …' She tossed the silver-plated Gero cutlery into the moving crate, using both hands.

He yanked a cloth from the hook on the wall and hit her across the face with it.

'Aloïs!' Silverware crashed to the kitchen floor.

'Maybe you're not married anymore,' he yelled, 'but I still am!'

In the living room, she knelt down beside Paul. She rubbed her teary face against his. He shivered with pleasure. From the kitchen came the noise of a cutlery drawer being dumped on the floor.

'Mama,' Paul asked, 'am I staying here?'

'Yes, love,' she answered, 'that's for the best. Believe me.'

'But why?'

'Because … because you and your father …' She struggled to smile, her voice grew quieter. 'Your daddy can't stay here alone, now can he? Can he?' She used the cuff of her blouse to wipe the tears from the corners of his eyes. 'Your daddy needs you, sweetheart.'

'But I want to live with you,' Paul whispered.

She caressed his head. 'That can't be, darling. Really not.'

'But why not?'

She took his face in her hands and held it against hers again. Her voice in his ear. 'This is the best thing for you. For you and your daddy. It doesn't seem like it to you right now … Later on you'll understand that it's for the best. Really.'

He wrapped his arms around her more tightly, but she squirmed out of his embrace and stood up. He held on to her leg. 'Ssh, ssh, quiet now,' she said, and caressed his hair. His eyes closed, he said *I don't want to be left alone, I don't want to be left alone*, and straight through it all there arose in him the memory of a fairy tale in which a little girl fell into a well and kept on falling, until at last she fell asleep.

Fourteenth

'We have to make do with what we have, buddy,' his father said sometimes in those first days, in the same absent-minded fashion that he spoke to the plants he tended, and also to the car when it wouldn't start. He had, he confessed later, thought about sending Paul to a Catholic boarding school. After all, what did he know about bringing up a child? What you needed in order to do that? The presence of a child kept him from throwing himself fully into his own unhappiness, which was perhaps his natural tendency. You had to have bread in the pantry and a warm meal on the table at night. Clothes in the cupboard and shoes on his feet.

Aloïs went to the shed and took out an old bicycle that had been his father's. The tyres were flat, the frame covered with a sticky layer of dust. When the summer holidays were over, he would not be able to take his son to school in the morning, the way Alice always had. He lifted Paul onto the saddle and saw that his feet couldn't reach the pedals. 'I thought you were bigger than that,' he said. The truth was that Paul was the smallest child in the class, and would never be taller than five feet and six inches.

He had the bike fixed up at Busscher's shop in the village. 'Solid material from the north of Groningen, the Fongers is,' Busscher said. 'They don't make them like this anymore.'

Paul got used to it, to standing on the pedals as he biked.

Sometimes he would rest by sitting on the crossbar.

His father cooked, Paul cycled to school standing up, and in the evening he peeled the potatoes. Countless sandy spuds passed through his hands in the course of time. After dinner, he did the washing up.

As time passed, he sometimes forgot what his mother looked like. Every bit as sad as her absence was the way her face faded; he could only make her translucent portrait adopt two or three expressions, a gross reduction that caused him pain.

In the autumn holiday of the first year of her absence, she was going to take him along to one of the Wadden islands. That day he waited in vain for her to show up.

She didn't come to his tenth birthday. On 20 July 1978, he turns eleven. The day looms up before him, massive, a glacial wall. It turns out to be a day like all the rest. He reads *King Ottokar's Sceptre*, cycles to the textile mill to see if there is anything of interest in the rubbish bins, and tosses stones through the windows of an old pig shed outside Huzink. When his father gets home, the potatoes are peeled and in the pan of water.

'Eleven,' his father says, holding him by his biceps. 'Eleven already.'

The box from the bakery shop contains two cream slices.

At nine-thirty he goes to bed. The last bit of sunlight slips through the cracks in his curtains. He buries his head in his pillow and calls for his mother the way a man in his hour of death calls for his mother.

In the autumn, after church one Sunday, they take a walk to the border. His father has heard that concrete blocks have been placed on the path, after two customs men were shot and killed earlier that week in Limburg by the Red Army Faction. It is a warm autumn day; Aloïs has his overcoat folded over one arm. They pass Kamphuis' pig sheds, from which emanates the biting smell of ammonia, and a cowshed where the animals rattle against the fence as they go by. The oak trees still have a few red and yellow leaves, the sandy path rises gradually in the direction of the border. Aloïs stops and looks around. Deep, golden light foams up around him. 'Sand ridge,' he says, and the sweep of his arm takes in the wide surroundings. For centuries, farmers have lived on the flanks of these rises in the landscape, like the one on which their house is built. The farmers who settled there first are still the richest ones.

Sometimes his father is in the mood to talk. He knows about things of which he usually doesn't speak; perhaps he saves them for his pupils. That an eternal storm rages on the surface of Jupiter, one that was already in progress when Paul was born and will still be going when he breathes his last. That the camel has two rows of eyelashes and can close its nostrils against the sand. That hares have no odour at all for a few days after they are born.

Sometimes those things suddenly rise to the surface, like old secrets.

On some evenings here on Grensweg, the sandy road running beneath these trees, you might see a Mercedes loaded with piglets or calves crossing the border, but the smuggling is fairly modest in scope. They can see the concrete blocks in the distance already.

The farmers who lived here in the olden days, his father tells him, sowed their grain along the high, sandy ridge and let their cattle graze on lower ground. For the peat cutters who came centuries later, even as late as the nineteenth century, there was room only down below. If you showed up with your belongings in the morning and by nightfall had built a sod cabin with four walls and a chimney that smoked, the peat boss would let you stay. It was a harsh existence. A plate of potatoes and a downpour, that was their diet.

The peat cutters drained the bogs and dug them; in their back gardens, they grew buckwheat and spuds.

Paul tries to keep up with his father's pace and thinks about the farmers who rule over the land from high atop their Massey Fergusons and John Deeres. Things have gone well with them, over time, although no farmer would ever admit that.

The concrete blocks are standing in the middle of the shaded path. There is just enough room for a cyclist to pass through. On the other side is a fork in the path — you can either turn right or go straight ahead into Germany, where the sandy paths lose themselves amid a web of paved roads.

Right on the border itself are three customs houses with wooden facades and a dip in the roof, built in the days that customs officials still patrolled the border canal. A car with the word *Zoll* on it is parked with its front bumper pointed into the Netherlands. Two customs officials are sitting in it. They have taken off their caps and stuck them between the dashboard and the windscreen. His father goes up and talks to them, bent over beside the window, which is open a crack. The driver stares straight ahead the whole time Aloïs is talking. Then a nod, they are allowed to walk on. Only fifty yards later does the servile smile slip from Aloïs' face.

In the back gardens of the customs houses, the cornstalks droop and the curly kale stands waiting for the first night of frost. They walk down the gently winding customs path along the border with Lower Saxony.

Whereas the Dutch landscape to their right has a roll to it, on the German side it has been levelled by brute force, a tablecloth without creases. On the Dutch side you can still see a section of a low, elongated hill, covered in brambles and low oak.

This is unique, his father says, look here. They examine the hill's innards, a cross section of gravel and rocks. His father describes to Paul the end of an ice age, a melting glacier covers the land. With great force, a river of smelt water races beneath the icecap, carrying rocks and stones along with it. Gradually the tunnel in the ice becomes clogged with stones, like a blocked artery. The temperature goes on rising until all the snow and ice has disappeared; in the landscape the stones in the river of smelt water remain behind, in the form of a long, meandering embankment. That is what they are looking at now, a river of stone, straight through the heart of the next-to-last ice age. It is the only esker in the country.

Paul takes in the sight and imagines life on earth without him in it. The earth turns cold and barren, the light is cold as a pane of glass. Inky blue storms roar across the polar desert. And the winter lasts a thousand years, ten thousand years, and when the cold finally gives way he is standing there in the silvery morning when everything creaks and glistens, in which drops become rivulets and rivulets streams.

His father is sitting on a tree trunk in the sun. Paul is hungry but they haven't brought anything to eat. A sand drift in the woods, glimpses of the fields and heath through the trees. In the sand, Paul finds a few potato plants. He pulls on them and pulls up red-skinned potatoes, attached to the plant by hair-roots. He digs them up one by one; the luck of the treasure hunter is with him. It is a whole pile of them. Excitedly, he roots through the chilly soil and collects them all. It's a mystery how they got there.

'Nice German spuds,' says his father a little later, and spreads his coat out on the ground. He places the potatoes in it, folds the coat, and lifts the load by the sleeves, which he has tied to make a handle. 'Whoo,' he says.

They cut across the fields towards their house. Hares run out in front of them.

They cross the Molenbeek close to the house of the Oude Wesselink brothers. Paul went in there one time, after picking damson plums beside the brook. They had a well in the attached stables and a humming kettle on a spirit stove. The dirt and cobwebs on the windows made it hard to look out. They were as old as trees, the brothers were, and just as friendly. 'We're so old,' they said in voices that creaked, 'that no one knows how old we are.'

Paul didn't know what to say to them. From a cupboard they produced a pack of glazed cookies from the Attent grocery store in Kloosterzand and watched as he ate; their thick grey socks shuffled over the flagstones. They had tinkered with time, the two of them, until finally it had stopped working.

Fifteenth

The Russian ate fries, Baptist said. He spoke a little German but didn't say much, just sat beside the fruit machine looking at his phone. After finishing his fries, he had ordered an XXL frikandel and a mexicano. Then he drove off in Steggink's Ferrari.

Paul kept looking at Baptist, but that was all he had to say.

'Can't be trusted,' Paul said.

'Couldn't tell by looking at him,' said Baptist.

'Just wait and see,' said Paul, reaching for the regional section of the newspaper. Baptist took the rest. Paul read about a man who was run over by a tractor while driving his quad bike. A family tragedy: the victim was the son-in-law of the man driving the tractor. Paul looked up. If you were to light a candle for everyone who died, at the spot where it happened, you wouldn't have room to walk. Dorpstraat would be a sea of tapers, the world an All Hallows' Eve of cosmic proportion, the planet a blazing torch hurtling through the universe.

Wen sat on her stool behind the display case, waiting till the fries were done. She smiled at her phone. Paul turned the page. A Bulgarian had been picked up at the border. They'd caught him slashing open truck tarps in the parking lot at the Avia station. His partners were still at large. On the next page, the number of burglaries and car thefts in the region had risen for the third year running. The police planned to set up a special mobile unit to deal with it.

Paul looked across the street. There was movement behind the windows at Shu. The first modular police station outside Mariënveen, he thought, was twenty minutes away. It was only during the weekend alcohol controls that they ever saw a police car. The people here paid taxes just like everyone else, but reaped only half the advantages. In the case of burglaries and robberies, it sometimes took an hour for the police to arrive; if you had a heart attack, the neighbour's car got you to the hospital faster than the ambulance.

'Do you have any idea what that is,' he asked Baptist, 'a "mobile unit"? Says here that the police are planning to set up a mobile unit.'

'That they climb into a car?' Baptist offered. 'And then drive around?'

'Yeah, must be something 'long those lines, yeah.'

Wen put his plate on the table. 'Taste wonderful, Paul.'

Sweet, pretty Wen.

'*Bon appetit*,' Baptist said. The corners of his mouth were inflamed. They looked red and painful. Back when he was fighting cancer, he hadn't come to the Happytaria for a long time. He said he couldn't tolerate the odour of dead meat. *Horror carnis*.

'And how's business, Paul?' Baptist asked.

That morning he had made sixteen packages ready for posting. German bayonets for America, an SS uniform to Norway, and a shipment of American gas masks to Belgium. Large packages for Germany he took himself to the post office in Stattau — that saved a pretty penny.

'The further in the past the war gets,' Paul said, 'the more business I get off of it …'

Baptist nodded. He told Paul about the Vietnam film he'd seen on television, and said: 'I think by now there have been pretty much more Hollywood soldiers in Vietnam than there ever were real ones, don't you think?'

'Pretty sure you're right,' Paul said.

Baptist was quiet for a bit. Then he said: 'There has to be someone who keeps track of that on the Internet. Some nut somewhere.'

'Bet there is,' said Paul. He jabbed his fork into a few fries and read about stretches of farmland being given back to Nature. The people left, perfectly good farmland returned to forest, swamp, flats. A little while back, there had been a wolf walking around close to the border. A couple of people had seen it. The photos were grainy and vague, but it did indeed look like a wolf. That was the status quo in this part of the country: a wolf, sure, but no ATM. They'd taken it away from the village. Too few transactions.

Baptist, who'd been living with his Chinese wife in the apartment across from the machine for the last few years, now had a view of a big piece of particle board they had screwed into the wall where the dispenser had been. 'Still, it's like a part of yourself's been taken away,' had been his comment. 'Some mornings there was people standing in line for it. And sometimes if you looked out the window at night, you saw a customer, too.'

If you wanted, you could now withdraw up to fifty euros extra at the Plus. In a shrinkage region, that's the way you lived your way around what was missing.

Baptist coughed. The sound was like something breaking inside him.

That afternoon, Paul drove his father to the hospital. The new Saksonia Medical Centre, shiny and square, had arisen between the wooded banks and stands of ash. In the corridor, Aloïs pointed the way. 'Don't worry, I know how to get around here,' Paul said. The wheelchair in which he pushed his father dated back to the days of the Russian. Paul had brought it in from the stable, cleaned it up, and pumped up the tires. The crackly rubber squeaked on the linoleum of the hospital floor.

The lift took a long time to arrive. This is my life, Paul thought, I keep the dying company.

An Asiatic nurse came to fetch them from the waiting room. She showed them the way to a little room off to one side. A Filipino, Paul figured. She spoke Dutch without an accent. Adopted, maybe.

She helped his father out of the wheelchair and, on the edge of the bed, removed his trousers. She was small, a silver crucifix gleamed at her throat. He watched her broad hips as she went to get the doctor. His lust was worrisome. It gushed out on all sides.

The skin on his father's thighs hung in folds. His lower legs were dry and scaly, fed upon by fungi. After a certain age, everybody looked like a photo from Auschwitz, Paul thought.

The tissue around the wound was red and shiny. Ronnie Steeghuis was right — good health was all you really wanted. Good health, a good woman, and a couple of euros in the bank.

It had started out as an innocent enough little cut; his father had paid no attention to it. By the time he first pointed it out to his son, it had already grown quite deep. Paul was frightened when he saw something white glistening at the back of it, fearing it was the bone itself. How it had happened, his father wasn't sure anymore; maybe he had bumped it against something.

In old age, the little details could suddenly bring you down. Paul thought about his father with only one leg. He feared that that would exceed his competency as 'informal care-giver'. Until now, he had not had to wash his father or put him to bed, but a future in which such bodily intimacies would be required of him loomed on the horizon.

'Gentlemen,' the doctor said. He shook their hands. He looked tanned and healthy, as though he had just hopped off his yacht to cure the ailing. Amid the grey hairs rising from his collar hung a Star of David in gold.

All we need now is a headscarf and all the revelatory desert religions will be in the room, Paul thought.

The doctor took a pair of latex gloves from a box and leaned over his father's leg. He gestured to Paul. 'Look here … And here. Can you see that? The blood circulation is very limited, the wound can't heal like this.' He stripped off the gloves and placed them in the waste bin. Turning to the computer, he consulted the patient dossier.

'You've had Broxil, I see.'

'Could be,' said Aloïs.

Paul nodded. 'He's had that.'

'I'm going to prescribe flucloxacillin right now; that's a narrow-spectrum antibiotic. And it's more or less our last resort. I expect it ought to do it. If it doesn't, then I'll want to have you admitted for a while, to see whether we can solve the problem here. Shall we agree on that?'

Before they had even stepped out of the lift, the memory of the nurse had begun to fade. A few years back her sweet face would have tormented him for days. It was better this way. Quieter and better. To Paul, this seemed like the first step on the way to accepting death.

His father's hands were folded in his lap. His scalp, covered in little cuts and scabs, shone through the thin white hair. A life without him was unimaginable. The Preacher of Ecclesiastes, Paul's favourite Bible character, had said that what is lacking cannot be counted. The Preacher's profane fatigue always made him feel happy, as though he had run into an old friend. Whenever Oswaldo Teixeira, the Brazilian priest who served Mariënveen and the surrounding parishes, read from the book of Ecclesiastes, it made Paul's day.

While Paul went into the pharmacy, his father waited in the car. The woman behind the counter performed her tasks without haste. The machine where one took a number had a calmative effect on the waiting, everyone sat back and relaxed. He looked at the posters for Vichy and Azaron, and examined the revolving rack of folders. What to do in the event of a cold sore. Of hay fever. Of intestinal parasites or fungus. Of cancer. He took a seat. Cold sores and cancer didn't go together. Neither did hay fever and intestinal parasites. Magnetic poles that repelled. Cancer and intestinal parasites were the only thing he was sure of. They went together.

The display above the counter jumped a digit — it was his turn. He pulled the prescription out of his back pocket, the pharmacist's assistant read it and looked at him.

'Krüzen,' she said, and nodded. Her hair was short and practical, it had a dark auburn glow to it. At the roots, the grey had grown out half an inch or so.

'*Paul* Krüzen,' she said then.

He smiled shyly.

'It's so nice,' she said. 'How are you doing?' She slid her reading glasses up onto her hair, the earpieces purple, the frames red.

'Fine, fine,' he said. 'And you?'

'*Comme ci, comme ça,*' she said. 'And where do you live these days? What kind of work do you do?'

'Mariënveen,' he said quickly. 'Curiosa.' A quick laugh. 'That's my business.'

'Still there? Man.'

He tossed a glance over his shoulder. Two old people nodded at him encouragingly.

'I'm so happy to see you again,' the woman said. 'And that I recognised you right away, funny isn't it?'

Absently, she scanned the prescription in her hand, then looked up again. She frowned. Then she blurted out: 'You really don't see it, do you? You just don't see it.'

He shrugged apologetically. 'I've never been very good at faces.'

'Ineke Wessels,' she said.

He smiled gratefully. 'Ineke Wessels. Now I see it.' But her face was just as unfamiliar to him as it had been a moment ago. Her name made him think of class pictures, the mixed groups formed after the merger of the local boys' and girls' schools. A girl in a blue, pleated skirt, always somewhere at the back. Part of the little army of the anonymous who remained in the background, even in photographs. That girl had become this noisy woman.

'But I definitely remember you,' she said resolutely. Her smile seemed to forgive him, but he was wrong about that. 'You had trouble keeping up. Anaemia, wasn't that it? At least I think that's what they always said.'

He nodded and relaxed. Her revenge had descended right away, there was a fair chance that she would now fill the prescription and be done with it. 'That's right, yeah,' he said. 'Slow. Still am.'

Now he saw himself too, in his memory's collection of primary school pictures. First at Sint Jozefschool, amid only boys in shirts with high collars and blazers in primary colours. The girls had come along later. With the girls, there also appeared the printed t-shirts and bellbottom trousers — the 1960s had taken ten years to get to Mariënveen. The powerlessness and revulsion of those days was what he remembered best; he was happy when it was over and never longed for it again.

Ineke Wessels had disappeared into the back of the shop. Behind a pane of opaline glass he could see her bent over her work. Beside him, the other assistant was helping a workman covered in a layer of white powder.

'Well, Paul Krüzen,' she said belligerently a little later, 'it was great seeing you again, you know.' She slid the box across the counter. 'Four times a day 500 milligrams with water and read the instructions carefully before use.'

He stuck the box in his pocket. 'Well, toodle-oo, okay.'

It was too bad he'd disappointed her, he thought on his way to the car, but she had brought down misfortune on herself by assuming that, as a woman of almost fifty, she differed little from the girl she had once been.

He slid in beside his father. 'It took a little longer,' he said. 'I ran into someone.'

Aloïs turned his head towards him, deliberately as a tortoise. 'Who was that?'

'A girl from my class, back then.'

His father nodded. 'I saw a woman, too,' he said. 'With a dog. The dog shat on the sidewalk. She thought no one was watching.' He grinned. 'Then she saw me … Those are the fun moments in life.'

One morning, a few days later, the phone rang. Paul answered it.

'Hello?' a woman's voice at the other end said questioningly.

'Krüzen here,' said Paul.

'Paul? Oh, hi! This is Ineke. Ineke Wessels. I got your number from the files at the pharmacy. That's not actually allowed, but necessity's the mother, right?'

It was silent for a moment. 'Yes, I suppose so,' Paul said then.

Her nervous laugh. 'I was sort of nasty to you, I think. I didn't mean to be.'

'Didn't notice,' said Paul. 'Don't worry about it.'

'That's the way it felt. I feel sorry about that. I wanted to apologise.'

'No need,' Paul said.

Once again, a brief silence fell.

'What I was wondering, Paul,' she said then, 'was if maybe you'd like to come by sometime for a cup of coffee? Chat a little about the old days and stuff. I live in Avermaten.'

'Sure,' Paul said.

They agreed that he would come by on Saturday afternoon. 'Goudsbloem 37,' she said. He jotted it down and hung up.

In the bedroom, his father was sitting on the edge of the bed. His big yellow feet looked stuck to the linoleum.

'Who was that?'

'That woman.'

'What woman?'

'The one from the pharmacy, day before yesterday or whenever it was.'

'And?'

'No ands. Just called.'

'Is she coming over?'

Paul grinned.

'Good thing, then,' his father said contentedly. 'I go out and she comes in.'

Sixteenth

He didn't see the Russian again until Club Pacha that Friday evening. The letters of the neon sign outside winked invitingly. As they turned the car into the car park, Hedwig said: 'Don't start clipping the girls' clothes off again, all right?'

He glanced over. 'All right, Mr Millionaire. Long as you pick up the tab.'

The Russian was sitting at the bar. His broad rear-end stuck out on both sides of the stool. Paul resisted the urge to turn on his heels and leave.

'Evening, gents,' Steggink said. Standing behind the high section of the bar, he took his tropical hardwood telephone from his ear for a moment and nodded.

'A coke and a beer,' Paul said to the Polish lady bartender. She had been working here for years, silent as a stone. The Russian glanced up from his phone. Had he forgotten that he'd seen them at Shu a while back? He turned back to the little screen. What's wrong, didn't your mother teach you manners? Paul thought. The man was just as impolite as the surly Russians who nearly drank themselves to death at the all-inclusive resorts in Thailand or the Philippines. They spent all day scarfing down food and knocking back drinks like machines, moving occasionally from the bar to the beach and from the beach to the restaurant. It was as though they had just been released from the gulag, and were celebrating their new-won freedom with this joyless bacchanal.

This Russian was that kind of Russian, Paul thought.

Hedwig nipped at his soft drink.

'So where are we going this year?' Paul asked.

Hedwig shrugged. 'As long as it's warm,' he squeaked.

'Remember Cambodia?' Paul asked.

Hedwig shook his head. Paul reminded him about their visit to Sihanoukville, a cheerless place with lovely, albeit polluted, beaches. The tall, slender Khmer girls in the massage parlours, with their slanted eyes and deep-brown skin, had been a good deal less cagey than their Thai colleagues.

But Sihanoukville had slipped out of Hedwig's mind completely.

Rita made her entrance in a black negligee.

'My my,' Paul said.

'*Mi amor*,' said Rita, kissing him lightly on the lips. '*Cómo estás*?' There were labels sticking out of her pants and bra, too. Why didn't anybody ever tell them that? They should no more have labels sticking out of their underwear than hair in their armpits.

Hanging from the little chain around her neck was the medallion of the Blessed Rita he had given her. He wore one just like it. He and Hedwig had once spent a holiday on the island of Boracay. They'd never been so far from home before. One day, Hedwig gave him a medallion he'd bought from someone on the street, with the Blessed Rita on it. Her portrait, surrounded by roses, a vine and the words:

STA RITA ORA PRO NOBIS

BLESSED RITA, PRAY FOR US.

'For me?' Paul had asked in surprise, because Hedwig had never given him anything before.

Hedwig grinned.

Not only was Rita the patroness of hopeless cases, but also of barren women and women who were unhappily married, as well as butchers and meat traders.

Later that afternoon, Hedwig showed him the little stand with Catholic paraphernalia, and Paul bought an identical one for Rita. She wore her name saint's pendant day and night.

He ordered a Bailey's for her and they withdrew to a corner of the couch. She caressed his thigh. They were so familiar with each other that he sometimes fantasised that she would move in with him, that they would have a life together. She had a son and daughter in the Philippines, his life would be the spitting image of Baptist's. But he'd had bad experiences before. Ten years ago, he had asked Lalita, from Thailand, to move in with him. They had met at a brothel in Nordhorn. He was head over heels in love; it took three months for him to discover that she was hooking on the side and stealing money from him. A phone and a car were all she'd needed to go on prostituting herself. She visited her customers in the little Renault Twingo he'd bought for her; after a while, Hedwig had laid it on him drily: 'So follow her next time, if you don't believe me. Like you're still wet behind the ears.'

It had cost him twenty thousand euros and a cherished illusion, but he finally took Lalita back to the brothel where he'd found her and never saw her again.

His father bore her presence patiently, saying only after she'd left: 'You're better off being rid of that one. She lies like a rug.'

With Rita it would be different. She was Catholic, like him, the homey smell of the Mother Church. He trusted her, but never asked her: the first whore in his house had barred the way for the second.

Steggink left his regular spot at the bar and sat down beside Hedwig. While Rita was tickling the palm of his hand, Paul heard Steggink tell Hedwig that he ought to let his money work for him; wouldn't he be interested in investing in the club? In becoming a partner? Sharing in the profits? 'You're stealing from yourself if you put it in savings these days, at 0.1 per cent,' was the last thing Paul heard him say before he and Rita disappeared into a back room.

In the room at the end of the hall, she closed the door behind them and bolted it. Her negligee slid to the floor. Her skin gleamed in the indirect light. The room had a low bed with a nightstand beside it, for the condoms and lubricant. Special services were available on request, but as he and Rita became closer the little perversities had made way for a form of conjugal intimacy, tracing out patterns of behaviour that they, just as in a marriage, could no longer avoid. She pattered over to the bed on her short legs and lay down on it. '*Du, komm,*' she whispered.

'Are you in some hurry, lady?' Paul said. He folded his clothes and laid them on the chair beside the door. Naked, he crossed the room to her. In the course of time, when it came to her, he had lost his shame. He slipped into her embrace. The warmth of her body was the greatest pleasure she gave him. He cupped his hand over her cunt, as though shushing it. It glowed in the palm of his hand. After she had put a condom on him, they fucked with no further ado, him on top, she on the bottom, her ankles crossed around his backside. She was close-shaven, the unruly hairs that remained scratched against his skin and aroused him further. His hands slid between her buttocks. Slowly, he pushed his nails into the soft flesh around her anus. Inside her, he became even harder. Her breathing at his ear, the moaning of a dog; he could smell the cigarettes on her breath.

He had never dared to ask her about her own pleasure. He could have, in the beginning, casually, but the moment had passed long ago.

She rubbed her breasts against his ribcage. He lowered his head and she raised them to his mouth. He took the left nipple — big and dark, as though she was pregnant — in his mouth and sucked it. His orgasm came not long afterwards, a sensation of extreme fluidity, as though he had cast himself off inside her.

He lay on her like a stone. When she tried to push him off, he made himself even heavier. '*Du, zu schwer!*' she groaned. He grinned and slid off of her.

She took the condom from his shrinking member, tied a knot

in it, and dropped it in the little galvanized Ikea bin. They smoked. Calm, sated.

Rita blew a jet of smoke at the ceiling and said '*weiß nicht*' when he asked, casually, what the Russian was doing hanging around the club.

Did he work here? Paul persevered, or did he maybe do other jobs for Steggink?

She repeated that she had no idea. '*Nur Freund, wie du.*'

Her children's father worked on a ferry between Stockholm and Tallinn, he came home twice a year, for a week. The children were growing up with her in-laws, sometimes she saw them on Skype. But that always made her cry, so she preferred not to call them.

Paul had helped her once to send them a huge package of Nikes, baseball caps, and brand-name clothing. He took it to the post office in Stattau and lifted the box onto the counter. There, safely registered, went a mother's love.

Rita sat up, grabbed the sheet that had slid down to the end of the bed, and shook it out with a handy flick of the wrist. The sheet slowly drifted down over their bodies, the flow of air from underneath it touched his face. Paul thought about the Blessed Rita. According to legend, a swarm of bees had draped a white sheet over her after she died. And so, in 1447, her life ended as it had begun — in the cradle, bees had crawled in and out of her mouth to feed her with honey.

She'd had a tough life, St Rita had. She wanted to enter the convent, but at a young age she was married off to a bully with whom she had two sons. When he was killed by a rival, the boys swore to avenge his death. In her prayers, Rita begged God to prevent this, because she would rather see her sons dead than have them carry out their vengeance — upon which the two suddenly died and the path was cleared for her to become a nun and dedicate herself to her love for Christ.

Rita of Cascia hadn't flinched at giving up her offspring for the sake of her great love, just like his own mother, Paul thought sarcastically.

Long ago, his mother and her Russian had ended up in Germany, in a small town between Nordhorn and Osnabrück. They ran, or so he was told, a little aerodrome outside Werdingen. On the day Paul got his driver's licence, he bought a Toyota Carina for four hundred guilders and drove to Werdingen, hoping to catch a glimpse of her. It had been ten years since he'd last seen her. He drove past the sign pointing to the aerodrome a few times, saw small planes taking off straight above him and others coming in for a landing, but didn't dare to take the turn-off. He chose instead to rely on pre-ordained coincidence — which would summon up her appearance at the local petrol station where he stopped to fill the car, or at the Cambodian restaurant outside the linear village where he sat at a window table late that afternoon, eating deep-fried chicken rolls and waiting impatiently for her arrival. The script was clear: all she had to do was turn into the car park at the restaurant along the canal and pick up a takeaway meal for herself and her Russian. There, sitting by the window, she would see a young man who looked at her and made her feel vaguely uncomfortable. She had the feeling that she knew him.

Those were the thoughts running through his mind as the time passed, and the chance that she would appear from his fantasies like a film star stepping off the screen grew smaller and smaller.

On the wall was a frame in which effect lighting created the illusion of a fast-moving waterfall. At the back of the dining room was an exercise bike and a portable table with empty hot plates on it, blinking like new coins. Mute was the world and deaf it remained to his pleas.

When dusk began to build up above the canal, he left the restaurant, watched by the Cambodian hostess and her elderly father. Wefts of mist hung over the water.

Was she still alive, he asked himself as he crushed his cigarette in the ashtray Rita held out to him. In August, she would turn seventy-six. He would have heard if she had died; Aunt Marion would have told him.

Seventeenth

The news of Horseradish Hedwig's millions spread like the flu. Petey Peep, wealthy as Croesus, who would ever have thought? The greengrocer's son as millionaire seemed so improbable that everyone in the village believed it right away. He lived in the shadows, his paltry dry-goods store was the perfect cover for boundless riches. It was the kind of story people can't get enough of. One had to make do with so much second-hand gossip and backbiting, this at last was something to put a gleam in your eye.

Did Hedwig notice it himself? Did he know people were talking about him? Paul doubted it — people had been gossiping about him all his life, about his voice, his predilections, the little store he defended with stubborn courage against the axe blows of time. Tongues had always wagged about him — he probably didn't notice anything unusual. He lived in seclusion, and although in twenty years the edge of the village had advanced almost to his door, the distance between Hedwig and the village had remained the same. The death of first his father and then his mother had made a loner out of him for good, a man with a private life about which no one knew the ins and outs. The last time Paul had been inside the house itself was years ago. The curtains remained closed, the front garden was a jungle. Paul was familiar only with the universe of his friend's shop, with Hak canned vegetables, Saroma instant pudding, and Dash detergent on the firmament.

Whenever the bell rang, Hedwig would emerge like a mole from the dark tunnel between house and shop, blinking at the light. Once the transaction was completed, he crawled back into his chamber. From safely behind the counter he had, by then, caught up on his customers' doings; back in the underworld he thought over the things he had heard and classified them according to their importance.

In the course of time, Hedwig's conversation had grown limited to illness and death. It was as though a radio were playing somewhere in the background, Paul thought — you didn't have to listen or say anything in return.

When they went on holiday, it was never for longer than two weeks. Paul could not stand Hedwig's company for any longer than that, and longer than that he was unable to leave his home. He thought he would die of homesickness every time. The farm, the land, the sky above it, every fibre of his being ached with the missing of it. Pattaya, Boracay, nowhere did one find places any more miserable. The dull heat, the remorseless light; he hated the tropics. What a blessing then were the moderate climes in which Mariënveen found itself, without insects that crawled into your shoes and gastrointestinal bugs that undermined your health.

After a few days, the nausea and panic would recede a little, only to rear their heads again towards the end of the holiday. He counted the days and longed for his bedroom in the shade of the lime tree, the wallpaper peeling off the moist walls and the odour of fungus in the blankets.

'And then if you go calling home every day, too …' Hedwig said.

A congenital disorder, his father called it.

As the years passed, his homesickness diminished somewhat in its intensity, but always when he was far away pursuing his desires, Muldershoek lay on the horizon of his imagination like the isle of the blessed.

He remembers most precisely how those desires began — a summer evening long ago, his father is mowing the grass, the television is on.

A feature film begins on Nederland 2. The actress has graceful fingers and slim arms, and a narrow, slightly cold face. She brushes her hair in front of the mirror; a bit later she makes a call. She places her long legs on the table, the silk peignoir falls open slightly. When she crosses her legs a bit of dark pubic hair can be seen between her thighs. Paul's throat goes dry. Jesus, isn't she beautiful. His father comes in and, standing behind the couch, watches a scene in which two men are being massaged by bare-breasted Asian girls. Paul's heart is pounding against his ribs.

'What are we watching here?' his father asks.

'A film,' Paul mumbles.

His father washes his hands in the kitchen and a few minutes later plops down on the couch — at this point, the leading lady is having sex with a stranger in an aeroplane. Paul is relieved when the story takes a turn for the normal: the woman and her husband are driving in a sportscar through an Asiatic metropolis. He brings her to a villa outside the city. With due haste they disappear into the bedroom to celebrate their reunification. They whisper things in French — the language of the angels — and during their copulation they are spied on by the Asian servants. A downy heat radiates all the way to Paul's fingertips. The servants, a man and a woman, stirred by their masters' copulation, chase each other amid the banana trees in the garden. The man overpowers the young Asian girl and frees a breast from her décolleté. She stops her struggling quickly enough, she pants, droplets of sweat appear on her forehead. Paul is fourteen, he never knew such things were possible. No prettier woman exists in this world, and the entire, terrible force of lust comes crashing down on him. How can something like this be on TV, on Nederland 2? It's a mistake, a terrible mistake — they are prisoners of the sex film and neither he nor his father know how to free themselves from the shame and paralysis.

Not much later, a pagan orgy takes place, and a flood of randy bodies, of legs, buttocks, pubic mounds, and breasts comes rushing into the room. His father rises from the couch, steps to the TV, and turns it off without a word.

Just as the test pattern was burned into the screen of his grandmother's television, because she never turned the thing off, so *Emmanuelle* was scorched onto Paul's retinae. The film was the start of and model for his own erotic imagination. The cleaving thunderbolt of that evening would stay with him for the rest of his life, in the days when the cruise missiles at Deurlo were pointed eastward but you had to go all the way to the city to buy a men's magazine.

'Time to get a move on,' his father said, and disappeared back outside. Paul stayed behind on the couch, shattered, and felt an immense sadness at the thought that such pleasure, such physical ecstasy as he had just witnessed, would never be his. He could look at it, long for it, but touch it, no, never. That was for others, and he hated life deeply for locking him out of the best it had to offer.

He was to discover soon enough that there was no lack of desire in the world; it was like oxygen, there was plenty for everyone — all of life was in fact a pushy incitement to desire as much as possible. But the sequel, the fulfillment, that's what it was all about of course, about that which was promised to all but available to so very few.

After they had seen the first part of *Emmanuelle* that evening, he realised that he and his father were actually in the same boat. After his wife left, his father never had dealings with other women. They were a bachelor household, and it seemed impossible that another woman would ever become involved in their affairs. With the loss of his mother, Paul understood, his father, too, had been denied access to sensual pleasure, perhaps for all time.

It was only ten years later that Paul took his first trip to Southeast Asia. 'There's absolutely no need for you to get bored there,' the female travel consultant told him, after summing up the attractions of Bangkok. Three days was the absolute minimum that the city deserved, and then two more at the end of the trip, 'when the two of you come back all relaxed from Pattaya'.

There, she had come out and said it: Pattaya. It was as though his desires had been laid on the table in front of her, ready for inspection. Hedwig was standing at the coffee machine, waiting for his second cup of hot chocolate. The travel consultant arranged the vouchers and stuffed the whole thing into an envelope. The tickets would be mailed to them later.

Hedwig was unaware of the trip's actual goal; sex for him was as remote a subject as space travel.

Before they left, Hedwig's mother had emphasised to Paul how important it was that Hedwig have absolutely no dairy products. She showed herself to be wondrously comfortable with the term 'lactose intolerance'.

So when Paul saw him spooning down a cup of ice cream on the plane, he said in amazement: 'But you're not allowed to have dairy products, right?'

Hedwig shrugged. 'She also says I have hypoglycaemia. All I have to do is cough and she's on the phone to Lamérus right away.'

Afterwards, Hedwig fell asleep with his head against Paul's shoulder. When he pushed him away, he soon fell against the man in the seat to his left, on the aisle, a Scandinavian who kept ordering one mini-bottle of Johnny Walker after the other. A little later, the Scandinavian, dressed in only a t-shirt, short trousers, and flip-flops, leaned over Hedwig and raised his glass to Paul in alcoholic loneliness. Paul nodded and smiled. For reasons impossible to trace, the only word he knew in Danish was '*hundelort*', which he had been told meant dog turd. He looked out the window. At 623 miles an hour, the plane was barrelling along over Afghanistan; his expectations for the trip swirled round and round in his head. The scenarios spun out over and over again. Suddenly, the whole mission seemed ridiculous. He had time and money, he would enter the kingdom of pleasure and take what had been denied him all these years, and now, closer than ever before, the whole house of cards seemed about to collapse, a treacherous illusion nourished by the chronic fever dreams of an onanist. He turned his gaze away from the dark night, but the howls of derision were everywhere.

The cabin lighting was turned off, here and there someone was still watching a movie. Hundelort the Viking, too, had called it a day and fallen asleep. Again, Paul peered into the deep darkness. Far below, an electrical storm was raging. Huge banks of cloud glowed from the inside, in stirring reds and yellows, as though a short circuit had taken place inside a row of hollowed-out cauliflowers. He wanted to go home.

The next day, Paul and Hedwig scurried around Bangkok like a pair of startled mice. They had absolutely no need to be bored, they were on the run. Within the walls of the great attractions was where they sought refuge. The golden Buddha was gigantic, as were the crowds that gathered round it. Flushed and sweaty, they wandered through the palace gardens.

That evening, they had dinner at a restaurant by the river. Tugboats were pulling a chain of heavy-laden barges. The cargo was covered with tarps and lashed in place with ropes. On the afterdecks a little lamp shone here and there, the barges seemed to be inhabited. The dark, floating settlement looked like a vestige of human life after a catastrophe.

The mosquitoes came for Hedwig. He raised a satay skewer from his plate and watched the sauce drip. 'Wijko sauce is thicker,' he said.

Paul knew his preference for thick satay sauce. Hedwig normally ordered fries solely for the mayonnaise, and chicken satay only for the peanut sauce. 'Otherwise they give you such strange looks,' he explained, 'if you only order the sauce.'

Across the river, the silhouettes of high-rise flats stood out darkly against the evening sky.

At three-thirty that morning, Paul awoke in a sweat. He needed to go to the toilet and he was thirsty, but lay there listening to Hedwig snore for half an hour before getting out of bed. After pissing, he went out into the hall in his pyjamas. It was a huge hotel, its floors centred around an atrium. He made a round, then sat in an easy chair and read *The Bangkok Post*. The horoscope was promising.

> *Cancer, 22 June–21 July*
> The tiny but erotically charged planetoid Juno brings you a visitor. Need we say more? It's not about a serious relationship or The Love of Your Life, but the passion is so intense that it may look a lot like it. It may leave you behind dazed and confused, filled with homesickness and sweet memories.

He was disappointed when it turned out that he had been reading a two-week old newspaper. His moment of passion had passed unawares.

Five o'clock, said the clock above the elevator doors. His father was watching television right now. In a few minutes, Aloïs would start getting ready for bed, after eating two slices of bread with chocolate sprinkles while standing at the kitchen counter. Then his false teeth would clatter in the sink and he would brush and floss what was left of his own. They had problem teeth, he and his father did, they developed plaque much more quickly than other people. The dental hygienist always seemed to precipitate a bloodbath in their mouths.

One floor down, a door opened. He saw a girl leave a room and close the door carefully behind her. The little pink skirt barely covered her behind. She slid her handbag up onto her shoulder and pinned her hair up as she walked towards the elevator. A little later, on his own floor, another girl came out of a room. She took the lift. Paul went to the balustrade and watched until he saw the two of them, in the depths of the lobby, heading towards the front entrance together.

The destination was approaching, it was coming closer for sure.

A waste of money, Hedwig thought, the two of them having separate rooms there in Pattaya. In the fridge in his own room, Paul found two condoms in a box, and saw that they were listed on the prices for the mini-bar. There was no need to feel embarrassed about it around here.

Every day, Paul and Hedwig went swimming in the horseshoe-shaped pool of the Shangri-La Hotel; the ends of the horseshoe led to a cocktail bar. The sound of Dutch came from some of the deck chairs. On the third afternoon, after a couple of laps, Paul swung himself up onto the pool's edge. Towel slung over his shoulders, he told Hedwig that he'd be back in a couple of hours.

Where was he headed, Hedwig wanted to know.

'Off for a walk.'

'I'll go with you,' Hedwig had said. He raised his sunscreen-whitened face to look at him and hoisted himself out of the pool. Paul placed a foot on his shoulder and pushed him back into the water. 'Buy yourself another piña colada, I'll see you in a bit.'

Hedwig, amazed, watched as he walked off. Then he crowed: 'Oh, I get it, off to do the deed! Dirty boy!'

'Thanks a lot,' Paul mumbled.

In the bathroom mirror he spread the water-resistant sunscreen over his face as evenly as he could. There was no way to get an accurate picture of it beforehand, of the available bodies everywhere, an entire city built under the sign of sex. Now he was on the verge of demanding his fair share, a pale little man with bad teeth in the sex capital of the world. He had resigned himself to having to pay for it, simply because that was the only chance he had.

He left the hotel and steered a course between the crowds and the deafening noise of scooters and trucks, looking for the street where the supply of girls was most concentrated. In the last few days he had seen countless massage parlours full of smooth-bodied young women who gave the glad eye to passers-by. It hadn't happened. When one of them came up and wound herself around Hedwig, he had uttered a flustered 'come on, get off it', and freed himself from her grasp.

Paul found his way back to the Soi Buakhao market and the surroundings streets filled with go-go bars, travel agencies, and restaurants; he envied the backpacking globetrotter who could get smashed in a pub with one of these doxies on his lap, then treat himself afterwards to a soapy massage or whatever those erotic specialties were called.

The girl he'd seen yesterday wasn't there. She had been small and buxom, and she wore hot pants. Now he saw another cute, round face; the girl herself remained sitting under the awning of the massage parlour while the others swarmed in and out. One of them took him by the hand, tried to pull him inside, but he remained standing before the girl he had chosen. Her name was Yindee, she said, pointing to herself. He nodded. The other one let go of his hand and asked for a cigarette. He felt around in his pocket and handed her one. With a smile, she disappeared. Yindee took him by the hand and in they went, down a dimly lit corridor and up the stairs at the end. She opened the door to one of the rooms along the upstairs gallery. Beside the massage table was a dish of aromatic oil, warmed by a tea light. She slipped out of her clothes and helped him to undress, removing his t-shirt last. Her mocha-coloured body brushed against his, he felt her hard little breasts. She came up only to his Adam's apple. The smell of shampoo. Dizzy spells. It felt as though he might faint any moment.

She patted her hand on the massage table. On his stomach, she gestured, then poured a little warm oil over his back. Her hands spread it over his skin, she kneaded his flesh for a long time. Then she climbed on top of him and rolled her knees back and forth over his back until the breath was knocked from his lungs.

A smack on his rear, he rolled over.

'You relax,' she said. She took hold of his wrists and laid his arms down alongside his body.

She massaged his thighs, her thumbs slid over his loins. From a different world, beyond the walls, came the muted sound of traffic, distant music, but he lay in the purple twilight of a temple and closed his eyes. Higher her hands slid, to his chest, he felt her pubic hair rasp against his stomach when she reached for his shoulders, the heat of her pussy. The shudder when she took hold of his penis; she oiled it, her hand slid calmly up and down. Just as he was about to come, she stopped. Using her teeth, she tore open the foil package of the condom. 'You love Yindee?' she asked as she rolled it onto him.

She straddled him, her hand reached down between her legs to his cock, she waited till he had said 'I love Yindee' before putting him in her. Her hands rested on his shoulders, she let herself come down on him and bounced back up until she had only the tip of his dick caught between her labia — she was an experienced horsewoman, and he was a little donkey weeping with pleasure; two viscid tears rolled over his temples. Juno's transit.

Later, when he came in powerful contractions, she laid her cheek against his and soothed him like a mother.

Eighteenth

Childhood. In the deepness of time. The days flow together without a ripple. He and Hedwig Geerdink usually cycle home together after school. His mother's leaving is rarely brought up.

At lunchtime, Hedwig's mother asks if he'd like a sandwich, too.

His stomach says yes, but his head shakes no.

'A glass of milk? Come on, have a sandwich. You have to eat something, don't you?'

He wants to, but can't. Something in him. It withdraws and rolls itself up into a ball.

Hedwig takes a slice of white bread with strawberry jam. A glass of milk. Another slice of bread with strawberry jam. There are more jams and fillings on the table than he has ever seen. All kinds of chocolate sprinkles, liverwurst, cheese and salami. Cottage cheese, kippers, apple spread, and peanut butter. Hedwig often brings ginger-snap sandwiches to school with him.

When the bell sounds in the store, Hedwig's mother disappears down the corridor. Quickly Paul grabs a slice of white bread and spreads a glob of jam on it. Hedwig knits his brow, but goes on eating without a word, his elbows on the table and the sandwich in his hands like a harmonica. There is a candle lit on the dresser, in front of the statue of the Virgin. A rosary has been draped over her praying hands. Hedwig goes on constructing sandwiches.

They bike to the textile factory. In the waste containers there they find half-empty spools of filament and stocking rejects that they pull over their heads. In the woods behind Paul's house they stalk lone pilgrims and convoys and shoot at them with arrows of young elder; at the corners of Paul's eyes, spiders with long legs and hardly a body to speak of go scurrying off. The earthy smell of forest soil is familiar, sourish. The top layer of beech leaves is dry, beneath that it is moist, and white hyphal threads weave through the packet of humus. When Hedwig pounces on the enemy with raised sword, it sounds as though a siren had gone off amid the trees.

After the massacre they withdraw to an old, low-ceilinged pig shed along the property's northern limit, where the mouldy smell of old dusty straw pricks at your nose and throat. Some of the windows have been boarded up, the last panes of glass are opaque as dull ice. Dust particles glisten in the light falling through the window gaps.

'I don't feel like it anymore,' Paul says after a while. They go to his house. His father is still at school. Paul sits down to read *Danny, the Champion of the World*. When he looks up a little later, Hedwig is gone. He puts the book away, gathers his pencils and paper, and starts drawing. The castles he draws are clammy and crumbling, bloodcurdling bats circle above them. The knight's chainmail looks like the carapace of a woodlouse.

Usually, his solitude is complete. The woods and the brook are his, he need tolerate no one else. Only in winter do strangers sometimes invade his territory, when there's ice on the Molenbeek and people come from far and near to go skating. A way upstream, close to the Oud Wesselink brothers' farm, they shuffle across the bridge on their blades and then skate on through the pasturelands, into Germany.

His father has taken the tie-on skates down off their nail. Waggling on the low wooden cheese cutters, he makes it to the first bend, comes back walking. The straps have frozen. He hates skating.

A latecomer ties on his skates, steps onto the ice, and disappears round the bend with his hands clasped lightly behind his back. It looks gentle and easy, at least like something you could learn quite quickly.

Every boy should know how to skate, even Hedwig can skate, and once again he pulls on the straps as tightly as he can and hobbles back to the bend. His ankles, it's his ankles, he can find no other explanation for it. They're weak, the way everything about him is weak; he makes a running start and glides all the way to the weir. Lying on the ice are the scrapings from blades. Grey light trickles through the trees along the banks, the powdery grey that comes before a flurry and makes everything inconstant.

Standing at the weir is his father. He watches and says nothing.

Paul tosses the skates onto the bank.

'You'll make them blunt like that,' his father says.

'They already are,' Paul says angrily. He picks them up off the ground and holds the rusty blades up for him to see.

'Always worked fine for me,' his father says. His scarf glistens at the spot where the breath leaves him. He turns and disappears through the trees, heading for home.

Just before nightfall, the skaters return, in little groups or alone. Paul can hear their voices and the scratching of steel from far away.

When the first snowflakes blow past the darkened trees, he has it all to himself once more. He lies with his nose against the ice and looks at the encapsulated air bubbles and sees how the current beneath carries leaves and twigs across the smooth, rust-coloured streambed. Behind him, close to the weir, the water fans out thinly from under the ice and disappears over the edge. In harsh winters, even the waterfall is frozen.

The brook that has twisted its way through the landscape ever since the last ice age has its source miles from here, along the slope of a lateral moraine. Back behind Muldershoek is where it is broadest. Aloïs dumps barrows full of rubble along the bends to keep them from eroding: tree roots tangle together just above the waterline.

As early as 1268, records showed a watermill behind their house, belonging to the Bishops of Utrecht, whose reach extended all the way to Mariënveen. Some six centuries later, in 1813, the first Krüzen became the owner of the mill and the farm at Muldershoek. The family would keep the millwheel turning for more than a hundred years, until that part of the property was expropriated by the water board and the mill was razed.

The mill began its long life as an oil mill and ended milling flour. In the water closet, beside a bit of doggerel by Paul's grandfather about the hard life of a miller, there is a photograph of the mill — a cosy-looking house with a tiled roof and walls of blackened oak planks. At the side of it you can see the waterwheel. The building tilts forward a bit, tired from years of work. When the millstones are turning, the deep rumbling can be heard in the wide surroundings. Jan Oude Booijink once described the sound as that of approaching thunder. For seven centuries the gears grind and the stones turn on their pivots. And then, thirty-seven years before Paul Krüzen is born, they put an end to its life. In its stead they built a concrete weir, below it the water broadens to a basin at the foot of high banks. Between a double row of poplars, it flows on to the bridge where, on a grey summer day in 1955, Aloïs Krüzen places a bouquet on the paving stones, and on again for miles to empty out into the drainage canal.

In summer, the foliage forms a ceiling of green above the brook and the water slips loudly beneath the overhanging bushes. Close to the concrete waterworks, Paul catches loaches with a net. They have whiskers on their lower jaw, their sensory apparatus in cloudy waters. The scour-hole is not deep, but moves quickly when the water is high.

From the mud there, Paul one day fishes up a coin which his father says is inscribed in Latin. He takes it to the priest, who puts on his spectacles in the doorway of the presbytery and thinks, at a first glance, that it may be a papal commemorative coin. To be certain, he'll have to leave it with him. Paul puts the coin away quickly and says that's not necessary. His faith in the benevolence of the infant Jesus and his mother Mary is implicit, but when it comes to the servants of God, one never knows.

The branches of the big linden tree behind the house scrape across his bedroom window; in summer the leaves swathe his room in greenish dusk. There is no bigger tree around; the arm spans of three grown men cannot circle its girth. A couple of yards above the ground, the linden forks to form a giant slingshot. There it becomes two trees, with a tall, dense crown that admits barely a drop of rain.

His grandfather had wanted to cut down that friendly giant. He climbed as high as he could with the chainsaw on his back, saw the awesome amount of work his resolution would entail, and climbed back down. He cooled his fury on the trees along the drive, close to the road, all of which he cut down, and then forced his son Aloïs to saw and split the wood. For weeks the owls flew over their lost hideouts, who-whoing sadly.

Losing the watermill had forced Paul's grandfather to take up farming, for which he had absolutely no knack. He had a hog shed built, and leased land from the farmers whose grain he had once milled, who now fleeced him by palming off on him their low-lying, swampy ground, acres which in earlier centuries had been boosted to a certain degree of fertility with turf-cutting and manure, and these days with artificial fertilizer.

Storms, lightning, and fits of rage, the linden had survived it all, and sometimes Paul sat with his back against its stubborn old skin and had the feeling that the tree comforted him by its mere example. The wind rustled through its leaves in summer, in autumn it blew bare, a period of rest dawned. Easy now, it seemed to say, just by standing there like that, everything will be okay.

To the right, Paul's bedroom window looks out on a little patch of grass, a recess in the woods, with a garden shrine made from rough pumice. The niche is empty, the statue of the saint that once stood there has disappeared.

At the arts and crafts club where Paul spends his Wednesday afternoons, waiting for his father to return from school, he fashions a statue for the niche. He wraps a long, slim bottle in rags drenched with liquid plaster. After adding many layers, the bottle assumes the shape of a woman with a cloak over her shoulders and her hands folded close to her body. The ermine cloak falls in long pleats behind her, like the royal mantle worn by Queen Juliana in the state portrait at the Rabobank. Mary's head is a bit on the long side, but that's not what the boys at the arts and crafts club notice. Quietly and teasingly, they sing: 'Miss Mary-Moo, Miss Mary-Moo, humungous art thy knockers.' But they're really not all that humungous, Paul thinks, and besides, the Virgin behind the altar at the church isn't exactly flat-chested either.

When the plaster has hardened and the paint is dry, he takes her home with him, his Mary with her flaxen hair and red cape. He frees the niche of ivy and puts her in it. Safe and sound, the Help of the Afflicted is back in the tabernacle, her eyes averted and her hands folded in prayer. He sinks to his knees and murmurs: 'Holy Mary, Mother of God, pray for us sinners, now and at the hour of our death amen.'

That evening, as he is mashing his potatoes with the back of his fork, his father says: 'She's pretty skinny.'

Paul looks up. 'She always is.'

'Oh really?'

Paul nods resolutely. 'You see that everywhere.'

'Didn't realise you were such an expert,' his father says.

Whatever the case, since then she goes by the name of Maria Anorexia, but Paul pays no attention to the mockery of her breasts and build, for he know that there have been appearances at Kevelaer and Heiloo, and that a woman in Amsterdam has even seen her dozens of times, so that it's very much possible that one day she may reveal herself in Mariënveen as a beam of light in the linden tree, the Queen of Heaven with her predilection for simple shepherd girls, housewives, and farm people, who showed her beautiful and comforting countenance to children often enough, so why not to a pupil of the Sint Jozefschool who has set up a shrine for her in the garden?

Every day before bedtime, his father reads the New Testament. He's a Jesus man, the fierce bloodlust of the Old Testament is less pleasing to him. 'There's nothing more you need,' he says of the New Testament. When he has finished it, he starts all over again, by the scanty light of his nightlamp, because it's not easy to follow Jesus' example.

'Jesus,' he says, sitting on the edge of Paul's bed, 'raises us to be good people. Not an eye for an eye, no, exactly the opposite. If someone strikes you on the right cheek, then you have to turn the left one.'

Paul sits halfway up under the clammy blanket and says: 'Geert Oude Voshaar says Mama's a whore.'

His father purses his lips.

'I pulled all the hair off his head.'

'What would the world be like,' his father starts in, 'if everyone took the law into his own hands?'

'Mama isn't a whore.'

'His hair?'

Paul nods and his hands pluck at the woollen blanket.

'You didn't hit him?'

Paul shakes his head. 'Pulled his hair out,' he says softly, confused by the undertone of disapproval in his father's voice. He can't punch, he shakes too badly; his punches either go wild or aren't hard enough. Geert Oude Voshaar's punches didn't faze him. He remembers the joy of grabbing a big handful of hair again and again and not letting go. The thatches of red hair that go flying.

'It's not right, really,' his father says. 'But what he did isn't either ...'

And right there, there's the rub, Paul realises. You can't both stand above it *and* take revenge. His father wants too much. That's his struggle. That he drives down the driveway in the morning with the peace of prayer in his heart, and the next moment finds himself yelling 'stupid cunt!' at a driver who comes screeching round the curve. That is the confusion that he tries to solve by following Jesus' example.

Sitting on the edge of his bed one evening, his father also starts telling him about one of his students, a boy named Viktor. A light breeze comes through the cantilever window. Paul hears the sound of falling water from the weir. His father describes his new student with so much verve that he appears live to him, right there in his bedroom. The kind of student, his father says, who a teacher encounters only once in a lifetime. And he's not the only one, all his colleagues think the same. Everything you tell Viktor finds fertile soil. It's as though he actually knows everything already, that all you have to do is activate it.

Paul thinks about his own struggle with grammar, with fractions, that he always mixes up the sine and the cosine.

For many summer evenings in a row, his father tells him about this boy wonder whose parents came from the West to settle here in the area. Viktor does judo, he's a blue belt. He used a trick to pin Mr Dobbe, Aloïs's colleague, to the mat. A boy this high — his father holds his hand up, about a metre and half off the floor.

He can't stop talking about him. Viktor plays the guitar and gave a rendition of *Blowin' in the Wind* to the whole student body, in the auditorium. And when they cried out for more, he went on to play *With a Little Help from My Friends*.

Viktor emerges from the stories more overwhelmingly each time. Paul goes to sleep exhausted and fearful.

'Does he really exist?' he asks one evening.

'Of course he really exists,' his father says a bit indignantly. 'What did you think, that I was making it all up?'

Paul shrugs. 'I don't know.'

'All true, every word of it,' his father says, and goes on with the adventures of Viktor the Wonderful. This time an episode about a field trip to Artis Zoo. After coming home, Viktor went upstairs and did not come back down, not even for supper. He locked himself in the bathroom and refused to open the door. His father picks the lock with a pair of pliers, in the bathroom his parents find their son in the bathtub. He is not alone.

'So,' his father says, 'can you guess what he had with him?'

'A book,' Paul tries.

'Guess again.'

'A friend of his.'

'Guess again.'

'I give up.'

'A penguin!'

Paul sits up straight. 'A *penguin*?'

'A real penguin,' his father says. His hands indicate the length of a good-sized carp. 'Stolen from Artis. In the bathtub.'

'That's impossible!' Paul shouts.

It wasn't all that difficult, his father says; Viktor just stepped over the little fence and fished the bird out of the shallow basin. He brought it home under his coat.'

Paul shakes his head. 'But you're not allowed to do that, are you?'

No, his father agrees, you're not. But the expression on his face tells Paul that an exception exists for very special violations, ones that attest to pluckiness and a sense of adventure.

Admittedly, his father says, it happened at Viktor's old school; he had told the story as an introduction to his talk about the black-footed penguin. And why would he lie about something like that?

'Weird thing to do,' says Paul. When his father leaves, he lies there for a long time, staring gloomily at the ceiling.

Nineteenth

Behind the doors' high, semi-circular archway, the sediment of the last century's three great wars lay piled. In the former cowshed, ten metres wide by thirty-five long, a hundred thousand objects from the First World War and the Second World War and the Cold War were to be found in cupboards and crates and laid out on trestle tables; Krüzen Curosia & Militaria comprised the largest collection of militaria east of the River IJssel.

Paul loved uniforms most. Scattered around the shed were a dozen display dummies, all dressed in authentic gear. The Tommy, the Kraut, the GI, and the *poilu*; the life-sized dolls stared blankly into space. He was also fond of the dully gleaming noses of torpedoes, the ridiculous *Pickelhauben*, the indestructible Swiss army post satchels, and the antique German field kitchen on iron-bound wooden wheels, but what he loved most were the uniforms. The sharp crease in khaki, the stiffly woven gabardine trench coats, the woollen uniform jackets that smelled every bit as musty as the blankets he slept under. Uniforms were what brought the man at war closer by. There, inside, a heart had beaten and a person had lived in mortal fear, boredom, and ecstasy. Nothing jogged his imagination like a uniform, and he felt admiration for the weavers and tailors who had made and shaped these durable textiles in such a way that they easily withstood the test of time.

Above the doors to the shed was a big white sign on which he had painted in black letters a sentence he saw once on a stand at an arms show in Aschaffenburg:

WAFFEN, BRINGT MIR VIELE WAFFEN
R. WAGNER

Saturday afternoon, one-thirty, he was printing invoices and waiting in the little glass office for the man with whom he had an appointment. In a baker's display case on his desk he kept the objects from his collection that were not for sale. They were of no real value: the cathedral fashioned from matchsticks — was it the Dom at Cologne? — made by a German prisoner of war, and the handwritten bundle of verse by an inmate who died at Neuengamme. In that same display case, he kept the coin he had found in the pool forty years ago, and the Russian's army compass, as corroded and encrusted as the Antikythera mechanism, which he had located in the field using the first metal detector he ever owned. These things had formed the beginning of his collection, which had accidentally become his livelihood.

A few months after the Wall fell, almost thirty years ago now, Laurens Steggink had asked him to go along on a business trip to the DDR, the country that had actually ceased to exist from one day to the other. It was a diffuse, wild time, an entire country had gone into clearance; characters like Steggink moved in like a flash to take their profits. Steggink's regular partner was ill, he needed an extra pair of hands. They drove east in a big Mercedes van, through West Germany, and crossed the border at Helmstedt — Marienborn. At Paul's request, they took a little time to visit the former *Sperrgebiet*. The vast ribbon of heavily guarded borderland was equipped with high steel fences, barbed-wire barriers, and guard towers. Paul stood quietly, taking in this manifestation of aggressive state power. In what must have been a gigantic tour de force, the state had thrown up a fourteen-hundred-kilometre-long barricade to stop the *Republikflucht*. A rampart against the thing within, rational and deadly. Now it was dead itself, this senseless pile-up of concrete and metal, now that the house of power had collapsed.

At a crawl, they drove into the land of the former enemy, against whom they had braced themselves with nuclear weapons and feet on the ground. As a conscript, he had been part of it, too; like Steggink, he had done his tour of duty at Seedorf. Paul had imagined the landscape differently, bare and grim, but it was green and pastoral; ancient tractors and hay tedders in the fields were sweeping the grass into long rows. The cows were skinny, the roads badly tended and empty. The image of the enemy had been many times more powerful than the enemy itself.

They drove to remote villages and farmsteads to buy up antiques and heavy oaken furniture. Steggink sometimes drove twice a week to East Germany to fill his van with Fichtenholz cabinets, sideboards, and escritoires, but also with mirrors, footstools, foot stoves from churches and for carriages, Cologne pots, washbasins, and birdcages. He bought up everything those people had. The avidity was mutual, but Laurens Steggink always got the better of the deal. Those Ossis sold everything they had for a song, and Paul cringed with shame when Steggink, like an SS-man at the entrance to the camp, pointed to the household items he wanted; copper coal scuttles, candlesticks, fire-irons, everything was merchandise. His wallet was almost too big to fit in his back pocket. Steggink's marks were hard, the people's hands were pleased to clasp them. So here they were, Paul thought, the enemies of yesteryear, these down-and-outers who hadn't owned anything new for decades.

In a little town east of Maagdenburg, Steggink held a bundle of marks under a woman's nose. When she reached out to grab them, he pulled them back. '*Diese Sachen noch*,' he said, pointing to a witch's cauldron hanging above the fire and a copper extinguisher. '*Dan haben wir einen Deal*.' Reaching back, he pulled the ponytail at the back of his head a knot tighter.

The farmwoman grumbled and growled, but gave in at last.

Steggink contentedly carried the booty to the van; once they were moving Paul said: 'Don't do that anymore, not when I'm around.'

'What?' asked Steggink, who was rolling a cigarette on the flat of his thigh.

'That thing with the money. That was pretty nasty of you.'

'That? That's the game, Paulie. That's the way it's played.'

The van grew heavier and heavier, hung deeper and deeper through its suspension, until nothing more fit in it and they drove home at last. Paul went with him a couple of times after that, then he bought his own Mercedes T2 and drove it east all by himself.

Each time he crossed the former German–German border, he was amazed to find that passing the guard towers took him fifty years back in time: the towers had guarded nothing but stubborn stagnation. Commodities production had sunk back to pre-industrial levels, the system had produced little more than apathy among the workers and corruption among the party managers; without an economic incentive, no one did anything anymore.

He mulled over the incongruence of an empire that had carried out the first manned space flight, but where the delivery time for a crappy little automobile was twelve years. The cows may have been skinny and the people may have lived in need of everything, but their engineers had actually gone and given them the first pictures of the dark side of the moon …

He went quietly about his business. He was a shrewd enough dealer. If necessary, he was willing to take advantage of a person's good faith, but he generally didn't push things to the bitter end. The profit margins lent themselves to leniency. He had an eye for antiques, it seemed. He furnished the cowshed in his father's yard as a salesroom; by appointment only, he received dealers from all over country, who sold the things in turn on the antiques markets at Weerselo and Zuidlaren.

Before long, Paul had to go further east each time, for the traffickers had descended like locusts on the former DDR and already 'sucked most of the country dry', as the first wave of cowboys put it contentedly. Down roads that grew narrower all the time, further and further from the provincial highways, he drove into the hinterland to find anything of interest. In desolate, deathly quiet areas he knocked on people's doors. He attended auctions and estate sales, and in Colditz, in the shadow of the notorious castle on the hill, he came across a complete SS uniform with the military identity card still in its inside pocket. The eagle on the canvas cover of the pass bore the swastika in its talons. The uniform's owner had fought on the front lines in the First World War and reenlisted in 1934, apparently caught up in the flush of the new German *élan*. The uniform lay neatly folded in its box, the boots at the bottom, covered with issues of the *Leipziger Volkszeitung* from 1949. Mao, Paul read at a glance, was engaged in heavy combat with the nationalists and, in a newspaper from a few months earlier, that the Soviet Union had given Yugoslavia the cold shoulder because it was evolving into a 'vulgar bourgeois republic'. He bought the uniform for a ridiculously low price and, seated in his van, took a good look at Dieter Soltau's *Wehrpass*. He had been born in Chemnitz in 1899, was 1.71 metres tall and weighed 75 kilos. In 1942, at a fairly advanced age, he had been promoted to SS-*Hauptscharführer;* the stamps in the booklet showed that he had served on the Eastern Front before joining the SS. After that he was stationed at Nice — a post on the Mediterranean as reward for services rendered? — and at the end of the war served in Mittelbau — Dora. A dynamic career, no question about it.

Paul could tell by looking at a chandelier how and when the crystal had been cut, from the looks of wood whether it was real or composite, all useful knowledge, but this, he sensed, this was the real work. The historical sensation when he opened the box, lying inconspicuously among all the household items beside the door, and saw the *Feldgrau* …

Dieter Soltau's uniform had been the kick-off for his collection of militaria. He had never sold it.

He crisscrossed the German countryside at random. When a fit of homesickness struck, everything in the surroundings through which he was travelling suddenly seemed to conspire against him. Evil, suddenly, were the trees, the grass, the roads and the houses. Nowhere in the world was it as filthy and dangerous as where he was at that moment. He sweated and shivered; sometimes he would pull the van over to the side of the road just to calm down.

One of the places where that happened was on the German–Polish border, where he'd been led by a tip about an old gunpowder factory. At Forst, he crossed the Neisse and entered Poland, where the factory had been set up in 1945. The Soviets had carried off most of the installations as the spoils of war, but there was, a trader in Halle had told him, enough there that was still of interest. The grounds of the Deutsche Sprengchemie plant covered some five hundred hectares, the factory buildings and hundreds of partially underground bunkers were connected by kilometres of rails and roads. There was still a risk of explosions, because a good deal of the nitro-glycerine had never been cleared; more than forty years after the war was over, the place was still filled with the caustic smell of gunpowder. Not long before his visit, a scrap merchant had been blown up after descending into a drain with an acetylene torch. A glove was all they'd found of him.

In the woods, Paul saw a man with a metal detector, eavesdropping on the soil inch-by-inch. Otherwise there was no one. The man didn't look up or around; it was, Paul thought, all in all an autistic hobby. He printed the overgrown ruins firmly in his mind, in order not to get lost. With factories like this one, the Third Reich had bolstered its brutish aggression, it was here that military supremacy came to a head. All the death and disaster that had spread like a plague across the continent had been prepared here. He thought about the energy it had cost to throw up hundreds of industrial complexes like this one — such a titanic enterprise could only be founded on forced labour and slavery.

Two hours he spent wandering around the abandoned complex, until, in the silence amid the trees, he was struck by a blow to the chest that knocked the air out of his lungs — home, he had to get home right away … He broke out in a sweat, at a trot he left the woods and found the van parked at their edge. It was three-thirty in the afternoon; just before midnight, he arrived home.

That was how he learned how long the leash was. The Neisse, when travelling overland, was the end of his world. Past that, he fell off it.

The German arrived half an hour late; he heard tyres crunching on the gravel. Slowly, on the drive that separated the shed from the stand of oak along the road, a Mercedes drove into view. The man entered the shed through the little door in the tall, semicircular archway. Paul turned on the light. The fluorescent tubes blinked and popped on, a flood of light washed over the immense treasure-chamber. The German whistled through his teeth. The racks were piled with field telephones, life rings, and binoculars. In the display cases, the medals and Zippo lighters glistened. A table filled with 25-pounder shells and rations kits. Boxes full of officer's uniforms, trousers, socks, suspenders, and neckties, heavy rubber boots as well as boots and shoes of leather, Krüzen Militaria had it all. Behind lock and key, he kept the Mausers, Lugers, and Enfields — the glass cases were opened only on request. The roof was shored up with torpedoes; from the rafters hung espionage balloons, as well as a makeshift hot-air balloon in which an East German family had attempted an ill-fated crossing in 1978.

'*Na sowas*,' the man said, impressed.

'*Ihre ganze Geschichte*,' said Paul. '*Kaffee?*'

'*Sehr gern, danke*,' the man replied.

Paul went into the office and turned on the percolator. Through the window he saw the customer wandering aghast among the armaments, all that lovely, deadly technology. He stopped for a time beside the Daimler Dingo, a British-made light reconnaissance vehicle. All his customers were impressed by his historical–thematic arrangement, and he let them take their time. Paul brought the man his coffee and went back to his books. A little later, the German appeared in the doorway, to ask for a little sugar. His cup was already half-empty. They had grown too unassuming, the Germans had. Paul placed his order on the table, the man looked through the cardboard boxes. Eight gas masks and army coats from the DDR, bought at the clearance sale of a military depot. From the golden age, back before the government set up their own agency, the *Treuhandanstalt,* to deal with the sale of state property.

A second box contained three Swiss nurse's uniforms. The man took one out and held it in front of him at arm's length. '*Ausgezeichnet*,' he said. '*Wirklich gut*.'

His wallet bulged like a housewife's at a clearance sale. They carried the boxes to the car, and Paul watched the Mercedes as it drove off the property.

His father was sitting with his leg up on a stool, messing with the radio receiver he used to follow the weekend services at the Maria Church.

'Drop your trousers,' Paul said. 'I need to get to it again.' He washed his hands thoroughly and dried them on a clean towel. His father worked his trousers down around his ankles and sank back in the chair. Don't say it, Paul thought, but there they were already, the words he'd heard over and over again: 'If it has to be like this,' his father sighed, and Paul chimed in: 'Then you'd just as soon be done with it ... Well hang in there for a while, okay?'

When the wound appeared from beneath the bandage, it startled him. Phosphor makes wounds like this, he remembered reading in the Dutch *Soldier's Handbook*. It ate its way through the skin, deep into the flesh, and one unique trait was that it didn't go out when you tossed water on it. The tip given in the handbook was to take a spoon and flip the burning phosphor out of the wound.

'Next week it's about time we went to the hospital again,' Paul said. 'Have you been taking those pills?'

'Sure.'

Paul rubbed antibiotic cream on the wound and put on a fresh bandage. Then he took a shower, shaved, and combed his hair with a part down one side.

'Where is it you're going again?' his father asked when he saw Paul making his supper so early and putting it in the microwave.

'Town,' Paul said.

'Oh yeah?'

'The lady from the pharmacy. Look at this for a minute, would you? All you have to do is push the start button. I've already set the timer. This button, here.'

'That one,' his father said.

'The one I stuck the little arrow next to.'

'Shouldn't be a problem.'

'Last time you actually turned it off.'

'There are worse things in the world.'

'Just push the right button this time, okay?'

Twentieth

Avermaten was the town's new housing development, where divorcees ended up and refugees started over. Living next door to Ineke Wessels was a timid Afghan family, she told Paul, across the street a troupe of uncouth Kurds had been assigned a house. She gave Dutch lessons on her days off.

'No, man, super-rewarding work, for sure,' she said when Paul asked if that wasn't hard to do. 'And the men are so courteous — Dutch men could stand to learn a thing or two from them!'

Perhaps, Paul thought, a Syrian or Eritrean man had recently sat in this very chair, as chivalrous as he was full of desire for an older Western woman with breasts like the barrels of a howitzer. He was glad he had stopped by the Plus for a box of After Eights.

Ineke Wessels was receptive to foreign cultures — that was the message broadcast by the living room of this house with the through lounge. African wood carvings, photos on the console of her in distant countries. In most of them she was wearing plus-fours and sandals. Sometimes she had a colourful shawl draped over her head and shoulders. She had only really started travelling, she told him, once the children had grown up and left home.

'And your husband?' Paul asked.

A fleeting laugh, the armoured good cheer was breached for a moment. 'Ruud,' she said. 'Ruud died in 2003. Fourteen years ago, already.'

'Oh,' Paul said. 'I'm sorry to hear that.'

'Suicide. Yeah, I won't beat around the bush, otherwise it sort of stays hanging in the air, you know.'

Paul looked around, his soul flew like a sparrow against the window.

'Just like that, in the prime of life?' he asked, because her frankness seemed to call for it.

'I don't want to talk about it for too long, if you don't mind,' she said. 'But yes, that's right, in the prime of life, you could put it that way, yeah.'

She poured them coffee from a thermos. 'And what about you, Paul? Wife, children?' And with a laugh that didn't burst forth but seemed inhaled: 'The white picket fence?'

'No, nothing,' Paul said. 'I still live with my father.'

'But that's not nothing, is it? That can be very valuable, exactly that, right? How old is your father?'

'Seventy-eight.'

'And is he still fit?'

'Welll ...' He rocked his hand back and forth, the old *comme ci comme ça*.

'So you're sort of his caregiver? He's lucky to have a son like you! And for you, of course, it's real rewarding, being able to do that for him.'

'Aw. The way it is is the way it is, right?'

'Still down-to-earth as ever, aren't you, Paul?'

The conversation took a turn — their old school; the Franciscan sisters who had run the girls' school; Mr Braakhuis, who had been headmaster of one of the country's last Catholic boys' schools. A potentate with a skull like a dinosaur bone. In his three-piece suit and necktie, he would sit on the little podium at the front of the class, smoking cigars and keeping an eye on his pupils through heavy, black-rimmed spectacles. They didn't make them like that anymore.

Along with the priest and the bank manager, Mr Braakhuis had formed the village triumvirate. Some people felt that the doctor belonged to that club, too: when push came to shove, you'd always choose antibiotics over the Lord's Prayer.

When they were in the fourth class of primary school, the girls' and boys' schools were merged. It was the mid-to-late 1970s, the end of an era. Mr Braakhuis retired and dedicated the rest of his life to the local history of Mariënveen. Gradually, the Franciscan sisters disappeared from village life as well.

Paul's eyes wandered around the living room. There was no hook in the ceiling strong enough to hold a rope. Whenever funeral notices in the newspaper gave reason to believe it was suicide, he always wanted to know how it had happened, the preparations, the act itself.

She made him look at one photo after the other. 'Here, Jenny, remember her? And Heleen? The school trip to Hellendoorn, remember that?'

'Ponypark Slagharen, if I'm right?'

'And Hellendoorn.'

He looked. Well-behaved children. A different century. Better. The second half of it, in any case. An incredible digital-technological time-rush had taken place since: without that revolution, even his own, fairly old-fashioned life would look very different. And the world had started moving. Russians, Chinese, Romanians, Poles, and Bulgarians, all those peoples you used to know only from the school atlas.

'The weird thing is,' Ineke Wessels said, 'that I don't really see you in any of these. Okay, in the class pictures, but even then, you always have to look pretty closely.'

'There's nothing about it that I miss,' he said.

'Really? Oh, I think back on it with pleasure. Those were wonderful times.'

He thought about the withdrawn girl whose unobtrusiveness was all that had kept her from being pestered. Who had her girlfriends been? He couldn't remember them. It seemed as though she had reshaped her past, modelled it after the person she was now.

'Oh, goodness,' she said, 'look at him, would you? What a pitiful little guy that was.'

'Hedwig Geerdink,' Paul said.

In a feigned huff, she said, 'You didn't remember my name anymore, but you remember his right away! He had such a scary voice, remember?'

'It's not that bad.'

'What ever happened to him?'

'Grocer. Just like his pa and grandpa.'

'You still see him?'

'We're friends. I think. But I don't know all that much about him. He keeps to himself. All he talks about is death. Who's on the point of dying, how so-and-so died, guess who just died this time. Even if someone was buried thirty years ago, he says: "Dead as a doornail." Graves, that's all he sees.'

She nodded gravely. 'Looking over your shoulder so much isn't good for a body. You have to keep looking ahead. Can I get you something else?'

'Naw. I think I'd better be going.'

'Oh, but I didn't mean it like that! You just got here. Aren't you hungry? Shall I toss a pizza in the oven?'

'Don't go to any trouble.'

But she was already on her feet. 'It's almost seven o'clock, you have to eat something, don't you? I know I do. I'm starving.'

When she disappeared into the kitchen, he leaned back on the couch. Talking took it out of you. A minefield is what it was. Still, he enjoyed the contact with Ineke Wessels more than he'd expected. She had a dead husband, and children who had left her. She wore her loneliness with dignity. Only the slight hysteria somewhere deep down in her voice told you how she was really getting along.

When she came back a little later, she gave him most of the pizza, and when he was done, she said 'That wasn't much, was it?' and hurried back into the kitchen to put another one in the oven. She brought him a bottle of beer and a glass of Moselle for herself. 'Would you like a glass?' she asked. 'Or is the bottle glass enough for you?'

The pizza had left him thirsty; he drank three-quarters of the bottle in one go.

'I'm glad I recognised you,' she said, 'even if you didn't recognise me. The past is a precious thing, we should cherish it.'

His mouth half-full, he said: 'I'm glad it's over.'

'It made you who you are, Paul, a unique and unrepeatable person.'

He burst out laughing. A corner of pizza crust flew out of his mouth.

'Well,' she said, 'come on.'

'I'm sorry,' he said. 'It's just a funny way to put it.'

Now she laughed a bit, too. 'That's the way I see it.'

For the first time, he recognised the girl she had once been, now that he had seen the photos.

'You're a cynic, Paul Krüzen. You know what a cynic is, don't you?'

'I think so,' he said, 'but why don't you tell me?'

'They say that a sarcastic person has a disappointed mind, and a cynical person a disappointed heart …'

There, now I've got you, her look said.

'And what about you?' Paul asked. 'Does that mean you're a cynic, too?'

'All cynical people have a broken heart, I guess, but not all broken hearts grow cynical.'

He slid the bottle across the table to her. 'Well then, how about another beer for me?'

She stood up. It seemed like she enjoyed being able to do something for him. He found it pleasant, too. Was this what marriage was like? he thought. So comfortable and easy? Was this the way it was for them, all those married couples? He would be in for something like that, he mused, like a car dealer smelling a potential sale.

'Cheers,' she said a minute later. She bent over the little glass table, the wineglass with its gilded edge in her outstretched hand. Her breasts hung heavily inside her tunic.

'Hup,' he said.

He rose to his feet and walked to the sliding glass doors, which looked out on a small back garden. The grass was high. Bags full of bottles, a grey rubbish bag with a knot in it. The branches of a maple hung over the fence from the neighbours' garden. She came and stood beside him. She was even shorter than him.

'At least one tree, fortunately,' she said, sliding the door open a little. 'I'm actually a real nature girl. A nature girl lost in the city, you might say.'

'Come by our place sometime,' Paul said. 'Plenty of trees around there.'

He thought about the linden behind his bedroom, that old heavyweight that survived the seasons with such constancy. It was important to have a tree around that you could relate to. Soon, people would be living as long as trees, but without the wisdom of their quietness.

The shadows lengthened, in a garden a blackbird sang. She came and leaned up against him. 'I can do that, can't I?' she said in another, softer voice.

He said nothing, didn't move. There were days that were complete shit, there were days you forgot had ever been days at all, and then there were good days. Don't let a happy day escape you, he had recently heard Yeshua ben Sirach say in the Maria Church, through the mouthpiece of Father Oswaldo Teixeira, and be sure that your share of happiness does not pass you by.

So they stood looking at the dusk in the garden, the little woman and Paul Krüzen, a man who knew how to tell the difference between a happy and an unhappy day.

'It feels safe,' she said after a while, and he remained silent in the hope that she would stop talking of her own accord.

Carefully, a little later, he laid his hands on her round shoulders. She curled into his grasp like a cat. The bra straps left dents in her skin. Old-fashioned soap was what he smelled, not the aromatic finesse of his *belles* at Club Pacha. When she raised her face to him, her reading glasses fell from her hair onto the floor. 'Doesn't matter,' she said quickly. 'One from the five-and-dime.'

Their kiss was eager and hard. A woman, he thought, a normal woman.

The bed was under the sloping rafters of the top floor. Through the cantilever window he looked out to the east over the stretch of arable land that had replaced the former wasteland of the Waarmanslanden, which separated the Avermaten from Mariënveen. Once a huge swamp, it had been drained in the 1930s by crews of the unemployed from the west. To cut off the flow of water to the swampland, the engineers had had a canal dug and let the old mill stream wash away in it.

The swamp was transformed into fertile fields, a winding road ran through it for kilometres.

They fell onto the bed. After a short time, Ineke Wessels drew back from their embrace and began undressing on the edge of the bed. Paul's shoes fell to the floor with a thud. He looked up. 'Just a quick call,' he said and thumped down the stairs in stockinged feet to the living room, where he took his telephone from the glass table.

'Krüzen,' said his father with a mouth full of bread and chocolate sprinkles.

'Yeah, this is Krüzen, too,' Paul said. 'I'll be back later.'

'Fine,' his father said. 'See you.'

Phone in hand, Paul climbed again to the bedroom beneath the eaves, where Ineke Wessels was waiting for him with a pillow at her back and the sheet pulled up over her breasts. 'Caregiving …' she said, watching as he hung his shirt over the back of a chair and folded his trousers over the armrest. Wearing only his underwear, he slid in beneath the sheet beside her. They fell upon each other like wrestlers, their flesh clashed together. First he was on top, then she was. 'This can go,' she said after a time, and hooked her thumbs under the elastic of his underwear. She grabbed at his stiff member, made it vibrate like a snare. His hands wandered, too. He felt a pluck of pubic hair; he wasn't used to that. Rita, Thong — they had adapted their body hair to the demands of the age. Ineke Wessels, though, had hair like he'd seen in sex films from long ago. One finger slipped between her wet labia. He slid down blissfully towards her loins, past her round, firm tummy; the sheet slid down along with him. Everywhere the smell of soap, but underneath that his nose detected an attractive hint, of something of the body's own that excited him. She grabbed him by the ears before he reached her sex and pulled him back up. He looked down between their bodies at his cock, resting against her pubic hair. It was mostly grey, grey as cigar ash. Arching her back, she took his cock in. Like a long wave, her pleasure rolled beneath him. Again he looked down, towards the pubic hair below her round belly. Her heavy breasts were hanging beside her torso. He took one in his hand and weighed the soft flesh. He closed his eyes. Little donkey, work your spell, he thought. Rita, come to my aid. Thong, Teresita, Luana, and Ludmilla, all you sexy sluts — but nothing got the train of his imagination back on track. Ineke Wessel's body spoke of the children she had borne and given suck, of a dead husband and the passing of the years, and grey as ash was her pubic hair. Nakedness had revealed an old woman. He pumped, but his strength flowed out of him, his hardness, he fought a losing battle. A happy day escaped him, his share of happiness dissolved before his eyes.

'It's the nerves,' she said a little later, trying to make things seem better. 'All things are difficult before they're easy.' She would laugh it off, apparently that's what she'd decided, and he sort of grinned along with her, embarrassed by his defeat. The older female body, he understood, was meant to be caressed with the hands and not with the eyes.

'I bought some saveloy sausages for breakfast,' she murmured, just before they fell asleep. 'I hope you like them.'

Twenty-First

Deep in the night — his phone. He sat bolt upright. *What did I do with that thing?* Where were his trousers, damn it? His father — he should never have left him alone. His trousers, damn. The phone rang without stopping. He stumbled around the room until Ineke Wessels switched on the lamp. A quick glance at the screen before answering. Not his father. 'Man, I almost had a heart attack,' he said to Hedwig. 'What's up?'

'Paul?'

'I'm here. What is it?'

'They beat me up, Paul,' Hedwig wailed.

'What happened?'

'I got robbed, Paul, you have to come over!'

'Goddamn it! Did you call the police?'

'You gotta come right away, Paul.'

'I'm on my way. I'm not at home. Half an hour.'

It sounded like Hedwig was crying.

'Are they gone?' Paul asked.

'Yeah.'

'I'll call the police. Turn on all the lights. I'm coming.'

He stepped into his shoes without untying them and said, 'I have to go.' She was standing beside the bed, in a faded nightgown stretched to formlessness. 'What is it? Something bad?'

'Hedwig,' he said. 'A robbery. Not good.'

'Go on, go,' she said.

By the time he got the emergency dispatch office on the line, he was almost out of the neighbourhood. He gave them the address and raced through the darkened Waarmanslanden to Mariënveen. He got there before the police. The house was beaming like a UFO in the night. Through the window he saw Hedwig sitting at the kitchen table; when Paul tapped, he opened the door. Clotted blood on his face, a deep cut beside his ear. He had fallen asleep watching TV, Hedwig said, when the two of them were suddenly there in the kitchen. Two men wearing balaclavas. The biggest one had pushed him hard against the wall, the cut on his face was from the plaster. The man had borne down so hard that his dentures had broken in his mouth. 'Here, right down the middle.' Hedwig stared in dismay at the two halves of his uppers on the kitchen table. 'Oh, oh,' he mumbled, 'oh, oh.'

The police car pulled up in front of the shop at a little before three, almost an hour after Paul had called. You could always count on them for the alcohol checks, but when there was a real problem they finished their coffee first, Paul thought. He let them in, a man and a woman. The whole story again, from start to finish — how Hedwig was beaten and then knocked to the ground with a hard object, once they had found what they came for.

Paul made a pot of coffee, his jaws clenched.

'The sum of thirty thousand euros, is that what you said?' the woman asked, jotting things down in a notebook. She was from the west, Paul could hear that.

'Something like that,' said Hedwig.

'You kept that in your home?'

He nodded.

'Why, if you don't mind my asking?'

Hedwig shook his waxy, damaged head. 'Well, we know by now how that goes with banks, don't we?'

'You don't trust the banks?'

'Robin Hood stole from the rich and gave to the poor. Banks do the exact opposite.'

'Did they speak Dutch?' the other police officer wanted to know.

'"*Geld, wo ist das Geld?*" again and again, the whole time.'

German, the ballpoint scribbled.

Paul stood leaning against the counter, listening with his arms crossed, while the coffee was brewing.

'Could you describe their builds? Skin colour? Unusual traits, things you noticed?'

Hedwig gave a description of large men, one wearing a bomber jacket and camouflage trousers like a soldier. The other one wore dark clothes, that was all he could remember. That they were white, he was sure about that. The balaclavas were dark-blue or black.

A coldness came floating down inside Paul like a bad drizzle.

'Was there any way they could have known that you had money in the home?' the man asked.

A quick glance at Paul, then Hedwig shook his head.

'But you say they were obviously looking for that?'

'That's the way it seemed, yeah.'

The ballpoint raced across the page, equally hungry for everything that was said.

On the windowsill there were plastic orchids, beside them a pile of *Story* gossip magazines and free local newspapers on which countless blowflies had met their maker. It was after Hedwig's mother's death that the dilapidation began. No window had been opened since. The house smelled as though meat were rotting somewhere. Hedwig no longer went to church, because he didn't feel like dressing up anymore; just like Aloïs Krüzen, he listened to the service on the shortwave set.

The lamp above the table blinked off and then on again.

The armchair in front of the TV was swaybacked, the filling stuck out through the upholstery. There must have been a moment when Hedwig had stopped putting things back in the kitchen cupboards, not the cutlery and not the apple spread either, just let it all pile up on the counter.

'That lamp keeps on blinking like mad,' the male policeman said.

'Always does,' Paul said. 'Out here, we're at the end of the wire.'

'Well, that ought to about do it,' the woman said after a while. 'Is there anything else you'd like to add to your statement?'

Hedwig shook his head.

Grimly, his arms folded over his chest, Paul said: 'Don't you want to know who did it?'

A moment of pure, salutary silence.

'Go take a look at Club Pacha,' he went on. 'In Stattau, just across the border. There's a certain Mr Laurens Steggink there, acting like a big man at the bar. And sitting beside him is Ivan, a Russian. A guy like this.' He held his arms spread widely. 'Go ask those two where they were tonight.' His voice trembled with rage. 'It wouldn't surprise me one bit if you found thirty thousand euros behind a baseboard, or under the floorboards. And maybe more than just that.'

'What makes you think that?'

'Let me put it this way,' Paul said. 'They knew damned well that he had money around the house. Yesterday I heard Mr Steggink ask whether he was interested in investing in the club.' He pointed at Hedwig. 'Yesterday evening, in fact.'

'You were there, at that club?'

'We were, yes. Go ask those two where maybe that money is.'

'Is that what you think, too?' the woman asked Hedwig.

'How could I tell?' Hedwig peeped. 'With those caps down over their faces and everything. I couldn't see all that so quickly.'

'You didn't have the impression that they might have known you?'

'No,' he said, 'in fact not, no.' He looked helplessly at Paul, who shook his head slowly.

'And what did you say was the name of this club?'

Paul spelled it for her, and then Laurens Steggink's name too. What the Russian was called, he had no idea.'

'Ivan, isn't that what you said?'

'The nickname they gave to the Russians back in the war,' Paul said. 'Ivan, Tommy, Fritz.'

'I see,' said the woman.

The police officers looked first at Hedwig, then at him, as though to see whether more was coming. 'We'll take account of your, uh, suspicion,' the man said. 'In the story.'

The woman laid a brochure from Victim Support Services on the table. 'A thing like this can affect you deeply,' she said. 'It can be traumatic. I'd recommend that you contact them, that's what they're there for.'

Hedwig stared dully at the folder on the tablecloth.

'We're going to take a little look around, if that's okay with you?' They left the room and fetched light batons from the car; a little later they were nosing about outside the house like foxes.

'*Thirty* thousand?' Paul asked quietly.

Hedwig was sitting bent over, his fingers jammed in his hair. 'Eighty,' he said softly.

Paul groaned.

'What a stupid shit I am,' Hedwig said in his high voice. 'What a stupid shit.'

'So why did you say thirty?'

Hedwig shrugged. 'I don't know. I was worried about the tax people.'

'Man oh man, how could you ...' Paul shook his head and fell silent.

Hedwig sat up, his sunken upper lip trembled. 'Oh, Paul, they really put the screws on me.'

'Steggink, I swear to God. What a flaming asshole. What an asshole.'

'Oh, how could I be so stupid.' Hedwig's eyes were filled with tears.

'We'll get it back,' Paul said grimly.

His friend looked at him sadly. They were two weak little men, powerless in the face of violence. They could hang up security cameras, install police locks on the doors, and call upon the Blessed Rita, but fight back, no, that they could not do.

Hedwig rose to his feet. He moaned quietly. 'Everything hurts,' he said. He opened the tap, waited till the water was warm and rinsed the blood from his face. A web of scratches appeared, along with the cut beside his ear.

The police officers came back into the house. The robbers had forced a window in the storage room, the back wall of which faced the field behind, and then broken through the door there into the house itself. 'There's nothing you can do about that,' the man said. 'If they want to get in, they'll get in. At most you can slow them down a little.'

'Where did you have the money?' the woman asked.

Hedwig showed them the way, up the stairs to the top floor. Paul stayed in the kitchen.

Fifteen minutes later, as they were leaving, the woman looked at the cut beside Hedwig's ear. 'You need to get that stitched, sir,' she said.

They remained behind, just the two of them, two miserable men in the dead of night. Hedwig turned on the TV. For a few minutes, he stood in front of the screen, where you could see the workings of a miraculous home gym. He looked smaller. Paul had read in the newspaper about the captain of a freighter hijacked in the Gulf of Aden — when he was freed, it turned out that he had shrunk five centimetres from sheer mortal terror.

Hedwig shuffled backwards, and when he felt the easy chair against his calves he lowered himself slowly, his hands pressed against the armrests. A little room full of people listened breathlessly to the instructor standing by the miracle machine, a physically fit, middle-aged man with glistening white teeth. After a while, his head resting on his arms, Paul fell asleep at the kitchen table.

Quivering grey light entered the room. Paul raised his head. Hedwig was still seated in front of the TV. Was he sleeping with his eyes open? 'Hey, old man,' Paul said quietly.

Hedwig blinked his eyes to show that he'd heard him. Paul poured himself a cup of bitter, old coffee and walked to the storage room. The blood began flowing in his arms again, with nasty, stabbing pains. He looked around for a drill and screws, but found only a hammer and a few nails, which he used to nail a couple of planks across the inside of the window. The lock would have to be replaced. In the kitchen he took a slug of coffee and said: 'I'll be back this afternoon, okay?'

'Okay,' Hedwig said flatly. 'Thanks for being there.'

'What did you expect, wuss?'

At the house his footsteps left a trail across the dewy grass. A few seconds later, he tiptoed up to his father's bedroom door and listened. His eyes were burning with fatigue. He turned on the Nespresso machine. For almost fifty years he had lived in this house, he had seen phantom flames chase across its floors and heard disembodied struggles above his head. Generations of Krüzens had been born here before him. The way a farmer examines his sowing seed, that's the way his father had looked at him, the last generation, when he was born, but the crop had remained less than par. With his daily instalments about the infallible Viktor, he had aired his disappointment. The son he did not have was presented as an example to the son he did. Only a few years ago, when Paul had suddenly recalled the series of stories about Viktor, did he understand the depths of his father's disappointment; he had proven a mere repetition of the family fiasco. And it was his grandfather who had penned the verse:

The miller it is who slaves and toils,
Risks life and limb and all earthly spoils.
Awake he works both day and night,
Complaints his reward, from left and from right.
Only when God's wind rocks the bower
And ditch and stream do their water bring,
Can his wheels grind the grain to flour
For our daily bread at the appointed hour.

Not only was the Krüzen dynasty under par, so was the bread baked from the flour that came from the mill at Muldershoek. The state's excises on flour were steep, which is why *mulders* like his grandfather ground sand and grit through the flour, making it fit only for animal feed. But the people, poor as they were stingy, made bread from it anyway; they came down with sand colic and grumbled that 'the sparks fly from your mouth at every bite'.

And so Paul's thoughts moved from forefather to forefather, like notes on a scale, while the sun rose from the milk of morning and lit the crowns of the trees down by the brook. His father's kitchen garden had fallen into disuse long ago. Paul had once turned it over and sowed a bed of his own, but the lettuce bolted and the caterpillars ate the curly kale, and that was the end of his involvement with the earth. He therefore bought his vegetables at the Plus, and canned and packaged goods at Hedwig's. They had really put the screws on him. Operas of blood unfurled in Paul's mind. To know your place in the food chain and to arm yourself accordingly. Bring me many weapons. Torturing Steggink, shooting the Russian in the kneecaps.

The day lay before him without direction, till he remembered it was Sunday and that there was a church service at ten.

Again, he listened at his father's door, and this time he heard him rustling about and coughing. He set the table and boiled two eggs. His glance slid over the bread knife and the Gero carving knife, part of his parents' *trousseau*. He heard his father's old, corduroy slippers shuffling across the floor, the rollator bumped against the doorpost.

'Well, back in the land of the living,' his father said as he entered the room. The bandage hung loosely around his thin white calf.

'Boy, am I ever,' said Paul.

Aloïs sat down at the table. Paul made coffee for him. The old man's worn-out bathrobe revealed a few scattered hairs on his snow-white chest.

Paul told him about the robbery, the nest-egg, the night he had just been through.

'So,' his father said when all was finished, 'Hedwig's got a problem with vermin.'

'Steggink knew he was flush. Hedwig was bragging about it in the cafe, about a week ago. How he was a real-live millionaire, oh yeah.'

'That was mighty stupid of him then,' his father said. 'Putting a price on his own head.'

'Exactly,' Paul said. 'And Steggink cashed in on it.'

His father broke a rusk into pieces with the tip of his knife. 'And you,' he said between bites, 'could stand to make your place here a little more secure.'

'It's already secure.'

'In what way?'

'Standard package. Cameras, infrared detection. Anything bigger than a dog gets recorded.'

The Maria Church was built to hold three-hundred-and-fifty souls. There were perhaps ten this morning, spread out over the pews. These days the wrath of God inspired about as much fear as Zeus' lightning bolts or the hammer of Thor. There was one priest left for all three combined parishes — an imported one, from Brazil, at that. Had the Europeans once set out with the Book and the sword to Christianise the savages in the sticks, the sticks were now Christianising back. Missionary work was coming back into style, but now it was the poor Europeans who needed help. The new pope was a Latino, too, just like their own priest. Paul sometimes noticed Teixera's concern for poor old Europe, a continent at odds with itself. People had no belief these days. Not in anything; above all, not in themselves.

In the past, the reverend may have resided like a monarch among his parishioners, but today he was doomed, like St Boniface, to a roaming existence and mission work among the heathens.

Back then, it was the priest himself who visited the ill to let them partake in the communion of the sick. They received the consecrated host, and the priest received a tenner. Those days were over now. Now you got the host in a gold-coloured box with a bas-relief of bread and sheaves embossed on it. And though as a boy Paul had once sat at the back of the church playing hearts, these days he was up in front praying for revenge. Oh Lord, punish them hard. Cancer and worms.

He looked at the Virgin above the altar, the one he had once used as his model for the plaster Mary. Maria Anorexia had first lost her colours, then her shape, and after that the ivy had once again taken possession of the garden shrine.

Today's sermon was about the phenomenon of struggle in the Bible, the struggle of all against all. Between rich and poor, man and woman, slave and master. But the struggle that sounded most grievously from the Psalms, the priest said, was that between the oppressed believer and his attacker.

In Oswaldo Teixeira's mouth the hard sound of Dutch turned soft and round, but today his message gave no quarter. Perhaps Hedwig was listening too, one kilometre away, and perhaps he threw the receiver across the room when he heard the priest say that a person who trusts in his earthly possessions has forgotten that his only true possession is the grave. Six feet deep in the ground, hard and dry in the country he came from, soft and wet in the peat around here. He had been told, Teixeira said, that they used to have to hold down the corpses with a stick to keep them from floating, because the groundwater rose more quickly in the hole than they could shovel sand into it. The rich lay high, the poor heard their loved ones go 'plop'.

'Ploop,' the priest repeated for good measure.

Uneasy and uncomforted, Paul took leave of the house of God.

Twenty-Second

At Hedwig's the curtains were shut tight once more. Paul walked around the house and saw that almost all the sills and frames had rotted through. Instead of replacing the wood, Hedwig had nailed lead flashing onto it.

By inches, both house and shop had become badly tattered; the best thing would be to tear down the whole building and build something new in its stead. The Venetian blinds were lowered in the display windows. Their slats hung crookedly, every which way; there were sun-bleached packages of Omo and Dash on the sill.

Only after Paul had knocked on all the doors and windows did Hedwig open up. His upper lip had receded like a toothless pensioner's; he was looking more like an old woman all the time, Paul thought. The two halves of his upper dentures were still lying on the table. It would have to go to the dental lab, if there was even a chance of gluing it. The room was still filled with the penetrating stench of decay.

When asked if he had got any sleep, Hedwig shook his head.

'Did you listen just now?' Paul asked. 'Church radio?'

'Hardly much felt like it,' said Hedwig. He looked up. His eyes were bloodshot. He blinked nervously. 'I want a pistol, Paul.'

Paul stared at him for a spell. 'To do what with?'

'I need a pistol. For if they come back.'

'And you're asking me for that?'

'You've got them. I know that.'

'I've got lots of things, but even so.'

'I want one.'

'You wouldn't know what to do with it.'

Hedwig made a pistol with his hand and pointed it at Paul. 'Boom, dead,' he said.

'They're not coming back,' said Paul. 'They're already having a party, with eighty thou in the bag.'

Mentioning the exact amount, he noticed, lent him a peculiar, sadistic satisfaction.

Steggink and Ivan were the only robbers in the world with a Ferrari Testarossa. Maybe they'd parked the thing a little further away, on the sandy road behind Hedwig's house.

'If I don't get one from you,' he said, 'then I'll have to try it some other way.'

Paul looked at him and saw that he meant it. There was enough available on the Internet. Ammo, deactivated guns, all simple enough to activate again.

Hedwig's cheeks trembled. 'I'm scared, Paul,' he croaked.

'It'll only get you even deeper into shit, really,' Paul said. 'They're faster than you. You don't know how to handle a gun. Invest in a security system. Cameras, movement detectors. That's of more use to you.'

But Hedwig wanted a pistol beside his bed, at any cost. To hold the instrument of vengeance in his hand and point it at the bedroom door. To exterminate the vermin.

'Man oh man, that is bad news,' Baptist said when Paul walked into the Happytaria around noon. 'So how's he getting along?'

'They smacked his head around,' Paul said. There was something shrill in his voice, he heard. Violence had struck an entirely defenceless man, a man of dough who had never hurt a fly. They sat at the window, Baptist beneath a poster of an XXL frikandel. Absentmindedly, at the end of his account of the night's events, Paul ordered a farmer's fries with gravy, peas, and bacon. 'I was just over there,' he said. 'That house … This was the first time I noticed what a wreck it really is. Inside and out. It's shocking.'

Baptist looked out at the street. Reflectively, he said: 'Hedwig has given up, Paul. It's not anything new. When I go by and see that mess over there, sometimes I think: the way it looks on the outside, buddy, that's what you look like on the inside. In here.' He tapped his index finger against his heart.

It surprised Paul to find that there was someone else who thought about Hedwig, he had always assumed he was the only one.

Wen slid a plate of fries in front of him.

Leaning back, Baptist folded his hands across his stomach. 'What's he got, three or four customers a day? And that's being optimistic, I think … He has nothing to care for, and no one to care for him. Then it can go fast.'

And what about me then, Paul felt like uttering in indignation, am I not my brother's keeper? He felt a flurry of reassurance inside at the thought of Ineke Wessels — she could always console him, once his father was no longer around. Anything better than dying lonely. Even with a wife who didn't know who Angela Merkel was, Baptist was happier, or in any case less unhappy, than he would be alone. Who would turn his back on salvation just because of a bit of grey pubic hair?

'It started with his mother,' Paul said. 'Once she wasn't around anymore.' He used his fork to spear the peas off his plate.

'What did they take?' Baptist asked.

Paul shrugged. 'Ask him yourself, if you run into him.'

No movement was coming from Shu Dynasty, the Chinese were taking a rest.

'If you hear anything,' Paul said then, 'anything, about who or what, then let me know, okay? Doesn't matter what. He's not getting away with this.'

'Who isn't?' Baptist asked.

'Steggink isn't, and that Hun of his either.'

'Whoa,' said Baptist.

'It's not that tough to figure out.'

'Mercy,' Baptist said. He slid back in his chair.

'So what else could it be?' Paul asked bitingly.

'That's a real mouthful, what you just said,' said Baptist.

'You know Steggink. He knew about it. One plus one is two; he'd had his eye on Hedwig for a while already, ever since that stupid business about him being a millionaire.'

Baptist looked at Wen and then at Paul. 'You be a little bit careful with this, okay?' he said then.

He didn't want to get involved, Paul understood, he was protecting his tribe — his adopted children, his grandson who would become a concert pianist.

'I'm going out to the garden,' Baptist said. 'The weeds are something terrible.'

Pressing his hands against the tabletop, he hoisted himself out of his chair. His leather slippers dragged across the floor as he walked away. At the door he turned and said: 'Keep your head on straight, will you?'

Paul watched him as he shuffled past the window, leaden as he was fragile; a frightened old man for whom a handful of safety weighed heavier than a handful of the truth.

He made a few luncheon sandwiches for his father, slept for an hour, then put on his work clothes and went outside. The sky was veiled in clouds, the afternoon was sticky and warm. He walked to the chopping block; in the semidarkness beneath the trees he saw the wispy green of low, feathery leaf. Diagonal stripes of sunlight fell on the forest soil in the clearing. The dead leaves cracked beneath his feet like the bones of birds. The water in the brook was so low that its rushing sound had stopped, a thin film of water trickled overtop of the concrete weir.

Rust had touched the axe head. He positioned a slab of oak and split it. The chopping block gave a little with the blow. He smashed an endless series of skulls. Blood, brain tissue, bone splinters. The blows drifted dully through the woods. The axeman's work soaked his shirt, sweat trickled down his face and along his neck. The dry wood flew. The woodland soil lay littered with it, pale and splintery where the axe had laid it bare. He fetched a wheelbarrow of new logs. One after the other, he placed them on the furrowed chopping block, each blow found its mark. The axe head cleaved the air like a verdict. Revenge was the purest form of justice. It was good and just. Like silent grey judges, the trees looked on.

'Did you go by Hedwig's again?' his father asked later that afternoon.

Paul was standing in the kitchen, chopping an onion. He nodded.

'How was he doing?'

'Badly. Scared.'

'I can imagine, yeah. Was there anything else they took?'

'A phone he never uses. I explained ten times how it worked. Hedwig isn't much for this day and age.'

'Not much for any age, if you ask me.'

Paul put two shot glasses on the table and filled them to the rim with jenever.

'*Prut*,' his father said, and dribbled as he raised the glass to his lips. He wiped his lips first, then dried the tabletop.

After dinner, Paul disappeared to his office. Lifting a panel in the floor, he opened the safe embedded in the ground there. Beneath a pile of stocks and bonds and bundles of fifty-euro notes lay a box covered in black moleskin. He placed it on the packing table, took off the lid, and pulled out a Luger P08 Parabellum. He held it in his hand. The weight was reassuring. During its long lifetime, the pistol had first served under the Nazis and then, after being fished from old army surplus materials and given a sprucing, under the Communists in the DDR, where it continued to be used until the 1970s. First the pistol had defended states and ideologies, now only a farmyard. Someone had offered it to him at a gun show in Dresden a few years back — he couldn't resist. The name Parabellum referred to the 9mm cartridge used with the pistol, and was taken from the Latin proverb *Si vis pacem para bellum* — if you want peace, then prepare for war. His thumb rubbed across the corrugated wooden grip. It was an atypical pistol, he felt. The barrel was short and slender, yet the grip was quite robust. In later versions, barrel and grip were more closely integrated, whereas with the primal model of the Luger they seemed to exist more or less independently. Even though Paul found the design rather unbalanced, and even though the system itself was prone to malfunction, many arms dealers considered the Luger to be the mother of all handguns.

Paul fished a cardboard box of cartridges from the safe as well. A kind of erotic charm emanated from the gleaming, rounded heads of the bullets. He sat down cross-legged on the floor. As though led by magnetic force, his fingertips slid over the smooth copper casings before feeding them into the clip. These bullets made only a small entry wound and caused little damage to the surrounding tissue. He could bring Steggink down with a 9mm, he thought, but the Russian was more of someone for a hollow-point, which tore an increasingly bigger hole in the body the deeper it went.

Placing the clip beside him, he cleaned the pistol, the way he had learned to in the army long ago. During his training as a medic, he had learned to use a Glock. He had excelled at marksmanship, unlike all other areas of military life. He cleaned the barrel with a rag drenched with gun oil, used a toothbrush to polish the chamber and the insides of the grip. Then he eyed along the sight and aimed at the door. Exhaling, he pulled the trigger. Click, said the Luger.

Twenty-Third

The car park at Club Pacha was full, except for a couple of spots. Paul parked outside the fence and remained seated for a time, with the final remains of daylight on the windshield. His phone trilled; leaving the message from Ineke Wessels unread, he placed it in the glove compartment.

Tonight would be his farewell to the place where he had been comforted and sated for years. Under his jacket he wore a black leather shoulder holster, pressed against his ribs. He used his thumb to pop open the snap on the retention strap. He took the pistol from its holster and put it back in. He repeated this a few times to make sure the gun wouldn't snag at the moment he needed it.

He climbed out of the car, his movements slow and deliberate. There was no room for mistakes, he was equipped with exactly enough courage for one action, it needed to be clean and careful; a single departure from the prescribed procedure and it would become an indescribable mess.

The red Ferrari was parked beside a Porsche Cayenne. He entered the club through the heavy, black front door; behind it was a little foyer with a string of coloured lights. Pasteboard, all of it, a backdrop. He heard music, voices and laughter, too. On Sunday evenings it was usually fairly quiet.

Steggink was sitting at his regular place at the bar, this time without the Russian; he raised a hand in greeting. Paul's gaze swept the room, sitting at the little tables beside the dance floor was a group of men in army coats. Some of them were wearing gasmasks, others had one dangling around their neck. Glasses tinkled, the music was turned up loud. Thong and Luana were wearing snow-white nurses' uniforms, Rita was wearing the same outfit and sitting on the lap of a German, while he fiddled with her breasts. At the pole in the middle of the dance floor, Ludmilla was doing a vertical split. *Shoot that poison arrow through my ha-ha-ha-heart …*

Paul stood at the door, frozen in place, incapable of doing what he had come for.

Luana shrieked when a man slapped her on the bottom as she wobbled on her high heels to the bar for a few more mugs of beer. They shouted at her as she went, tongue protruding from wet lips. It was party night; Steggink gave him the thumbs up. Paul remained standing at the door for just as long as it took for all the courage to drain out of him and his knees to become shaky and weak. And Steggink just sat there grinning like a monkey, till Paul turned and left the place.

He drove back to Mariënveen benumbed, defeated by the hellish charade of horny Krauts and loose women; this would be his last image of Rita, in a nurses' uniform that was both too big and too tight for her; her body had grown in breadth and not in length, not the way that went with Swedish nurses. He took it up to a hundred and fifty under the trees, the wheels barely sticking to the curves. The yearning to feel a rain of bullets go flowing from his hand, straight into Laurens Steggink's body. To stomp on the dying man's body. To wipe away its expression, its *Steggink*ness.

Slowly, the tremors ebbed out of his body.

Through a crack in the curtains he could see the reflection of TV light on the sill; he went on knocking at the window till Hedwig opened up. Two chairs were set at the foot of the hallway stairs, as though to keep someone from climbing them. Hedwig dropped back into the wingback easy chair and turned down the volume on the German gameshow. 'What's up?' he asked in the lowest register his voice could do.

Paul's elbows rested on the red plush tablecloth, his chin on his fists. 'Got a drink for me?' he asked.

Hedwig fetched glasses from the console, and a bottle of full-grain jenever from the vegetable drawer in the fridge. He poured, Paul drank it down. He pointed at the glass. Hedwig poured him another one. The gameshow host slapped his hand against the roof of a BMW 1 Series.

'I was there,' Paul said. 'At the club. It was easy as all get-out.' He finished half of the second glass. 'Steggink was supposed to go along to the office, that's where it had to happen.' He closed his eyes and shook his head. 'I froze up.' From out of nowhere, Viktor suddenly appeared in his mind's eye. He would have been the right person to do something coldblooded like that.

Paul avoided Hedwig's eyes, looking instead at his parents' portrait on the console. Had the picture been taken at their golden wedding anniversary party? Beside it stood the statue of the Virgin that had held a rosary in its folded hands for as long as he had been coming here. Time had not stopped here, not completely, not the way he had thought: it gnawed. It ate away at everything. The paint, the woodwork, Hedwig's heart.

'I fucked up, in other words,' he ruled.

'Listen, Paul,' Hedwig said in a voice that spoke of abysmal fatigue, 'did they almost kill you? No. Are they going to do that? No. You can fire a tank at them for all the good it would do. Let me arrange this. Tomorrow I'm going down to report the robbery formally and then I'll tell them about Steggink.'

'Tomorrow the police station's closed,' Paul said. 'Be open Tuesday again.'

'So Tuesday then.' Without stitches or surgical glue, the cut beside his ear had sealed itself beneath a black scab. 'Stay away from there, Paul. That's not your kind of thing.'

They fell silent.

'And bring me a pistol,' Hedwig said then. 'Please. I've got nothing. No family, no kids. Nothing, no one. No one to hear me if something goes on here. You've got them. I know that. You feel like the top dog. But I can't sleep because they could just show up in the room again, like that.'

'Not going to happen.'

'Says you.'

'You wouldn't even know how to load the thing.'

'I know how to pull the trigger.'

'So show me,' Paul said. Reaching under his coat, he took out the pistol and laid it on the table between them.

Hedwig looked at it as though he had pulled a viper out his pocket. 'Well I'll be,' he said quietly.

'Well?' Paul said.

'Man,' Hedwig said, 'you tell me.'

Paul popped the clip and showed him the safety. '*Gesichert*,' he said, 'you see that, right here?'

Hedwig took his reading glasses from the buffet and peered at the word Paul was pointing to on the side of the weapon.

'And if I push that up — look, like this — then he's ready to go.'

What made the Luger so unique, he went on dreamily, was that the barrel rocked back after the shot and activated a system that was as ingenious as it was vulnerable; constructed by the designers as a sort of knee joint, it ejected the spent cartridge and then chambered the next round. This information for gun buffs, he saw, went right over Hedwig's head. His friend stared at the pistol, entranced. His hand slid over the tablecloth and picked up the gun. Paul put out his hand and pushed the barrel aside. 'Never point it at anyone, dipstick. Not even with the clip out.'

'Sorry.' His finger tightened around the trigger.

'Try it,' Paul said, 'it's empty.'

When the gun produced its dry click, Hedwig blinked.

'Well,' he said. 'Boy.'

Paul demonstrated how to insert the clip and had him repeat the steps one by one.

'Remember, you didn't get it from me,' he said. 'That would be the end of the whole she-bang.'

'Not from you,' Hedwig repeated mechanically.

Along with the gun, a bit of life seemed to have come into the room. They drank another jenever and kept half an eye on the TV. Paul's phone pinged again.

> Everything okay??? So frightened!!!hope everything okay with you!!!xxxineke

A vague weariness came over him. He started a reply, but stopped halfway. Hedwig changed the channel. Lying on the table was a Luger P08, manufactured in 1939 at the Mauser plant in Oberndorf am Neckar. Both barrel and frame had once been decorated with a minuscule German eagle with the swastika in its talons; those had been removed when the gun was refurbished under the DDR regime.

More than three million had been manufactured worldwide, original specimens went for a pretty penny.

Twenty-Fourth

Once upon a time, the higher cropland had all been covered in rye — for five hundred years, a thousand, two thousand, who could say? All that time the friendly grain ripened in the summer sun, long before domesticated buckwheat arrived from Central Asia, or before the potato crossed the Atlantic in the homebound ships of the conquistadors, crops that competed with rye but had never elbowed it out entirely. Only when fodder maize appeared did the golden sheaves on the high-lying fields become a thing of the past. Somewhere around the mid-1960s, shortly before Paul was born, rye had disappeared almost from one day to the next. The tillage changed colour, the warm yellow of ripening haulms made way for the uniform green of maize leaves. By this time of year, the stalks had grown so high that the farms disappeared in their midst; the country roads meandered through a labyrinth of maize.

It was early July. Standing at the top of the rise, Paul looked out over the maize fields below. A gust of wind blew through the tops, the stalks bowed like a market square full of believers. Later in the season it would all be chopped and ensilaged, to feed the animals on winter days. A wood pigeon burst from the foliage at the forest's edge and skimmed over the rust-coloured tassels.

From far away, he caught the high, hoarse whine of cross-country motorbikes in a sandpit.

He walked home. Parked along the drive, a man sat waiting from him in a van, adamczyk security printed down one side. On the phone he had briefed them about what he needed — the possibilities were endless. Since shops had started installing better security equipment, Adamczyk said, there had been a rise in the number of robberies at private homes; the Pole swore by Sony equipment.

Paul pointed out to him where he wanted the new system installed. The doors and windows would be equipped with vibration sensors, and Adamczyk was to mount motion-detection cameras on the outside walls of the house and shed, linked to spotlights that gave off a blindingly bright, 8,500-lumen light at the slightest movement. When the alarm was tripped, Paul would receive push messages by way of an app and could view the images in high-definition on his phone. The images were sent on to a central server and saved there.

The old security system was taken down; he could try selling it on an online forum, Adamcyzyk said.

The historical role of the Pole, Paul thought while he watched the man work, is to protect us from the Russian. Pilsudski's troops fighting against the Bolsheviks, the unexpectedly stiff resistance after the German–Russian invasion — heroic and futile was their courage. Paul had seen photos on the Internet of mass graves where Polish officers were dumped in the forest by Katyn.

'You've got enough work to keep you busy, I suppose?' he asked Adamczyk, who was up on a ladder against the outside wall of the shed.

'Busy, man!' the Pole shouted down at him with unexpected camaraderie, probably prompted by an insufficient command of Dutch. 'Afraid, everybody afraid!' He laughed. 'I say like this: lots of foreigners, lots of work for Szczepan Adamczyk.' The ladder shook under his laughter.

Paul pointed to an imaginary line at his feet, two metres in front of the shed door. 'I want infrared detection here, too.'

The system was extremely sensitive, the man explained, it was easily tripped. A passing cat was all that was needed.

'That's what I want. An alarm for hedgehogs, bears, everything.'

'No bears in Holland!'

'Sometimes there are. Russian bears.'

His phone rang. The hospital. His father would be admitted on Thursday, the day after tomorrow; on the website he would find a list of things he should pack for the stay.

Adamczyk wasn't finished with everything by the end of the day, he said he would come back tomorrow.

When Paul opened the microwave, he found the meal he had put there three days ago. The pasta was covered with a downy haze of mould. He slid the whole mess into the bin. His father sat at the window, staring into the garden.

Paul peeled the potatoes and tore open a plastic sack of chicory. Raw chicory hotchpotch was not his father's favourite, but the vegetables were good for you and you could get them for next to nothing at this time of year. He fried up cubes of bacon and sautéed an onion, while the Unox smoked sausage was warming up nicely in its pan of hot water. He had tried a smoked sausage from Hemmer, the butcher, once, but in the end nothing could beat the mix of flavourings that Unox put into its sausage. He added some fluid to the bacon and onion and flavoured it with a bit of ketchup, mustard, and a shot of unsweetened coffee creamer — Krüzen's Miracle Gravy.

'Thursday,' Paul said as they were sitting down at the table, 'we're going to the hospital. You're going to stay there for a little bit, I think.'

His father nodded. His face bore no clear expression.

'I'll order a new pair of pyjamas and a bathrobe for you. A new pair of slippers wouldn't hurt either. Any more requests?'

His father shrugged. 'Nothing with Mickey Mouse or something on it.' He slid a forkful into his mouth and began grinding slowly. The chicory cracked between his molars.

Back when he was fifteen or sixteen, Paul recalled, he had once fallen asleep with a porno magazine in his hand. Sleep had overpowered him before he'd had a chance to wipe himself clean. Which was how it happened that he failed to set the alarm and his father had to wake him the next morning. The sperm had dried on his abdomen, there where a stripe of hair had appeared some time earlier, connecting his pubic hair to his navel. He was too late to pull the blanket over himself. Light was visibility, light was shame.

'Admit the error of your ways and sin no more, print it in your mind before going to sleep, know thyself,' that was what he heard at church on Sunday, and he felt deeply miserable because he knew that the only thing he would print in his mind before going to sleep were Asian beauties who, wearing a grievous expression all the while, let themselves be fucked by some ugly goon kneeling between their thighs.

In the meantime, perhaps, that humiliating moment may have slipped from his father's memory, Paul thought, like so many of his memories had. Sometimes Aloïs said: 'I can remember things really well, only not for very long.'

Paul took a bite and wracked his brains about whether there was anything he needed to ask him, in case he died, but came up with nothing. He knew where the insurance policies were, and he had a general idea of the crucial events that had taken place in the past. There was nothing more that needed to be said, and no forgiveness to ask. The farewell would be beastly, brief, and unsentimental. He had been in his father's life for half a century, longer than any other welp in the animal kingdom; they had become intertwined so firmly that it would be more like a shedding of the skin than any disastrous parting.

'Did you have a good time,' Aloïs asked, 'at that woman's house, a couple of days ago?'

Paul grinned and sat up straight. 'She's a little too old to give you grandchildren anymore, if that's what you mean.'

His father nodded. 'But otherwise?'

'She's nice.'

'That's nothing to sneeze at, these days.'

'Maybe we'll see each other again sometime, could be,' Paul said as he poured more gravy into the crater of hotchpotch. He didn't know what else to say about it. Hunched over, they went on with their meal.

Hedwig still hadn't opened the shop. Paul felt a certain revulsion at the thought of that closed house, of the soul inside there struggling with his demons. There was no comfort he could offer him, only a Luger by way of reassurance. He decided to avoid him for a few days, the way you avert your gaze when you see someone who has recently lost a loved one; to keep from being pulled along into the maelstrom of sorrow, you look at your shoes, or at a buzzard drifting against the blue sky.

Adamczyk didn't show up on Wednesday. That evening, Paul drove right on past Hedwig's house again, assuming that his friend wouldn't feel much like hanging around the bar. First, he went into the Happytaria. Baptist was sitting at the window, Xi put two tins of Grolsch on the table in front of them. When Paul popped the tab, a squirt of beer foamed through the opening.

Baptist rolled his tin in his hands. 'A fine Japanese pilsner,' he said, 'Grolsch is.'

Paul nodded. He recalled the feeble, somewhat formal protest against the sale of *cultural patrimony* a few years back, when Grolsch was acquired by that Japanese brewer.

'They're leaving, y'know,' Baptist said, nodding at the building across the street.

'Who's leaving?' Paul asked.

'The Shus.'

'What do you mean, leaving?'

'Up to Arnhem, somewhere. Closing down the place.'

'Oh, come on.' Dumbfounded, Paul looked first at Baptist, then across the street and back again. 'That's impossible.'

'Oh, I don't know.' Baptist shrugged. 'When I'm not around anymore, I don't know how long they'll stick around either.' He glanced over at Xi, who was filling the display with deep-frozen gravy rolls. Xi looked up with a laugh and said: 'How Long is a Chinaman.'

'And Hu is his brother,' Baptist finished the joke resignedly.

Paul looked across the street in silence. Ming, Mama Shu, the old father, they had become as natural a part of his life as his own family. Baptist observed his bewilderment with amusement and said: 'Nothing remains the same, Paul. Did you think it did? That all this will still be around a hundred years from now? That tree? Those houses? By that time, everybody in the world will have been replaced by someone else. What did it used to say here on the wall, back then? You're the only one who still remembers.'

'Alferink's Fish, So You're Sure It's What It Is,' Paul recited automatically.

From here on out, the words shu dynasty would slowly flake off the windows across the street, and the Chinese characters underneath that, which Ming said actually meant something very different from Shu Dynasty. What exactly, she never wanted to tell them. He should remember to take a picture of the ideograms, maybe Google Translate would be able to figure it out.

Did the Shus' departure signal the start of a Chinese exodus out of Mariënveen? They had watched them arrive with suspicion, and their presence had often been the subject of bitter comment; he had not expected to feel such sincere sorrow at the news of their departure.

It was a balmy evening, the leaves of the lindens hung deep-green and dusty from their branches, it needed to rain again soon.

Dispirited, he sat in his niche at the bar. The only other person in the place was fat old Ewald Bruins, who owned a body shop and never missed a meal.

Mama Shu put a bottle of Grolsch down in front of him. 'Everything okay, Paul?' she asked.

He shook his head. 'What's this I hear?' he said. 'You folks cutting out on us?'

She didn't understand.

'Going,' he said, 'you people. To Arnhem or something …'

Her face lit up. 'Restaurant of family of my husband. Old people, good for us there, you know!'

'For us it's not that great, Mama.'

She smiled, the way she always did when she didn't understand something.

'Sure it is,' said fat old Ewald Bruins, without taking his eyes off the porcelain dragon behind the bar.

Paul looked at him, but Bruins said nothing more.

'So why's that?' Paul asked at last.

'What business do these people have here anyway?' Bruins said.

Mama Shu was arranging bottles in the fridge under the bar; she had made a strategic withdrawal from the conversation.

'For as long as they've been here,' Paul answered, 'you've been sitting here wolfing down half chickens. For as long as they've been here.'

'So what?' Bruins said tonelessly. 'I don't need them for that, do I?'

'Do you think there's anybody else who'll be willing to do that here? Seriously? With idiots like you at the bar?'

Bruins turned his torso a fraction in Paul's direction. 'Hey, keep your shirt on,' he said.

'Not a businessman around who would come to Mariënveen for a half chicken and a blabbermouth,' Paul said. He took a slug of beer. 'Or do you see things differently,' he added mockingly. 'When they're gone, there won't be anyone else willing to fry up half chickens for Ewald Bruins. You can stay at home nice and cosy and take them out of the freezer yourself. Well, have fun.'

Mama Shu looked at him in amazement. Never in all those years at the bar had he lashed out like this. He couldn't figure himself out. He felt abandoned, betrayed. The Chinese had somehow been a window onto the world, without them it seemed like a possibility had been cut off. Even though, he realised, their arrival hadn't really changed anything at all. They hadn't mixed with the people of Mariënveen and had established no intimate bonds of friendship. The interior of the cafe they had left unchanged when they moved in — the billiard table hadn't moved an inch, the shelf over the bar still held the same consolation prizes as when Kottink ran the place. The party hall was the only place where they had added their Chinoiseries — airbrushed photos of waterfalls and the life-sized, jade-green Buddha. A Chinese marquee had been built over the entryway, with green, scalloped roofing tiles on top and red woodwork below, the golden lions guarding the entrance.

He remembered how, long ago, the news had gone around that Chinese people were coming to Mariënveen. That people from so far away would see any reason to come to them seemed unthinkable. Still, they came, the first wave in Baptist's wake and then the second, drawn by the first. There was something here they wanted, the village actually amounted to something.

That the Chinese from Shu Dynasty didn't fraternise with the ones from the Happytaria had always surprised him.

Now the moment had come for them to turn their backs once more on Mariënveen. Somewhere else there was a future that was lacking here. They put down shallow roots, the Chinese did. He had hoped they might become just as bound up with the soil as he was, but without so much as a glance at the stay-behinds, they were tumbling on before the wind. Hither, thither. There where they prospered they remained for a time, when things took a turn for the worse they were gone again. He had actually talked himself into believing that they had become fond of Mariënveen. That they had developed an appreciation for both the landscape of mixed woodland and pasture and the people's roughhewn manners, and learned in the meantime to recognise the specific transitions between turfy soil and sand. That they knew the difference between an esker and a drumlin, but no, forget it, all they did was sit around peering at those damned phones and then take to their heels as soon as it was convenient. Faithless gooks, no sense of honour and no stamina. They'd been right after all, Abbink, Oliemuller, Bruins, and all the rest: you couldn't count on them for a thing. Thankless dog-eaters and fried-chicken swindlers.

And so his reproaches went round and round, rancorous and distressed, the lamentation of a stay-behind.

Paul was roused from his thoughts with a start when, around nightfall, Laurens Steggink walked into the cafe. He was alone. On a Wednesday, a night when Club Pacha was open. Paul hadn't expected him here — Monday, after all, was Steggink's billiards night.

'Yo,' said fat old Ewald Bruins with a quick glance to one side. Steggink kept his own eyes straight ahead. He zipped open the case and screwed together the two halves of the cue. Meticulously, with moves of devotion, he chalked the tip. Paul's heart pounded, Steggink had seen him, but apparently decided to ignore him for the time being. Straight through his fear of a confrontation, Paul thought about the word 'baize', and what a pity it was that a word like that was reserved for something as petty as the felt on a billiard table. He stared at his enemy as he piled up coins on top of the time clock. With eighty thousand guilders you could play billiards for the rest of your life, and longer, too. Paul clenched his jaw, he felt his eyes turning dry and irritated.

Steggink arranged the balls on the table as casually as though only a few nights back he hadn't left Hedwig for dead, with smashed dentures and his head bloodied and covered in cuts. His plait was bound up tightly at the back of his balding head. He bent his knees and leaned on the bumper, the lamps above the table lit his tawny face. Along the line of sight from eye to cue tip and ball, their glances grazed each other.

He played the first shot from the cushion, the white touched the red but then rolled on aimlessly, without touching the yellow, across the felt until it stopped. Steggink stood up straight and stretched. His grip on the cue tightened. He had big hands and broad wrists, his wiry body was tough as a bull pizzle. The girls at the club feared his strength.

How he wished he could feel the Luger against his body now, Paul thought, its metal warm as he was.

Steggink took a few steps in his direction and, behind the back of fat old Ewald Bruins, held out the cue, pointing it at Paul.

His name had been put in the police report by now. Had they already stopped by to talk to him? Had he been questioned?

His lips formed a word Paul couldn't make out — a couple of words, a sentence. His look was rigid and cold.

'I can't hear you,' Paul said hoarsely. 'You need to speak up.' He picked up his bottle by the neck and raised it to his lips. Displacement behaviour. He put it back down on the bar but kept a hold on it, to strike back with if Steggink took a swing.

'You keep your mouth shut about me, Paul Krüzen,' Steggink barked. 'No more lies anymore. Otherwise it's your turn. Simple as pie.'

Fat old Ewald Bruins looked over his shoulder in surprise.

Mama Shu came through the swinging door, which saved Paul for a moment. The cue stick was lowered. Paul felt around in his back pocket and took a ten-euro note out of the money clip. He put it on the bar and stood up.

'As you wish,' he said to Steggink as he walked out. At the door he turned and said: 'I'll wait and see just how much truth you can take.'

Twenty-Fifth

Another shiver ran through him. Clouds of insects hovered up and down above the road between the trees. He rolled up his window. So it's war, he thought, war between me and the biggest criminal in the village. And his Russian.

He could never go back to Shu again, just like he couldn't go to Club Pacha; his world was shrinking with each passing day. He had ended up in the Waarmanslanden unawares; the sky turned pink and purple above the wide fields of maize. He would have to find a new cafe and a new nightclub. There would be new girls with detached bodies and labels sticking out of their underwear, but Rita they could never replace. He felt a stab in his chest. He was going to miss her, her reassurances, her soft wetness, the goodness of her heart.

Steggink had taken away his two ports of call, and his rage flared up so large and impotent that he felt like smashing into a tree or an abutment, just to be rid of it.

The houses of the Avermaten, the dark accretion of stone and glass, appeared on the horizon. A few minutes later he drove into the neighbourhood. The lights were on in the living rooms, the swings hung vacant in the gardens. Behind these front windows the people were doing their best to bring their desires into line with their possibilities.

He drove at a crawl past Ineke Wessels' house. The curtains in the front room were open, there was no light on. He looked up, but the cantilever window on the top floor was dark, too. Maybe she was lying there with an Eritrean or an Afghan; ignoring the unforeseen swell of jealousy, he turned the car round at the end of the street. The fluorescent lighting was on in the living rooms where the refugees lived. The houses glowed like greenhouses, the TV screens flickered nervously.

Between walls of maize he drove back to Mariënveen, the light of town behind him.

At home the headlights swept over the oaks along the drive. He climbed out and listened. The engine cooling, a breeze between the trees. Far away the exultant cries of lapwings above the fields. After a minute, the headlights went out automatically. 'It's safe,' he said to himself. 'I smell honeysuckle, I see the stars. I'm not afraid.'

Upon waking, his nightmare had already paled to translucence, but the feeling it had summoned was as strong as ever. There was enmity and mortal fear, the ending was certain.

He fried eggs with bacon and, after breakfast, packed a small suitcase. The new pyjamas had been delivered by the package courier in his clapped-out Transporter, the slippers hadn't arrived yet. He stuffed the old slippers in the suitcase and put the whole thing beside the door. All these actions had something ill-fated about them, something definitive, although not necessarily portentous in and of themselves. At the hospital they would treat the leg with a regimen of hygiene and antibiotics, his father would come home healed, they would live together under the same roof for a few more years until he was struck by a brain haemorrhage and died on his way to the hospital.

'The shaver, have you got that?' his father asked.

In the bathroom he clicked open the foil and knocked the hairs out of it above the sink. As a boy he had been amazed by the greyish powder that collected behind the razor heads. Fine as ash it was, even though the hair on his father's cheeks and jaws was still stiff and hard, and darker in hue.

He rinsed it down the drain.

In the shed he opened a display case and took out a Walther P38. The gun had been deactivated with weld points in the barrel and chamber. Accompanied by a certificate, it could be bought and sold freely in accordance with Article 18 of the Dutch Arms and Munitions Act. Although he also owned a Walther PPK, the same *Polizei Pistole Kurz* that Hitler had put to his head in the *Führerbunker*, he chose the P38 because all he had was 9mm ammo.

Using a Dremel tool, he carefully ground away the weld point in the barrel. Damage to the rifling inside the barrel could make the shot go wide. He ground away the point in the chamber as well, then cleaned the caked-on, burnt gunpowder from both barrel and chamber. The insides of the pistol had some corrosion damage. Sometimes that could render a gun useless, but he would get this one going. He oiled it, filled the clip, and slid it into the grip. It felt compact, effective.

Removing the planks in the floor, he tapped in the safe's six-cipher code — 07-08-42, his mother's birthday. He wrapped the pistol in a cloth and placed it on top of the undeclared cash and securities. Then he answered a few emails and prepared a few orders on the packing table. A Slovakian customer had placed an order for twenty antenna mounts. That you might need one antenna mount, Paul could feature that, but what anyone would do with twenty of them was a mystery to him. Then he put together a box of canteens, rain ponchos, and six SS daggers. The daggers were a later production model, the original ebony handle had been replaced with oak. The blade bore a text, in Gothic letters, reading: *Meine Ehre heißt Treue*. My honour is loyalty. The mailing address was in Liège; undoubtedly a group of young neo-Nazis who would spend a weekend in the Ardennes, parroting revisionist theories. A swastika gave them a hard-on, and being able to freely perform the Nazi salute amid the dripping conifers made them drool at the mouth.

He put the boxes on the back seat. On his way back to the shed, his phone rang. Adamczyk, asking if he could come by that afternoon.

'As long as you finish it up right away,' Paul said curtly.

Pushing his father's wheelchair through the gravel wasn't easy. Paul held the car door open for him.

'You buckle up?' he asked.

His father fastened his safety belt.

On the fifth floor of the hospital, Paul looked around the waiting room. The ill and the dying were just as absorbed in their smartphones as the sound of body were; no one was reading a newspaper or a book, only one or two of them leafed through a well-thumbed magazine from the bi-monthly portfolio.

They waited for a long time. He walked around, stared out of the big plate-glass window at fields, the trees, and the farms with their orange-tile roofs. Not a cow or a sheep in sight. The landscape was empty and sterile. The animals had disappeared from sight once and for all, and he realised that he had become a man who remembered animals in the fields and who felt loss when they were not there.

Their name was called by a nurse wearing green Crocs, and Paul pushed the wheelchair into the little room into which she had vanished. The strand of events spun out calmly, up to and including Dr Levinson saying that a bed was being prepared for Aloïs, one floor down. Nodding, the doctor examined the rotting flesh on his father's lower leg. Then, as though his father wasn't in the room, he explained to Paul what gangrene was, and removed some tissue for testing.

The void in the house blew its cold breath down his neck, the way it had when his mother left. As the kettle began to whistle, he realised that everything had to go on the way it had always gone; he needed to stick to his routines and await his father's return as though he had never been gone at all. He would cook meals, spread sandwiches, make tea, wash the dishes and put them away in order not to end up like Hedwig, isolated from the outside world in a grimy house.

When Adamczyk finally showed up after four, Paul said tersely: 'I want everything to be arranged today. Otherwise you can take down all that junk again.'

The Pole nodded, he understood Paul's mood.

At the front door to the house, too, and at the back, close to his bedroom under the linden, he had him mount cameras, movement detectors, and floodlights. In both bedroom and office was a display on which Paul could watch the remote images.

At eight in the evening, Paul brought him a can of beer.

Once he was finished, Adamczyk said, Paul would be able to see every movement on the grounds, with eight split screens. If he wanted, he could also summon them up on his smartphone. The Pole knew the word 'failsafe', he used it two or three times himself.

Twenty-Sixth

When he went by later that evening, he saw that the cut beside Hedwig's ear was healing well. Flies were whining around the stack of dirty dishes. Paul poured himself a drink and said nothing about last night's run-in with Steggink. He asked if Hedwig could turn down the TV a little. He pointed the remote at the screen, and the noise sank to a tolerable level.

'So, how are things here?' Paul asked.

'What can I say?' His rasping voice sounded more horrible than ever.

'When are you going to open the shop again?'

The easy chair creaked. 'Maybe never.'

After a short silence, Paul asked. 'And then what? What's Plan B?'

'Plan B?'

'Yeah, what then, I mean. Without the shop.'

'Oh. Sit around a bit. Watch a little TV.'

Paul turned the shot glass in circles on the tablecloth and nodded as if he understood. 'Did you,' he asked then, 'get around to calling Victim Support? Like it said in that folder?'

Hedwig glanced over at him. 'Why would I?'

'Well …' Paul said. 'Because maybe it would help, something like that. Against the whole business. Here …' He tapped his index finger against his temple.

With a sorrowful look on his face, Hedwig said: 'And then what? One of those people who tells me things I already know? That's not my kind of thing, Paul.'

'They almost killed you. People at places like that have gone to school for things like that, how you should deal with it. I'll take you there. I'm driving back and forth all the time anyway.'

He told him that his father had been admitted to the hospital that afternoon. It could take a while, gangrene was hard to cure. Hedwig nodded, his gaze fixed the whole time on the RTV East news bulletin. He had lost his interest in the suffering of others and curled himself up like a frightened woodlouse around his own injury. His reasons to go on had received a vicious stomping, it would take all the resilience he had to scramble back up.

How passionately Paul hated Steggink and Ivan, who hadn't cared a whit whether Hedwig lived through their attack or not. Their casual destructiveness, the indifference concerning his survival.

From an old comic book about the youthful detective Rik Ringers, Paul remembered a character whose hair had turned white as snow from fright — could an existential shock cause something like that too? The soul that turned ashen-grey on the spot?

As he came up the drive, the floodlamps on the shed and house bathed the car in bright light. The system worked like a charm, the place looked like a major anti-aircraft battery.

He took the pistol out of the safe, put on the holster, and stuck the gun into it. It weighed almost a kilo. He put on his sportscoat over the top of it. Walking along the old stables to the front door, lamps popped on everywhere he went, eruptions of light energy in the darkness. It chased away the shadows beneath the linden and reached all the way to the chopping block.

Inside the house, he left the lights out, finding his way to the dining room table in the dark. He sat down, and the shuffling and rustling that he produced himself came to a halt. He heard his breathing, his pulse settled to a state of rest. He was alone with the household ghosts. He listened.

After a time, he got up and felt around until he found a shot glass in the cupboard. He filled it with full-grain jenever from the freezer, until he felt it running over the rim. Slurping the spilled jenever from the countertop, he wondered to himself if they had given his father his bedtime bread with chocolate sprinkles. The jenever burned against his inflamed gums.

For a long time, he sat in the dark. To be invisible to the enemy, he had to become a shadow himself. When he stuck his hand out, he saw a vague smudge. It was as though he were slowly dissolving and leaching into the darkness.

When he'd had enough of this, he stood up and took the light baton down off the plank in the hallway leading to the stables. Still operating by feel, he found the key and opened the stable door. The stagnant air with its odour of creeping corrosion caught him unaware, amplified by the darkness in which he made his way only by touch. He knocked over a milk can, which rolled with a maddening clang across the concrete floor. He cursed and clicked on the baton. A strip of yellow light fell across the floor, slid over machinery and building materials. From the beams above his head hung greyish-brown veils of cobweb, dust and hay.

He climbed the tall, narrow ladder. The wooden rungs felt soft and weathered. In the front loft the rolls of hay had with time dissolved completely to dust. He picked his way carefully across the planking, not knowing whether it would still hold after so many years of disuse. The latch on the door to the big loft always stuck, he knew that, it had to be opened with force. Behind it the loft stretched out into pitch-blackness. His heart pounded in his ears; there was no difference between the fears of an eight-year-old boy and a forty-nine-year-old man. But the boy, Paul thought, was now bringing the man along with him. Carrying a pistol. If the ghosts were to manifest themselves in all their horror, he could always shoot himself with it.

The bundle of light cut through the darkness. All the way against the back wall stood his grandparents' suite of furniture; easy chairs, an oaken table, a few kitchen chairs. The beams supporting the roof were decked out with the same sticky webs as downstairs, in the stables. The ray of light swept over the bottoms of the roofing tiles. He relaxed his grip on the lantern. Carefully he stepped out onto the grey floorboards and walked between piles of roofing tiles and rusty paint cans. The leather hood of the antique pram had rotted away, where the eaves met the floor lay piles of planks and beams from the old watermill. He took a wooden kitchen chair from the table at the back and placed it in the middle of the loft. He sat down in it. He clicked off the light, the darkness reassumed its rightful place.

It was as though he was tumbling head over heels into a deep, black hole. His eyes found nothing to clutch at, nowhere did even the night sky leak its way in between the tiles. It made no difference whether his eyes were open or shut, the darkness was equally deep; he was buried alive. His breathing went in and out agitatedly. He murmured snippets from one of David's psalms — *The Lord is my shepherd … I shall not want … He maketh me to lie down in green pastures … He leadeth me beside the still waters … Yea, though I walk through the valley of the shadow of death, I shall fear no evil. For Thou art with me …* Along his back, where he expected to feel any moment now the touch of something clammy and dead, ran a long, cold shiver. Here, in this darkness, was where the fights took place that had kept him and his father awake, the life-and-death grappling.

Mechanically, his lips repeated the words *For Thou art with me …*

He cleared his throat and said: 'If there's something or someone here, come out now!'

How weak and ridiculous his voice sounded in that huge loft.

'Whoever or whatever's here, show yourself!'

Perhaps he expected some shifting creature to actually rear up, transparent and ectoplasmic. Nothing, he used to think, would comfort him more than physical evidence of their existence. It had been precisely the lack of *substance* that terrified him so about the struggles going on above his head.

Nothing happened. The silence pressed against his ears. He was alone in a huge, empty loft. All his life, the ghosts had manifested themselves with terrifying thuds and tumult above his head; tonight they were keeping to the shadows. He turned on the light again and rose cautiously, as though expecting to be pushed back down into the chair. Shuffling his feet, and looking over his shoulder the whole time, he moved towards the loft door. One last time the beam of light slid from the ridge to the back wall and lit up the dark corners, but whatever it was that lived up there, it wasn't allowing itself to be provoked. He closed the door behind him and pushed the latch firmly into place — and divided the house once more into his territory and theirs.

He washed the dust from his hands and brushed his teeth. His hair, he saw in the mirror, had not turned white. A little grey at the temples, but that was nothing new. He examined the cracks around his mouth and eyes, most of which had simply appeared on his face unannounced.

It was past one. He folded his clothes over the chair. He rarely prayed these days before going to bed, but now he sank to his knees and silently murmured the Lord's Prayer. He addressed a prayer of intention for his father's recovery, and crossed himself.

Straight as an arrow, he lay beneath the blanket, hands folded on his chest. The crack in the curtains admitted faint starlight. He missed the hissing out by the weir, the voice of the brook that murmured him to sleep when the water was higher. Slowly he went under, the zigzagging fall of an autumn leaf, until a loud thud in the attic pulled him back from the gates of sleep. He panted in shock and peered into the darkness with wide-open eyes. The sound had been crisp and isolated. He lay petrified, waiting for the sequel, the retaliation for disturbing the quiet up there. But that one sound was all there was.

A paint can or a roofing tile, he told himself, something he had moved inadvertently had now fallen to the floor. That was how he comforted himself, knowing all the while that he had touched nothing but that one chair.

Twenty-Seventh

The next morning he made his own bed first, then his father's. The closet exhaled Aloïs' smell when he closed it.

At nine he called the ward. It took a few minutes to get his father on the line. He had, he told him, watched TV till past midnight. Then he had drifted off with the earplugs still in.

'You need anything else?' Paul asked. 'I can bring it by this afternoon.'

'Nah. I've got everything here.'

'Did you get a sandwich before you went to bed?'

'Everything's dandy here, what else can I say?'

His father seemed to be getting along fine, while he himself wandered the rooms here at home like a cat on hot bricks. There was no breakfast to make for anyone, no box of pills to put beside the plate, those acts of routine without which his morning seemed somehow amiss.

Paul took the newspaper from the letterbox out along the road and read the news and background stories till ten-thirty. Then he went back to the stables and climbed the ladder to the hayloft again. Reaching the door to the big loft, he swung it wide open. His gaze was drawn immediately to the middle of the loft, to the spot where he had sat that night. A shiver, cold as an eel, rolled down his back when he saw the chair knocked over on the wooden floor. Above it, for a moment that went on forever, he saw a rope fastened to the anchor beam and the motionless body of the man in the grey void, the fallen chair beyond reach of his feet. The hallucination vanished as quickly as it had come, and he was staring again into the empty space beneath the rafters, which reminded him of a whale's ribcage.

He closed the door and picked his way down the stairs again. He would, he decided, once his father was no longer around, have the farmhouse torn down and build a new one in its place, a thatch-roofed Saxon pseudo-farmhouse like so many others. If your hand offends you, cut it off, if your house is full of ghosts, burn it down. This mausoleum, with a memory hanging from every nail. He knew almost no one else who had lived for fifty years in the same house. Only him. And Hedwig. It would be a pagan bonfire, away with everything, all the household goods, every mute object augmented with remembrance, and from that fire a purer person would emerge, purer and lighter, relieved of the burden of everything that had riveted him to the past.

It was with these thoughts of demolition and catharsis that he began his working day; he sent reminders for payment and answered questions from a costume designer who was looking for uniforms with *Totenkopf* insignias and weapons for a film. In everything, he thought, he was a man of the past. Only now, now that it was too late, did he understand the importance of children — they were *future-bearers*, that was the kingdom they would inherit. As a parent, you could look at them and be at peace with the way things went. He, on the other hand, increasingly had the feeling that he had done everything wrong. Like a reckless gambler he had wasted fortunes on faithless women, and on women who had been worth every penny of it, on mixed drinks that made their breath sweet and their lips sticky and watches and jewellery with which he had tried to open up their hearts — but he had built his house upon the sand. And now it was too late. Mechanically, he filled the orders, closed boxes and packages, and taped them shut. Childish, he thought, I've remained childish all my life. As though no loss and adversity would come with the years, things that were so much easier to handle with a woman at your side. A single man died on the average of five years earlier than a married man. Loneliness was just as bad for you as smoking or excessive drinking; he who lives alone, out at the world's edge no less, dies a lonesome, dismal death.

Write this man down as childless, Jeremiah said, a man who shall not prosper all his days. That was how a pre-Christian prophet put Paul in his place, like an irresponsible child who has ruined his chances of happiness.

And at that very moment, will wonders never cease, he received a text message from Ineke Wessels.

PAUL?? IS THIS YOUR NUMBER? IS EVERYTHING OK?
SEND ME A MESSAGE, PLEASE??!! XXX INEKE

Someone should really explain the caps lock function to her, he thought, fatigued. It was like she was throwing bricks at him, with all those punctuation marks and capitals. He applied all his powers of fancy to imagine a life with her in a newly built farmhouse, she vociferous and dedicated, he quiet and tolerant, both in the realisation that this was the best life had to offer them. If he became ill, she would go with him to the GP and remember what the doctor had said. On occasion they would spend the holidays with her children, and on the day after Boxing Day they would eat a crepe at the old mill in Eshuis. They would grow old together as an exercise in thankfulness, in the same way one should thank God for a crust of bread.

He put down the tape roller and sent a message back.

Hi. Big mess here, my father in the hospital. Cup of coffee when things quiet down? Paul

Her reply came almost immediately.

IF THERE'S ANYTHING WRONG JUST SAY SO RIGHT AWAY. I DON'T LET MY LIMITS BE CROSSED ANYMORE. I DID THAT FOR TOO LONG.

Even after reading the message for a second and third time, he still didn't know what she was talking about. He typed 'ok' on the screen, sent the message, and turned off his phone.

'What do you figure?' he asked Baptist that afternoon on his way to the hospital. 'Can you fall in love even when you're older? Or is that more something for young people, like top-class sports and good health?'

Baptist grinned. White slime gathered at the corners of his lips. 'Out courting are you, my boy?'

'Can something like that grow,' Paul went on, 'or does it have to be there like wham-boom?'

Baptist scratched at his unshaven cheek, the white whiskers rustled against his fingernails. 'I'm not really an expert, y'know,' he said.

'It seems,' Paul went on, 'that romance, infatuation, all those things, that you have to go through that first before you get to the next level, or something. But can't you just start with that, I've been wondering, and skip the first part?'

'Well,' Baptist said, 'with Lihua and me — we just started somewhere, of course, when her brother dropped her off at the shop that day. Romantic, no, not that. And whether he was even her brother, in fact I'm still not sure, in any case I've never seen him since.'

He stared at his nails. He had strikingly handsome hands and nails, Paul thought, that didn't seem to fit with the rest of his body. Baptist looked up, his eyes floated a milky blue behind the lenses of his specs. 'To be honest, I don't really know if I love her or not. But when I haven't seen her for a while … then I miss her … So what does that say?'

A silence descended between them. It was as though they were both thinking deeply about a chess move. A tractor drove down the street, the contract worker driving it wore his baseball cap turned backwards, the latest fashion blown in from the big city.

'Boy,' Paul said, 'I don't know either.'

'See, there you go,' said Baptist.

Before that night with Ineke Wessels, Paul had never had erection problems. It was the handwriting on the wall: the days of unbridled pleasure were over, if he had ever known them at all. He would have to order Viagra pills on the Internet and after that — when he couldn't stand the disgust in the girls' eyes any longer — give up on it completely. Maybe, he thought, it was even possible to arrive at a kind of harmonious cohabitation with a woman like Ineke Wessels, once lust no longer played a real role. Their sex glands becoming inactive, their bodies serving only to keep each other warm.

Paul turned his gaze to the far side of the street, where old Shu stood smoking a cigarette in the alleyway between the houses, his eyes closed and his face raised to the sun like an iguana. That wouldn't last much longer either. Worse than the barbarians who were coming were the barbarians who left again.

'Might I ask,' Baptist said, 'what makes you actually want to know?'

Paul nodded and said thoughtfully: 'A woman, she lives in the Avermaten. We know each other from school. I don't know, it seems like she's wanting to start something. Or maybe not, it's not clear to me.'

'Well-well,' Baptist said. 'And a Chinese girl, ever think about that?'

Paul shook his head. 'I have a hard time reading the instructions on things that are made in China.'

Baptist burst out laughing. 'That's a good one,' he said. 'That's a good one. I've got exact the same thing.' His laughter trailed off. 'Exactly the same.'

They'd been haying — the grass lay in rows on the fields along both sides of the road. The smell of it floated through the open windows, insects ticked against the windshield and left yellow splatters behind.

His father was lying on the neatly made-up bed, reading *De Telegraaf* — 'that worthless rag'. Paul took half a loaf of bread, a tub of margarine, and chocolate sprinkles from a plastic bag and put it all away in the nightstand.

The hospital was quiet, it was obviously the holidays. Life seemed to have slowed down, a bit like the way he imagined the 1950s, long before the great rush of time had begun.

His father was on an antibiotic drip, the needle was stuck in his elbow and covered with an elastic bandage. Paul stood by the window and looked out at the sun-covered landscape. A kestrel seen from behind, hovering over the empty fields. If his father had had a room on the east side of the building, he could have seen the Avermaten.

Paul turned on his phone: Ineke Wessels had sent nothing else.

His father looked at him from behind his newspaper. 'You're supposed to turn your phone off here. You expecting something?'

'Not really,' said Paul, and put his phone away again.

He considered telling him about last night and the knocked-over chair he'd seen that morning, but didn't, because all things considered it was rather eccentric to go summoning up ghosts in the attic in the dead of night. Maybe he believed more soundly in ghosts by now than he did in God. Instead of the unshakeable conviction of his youth, God had become in any case more of a regulated chain of actions, of rituals that swelled or ebbed away in proportion to how things were going with him. God, he thought, had in any case never knocked over a chair in the attic.

'So they're taking good care of you?' he asked.

'Brilliantly,' his father said. 'Staff's magnificent.'

'Ah, that's good to hear,' Paul said.

'Come right away if you need them, and always nice as can be. Nothing like what you read in the papers.'

'That's more about nursing homes, I think,' Paul said. 'That they leave you sitting around all day in your nappy.'

'And if you need anything: no problem at all, Mr Krüzen. No, the service here is tops, no two ways about it.'

Sort of like at home, Paul thought bitterly, who couldn't remember ever having heard a single word of appreciation. He folded up the plastic shopping bag from the Plus market and stuck it in his back pocket. 'Okay,' he said, 'well then, I'll be getting home.'

Twenty-Eighth

The nights used to be so cold that, early one morning long ago, he had seen frost on the counterpane. His mother had turned on the light in his room and slid the curtains aside. He lay buried under the blankets, shivering at the prospect of getting out of bed. 'Paul!' he heard his mother say. 'Hurry up! We'll be late!'

It was infinitely long ago that he had heard her voice. Now, suddenly, as he was lying in bed and reading the Gospel of Matthew, he heard it again, as clear and strong as when he was a child.

Usually her voice lay tucked away in some inaccessible fold in his memory, but now, at an unguarded moment, she had appeared and she had called him. A huge and powerless longing rose up inside him, followed on the heels by the same sorrow as forty-two years earlier, when he had clamped on to her leg and begged her to take him with her. He couldn't figure himself out, so moved as he was at this late hour, while the reading lamp shone on the pages of his Bible.

For forty days and forty nights, he read, Jesus had been alone in the wilderness. He was very hungry. Then the devil came and beset him. He dared him to change the rocks into loaves and to jump from a tall temple. He promised him 'all the kingdoms of the world, and the glory of them', but Jesus withstood the temptations and simply said:

'Get thee hence, Satan!'

'After that,' Matthew wrote, 'the devil left him, and behold, angels came and ministered unto him.'

Paul looked at the ceiling. '*Vade retro, Satana,*' he whispered, even though it was quiet up there tonight. He leafed through the gospel for a while, then put the book down beside the pistol on the night table and turned off the light.

He remained awake for a long time. Still lay the forest beyond the windows. He thought about the night when Danny, the Champion of the World, went looking for his father. It was after midnight; his father should have come home hours ago. Danny, who had learned to drive at a very early age, was able to start a car and drove between high hedgerows to the place in the forest where his father was poaching. He was alone in the dark woods. He called for his father, his voice thin and faint amid the trees. 'Father? Father, are you there?'

No reply came, there was no one.

Only now that Paul lay staring wide-eyed into the darkness did he see the correspondence with Christ's dying moments. Alone on the cross, abandoned by one and all. Couldn't the three crosses atop Golgotha also be seen as a forest, a *sparse* forest? He too had called for his father. *Eli, Eli, lama sabachthani* were the loneliest words in the Good Book, the priest had once said during Sunday school, all the more because those close by misunderstood Him and thought he was appealing to the prophet Elijah.

Paul crossed his arms over his chest and tried to recall what Danny's failsafe method for poaching pheasants had been, for god sake, but there his memory failed him.

He looked at the clock radio and saw that it was four past twelve. He had just turned fifty.

Twenty-Ninth

A Saturday morning in late July, the sun remarkably bright. His birthday, nine days earlier, had gone unnoticed; his father was still in the hospital. The first ripe elderberries dangled from the bushes at the forest's edge, the bird shit on his car would soon be turning purple. Paul drove in circles on the ride-on mower, a powerful machine that the Honda dealer said could handle a hundred square metres of lawn in only two minutes. But the grass was high and still wet with early dew, and it took a lot longer than that. As a boy he had mown the lawn with a simple push-mower, the rotating blades jammed in clumps of grass and sorrel, it had taken him hours. Then there was a rotary mower with a gasoline engine, which was already a vast improvement, but which still stalled when it hit tall grass. Somewhere in the early 80s his father had bought his first ride-on mower. Paul couldn't remember the make, but he remembered its powerful Briggs & Stratton engine. The accelerator handle switched back and forth between turtle and hare, with neutral in the middle. From then on, regardless of how badly he wanted to sit on that machine, he never had to cut the grass again; his father always did it. And the accelerator always remained on turtle. 'The turtle can tell you more about the road than the hare,' his father would say, and go on calmly turning circles across the lawn around the house.

That ride-on mower had been replaced long ago, and in the meantime the cells of Paul's own body had refreshed themselves a few times over, too, only those faithful old brain cells went on stubbornly broadcasting signals from long ago, clear as starlight.

On his way to lunch at the Happytaria, he stopped by Hedwig's. The shop was still closed, the curtains still drawn. Hedwig didn't open the door. Paul put his ear to the window and heard the sound of the TV. He went back to the car and called him. He tried twice, to no avail.

Once again, he knocked on the windows. 'Hedwig!'

He expected to see him appear in the doorway any minute, blinking his eyes against the light. He rang the bell again and decided to let himself in the same way Steggink and Ivan had. With a brick, he knocked loose the planks he himself had nailed to the inside of the window frame just two weeks ago. He pulled himself up until he was hanging from the waist up in the storeroom, lifted one leg onto the sill, and dropped down on the other side. A sense of foreboding crept up from his abdomen.

'Hedwig!' he shouted to announce his presence, to make sure he didn't shoot him with his own weapon. Shouting and crashing about, he entered the house itself. 'Hedwig! Don't shoot! It's me, Paul!'

In the hallway, stronger than ever before, hung the odour of decay. Things weren't right, he knew that; he braced himself against what he would find. 'Hedwig!' he shouted again, and tasted the heavy stench on his tongue. He gagged.

The television was showing webcam footage of an RTV East radio broadcast. Hedwig was sitting in his chair. Paul took a few steps into the room. 'Hedwig?' One look at his face was enough. His greenish skin, the flies taking off from his open mouth. *Santa Rita ora pro nobis.* A sob of horror welled up in his throat. They were walking across his eyelids, his sunken eyeballs, with their disgusting legs. Big, slow flies gleaming bluely in the sparse light that fell through cracks in the curtains — they covered his face, his reddish-pink marbled hands, his swollen ankles protruding from the slippers. Paul threw up on the carpet.

Under the chair he saw a large stain of fluid. Blood? Could a person bleed that much? He registered the maggots crawling over the floor in search of a sheltered place to break open the pupal case, and a cardboard medicine box, stained at the edges with the pinkish moisture it had absorbed from the carpet.

Paul took the remote from the floor and turned off the TV. The zooming of the flies was all around him, an undulating fabric of sound. Again he threw up, and stumbled out of the room. In the hallway he twisted open the deadbolt — flaming sunlight fell through the doorway.

Panting, he sat in the driver's seat for a moment, then picked up his phone.

While calling the emergency line, he went back into the house, the other hand held tightly over his nose and mouth. 'Police,' he replied when the operator asked which service he needed. He slid the chairs at the bottom of the staircase to one side and went up with the phone against his ear. Stiffly, while searching the bedroom for the Luger, he reported the death of Hedwig Johannes Geerdink, and gave them the address on Bunderweg. The stench of rotting filled the house. He could find the pistol nowhere, not beside the bed and not in the half-empty closets or on the little desk where the computer was.

Empty-handed, he went back down the stairs and waited outside for the police to come.

Half an hour later, a patrol car pulled up from the direction of the village. Two policemen climbed out, stony-faced. 'Good afternoon,' said the youngest of the two.

Paul nodded.

'You're the one who found him, sir?' The youngest cop glanced at a note he had in his hand. His face was strikingly brown, his eyes bright. 'Mr Krüzen?'

'That's me.'

The policeman looked up in surprise. 'And the deceased is …?'

'Geerdink. Hedwig Geerdink.'

'And you are?'

'Paul Krüzen.'

'What I meant was, your relation to the victim.'

'A friend.' Paul's eyes wandered across the pasturelands beside Hamriksweg. 'We're friends.'

'My condolences, sir.'

'How did you get into the house?' the other officer asked. 'Do you have the key?'

'There was a burglary two weeks ago. The window hadn't been fixed yet.'

The older policemen held his gaze. 'My condolences,' he said then too. 'And how was he when you found him?'

Paul sniffed and jerked with his shoulders. He felt tears burning. 'In his chair. Flies all over the place.'

Just then the GP arrived in his old Saab. 'Good afternoon, gentlemen,' he said, and introduced himself to the policemen.

'Dr Lamérus,' Paul said when the doctor held out his hand in greeting.

Lamérus held on to his hand for a few moments, then said: 'I'll talk to you in a bit.'

He entered the house with the policemen.

About ten minutes later he was the first to re-emerge. He put his leather bag on the ground, raised his face to the sun, and pulled a pack of Gauloises from the breast pocket of his short-sleeved khaki shirt. 'You?' he asked, holding up the pack to Paul. They blew smoke at the sun. 'You never get used to it,' Lamérus said. 'no matter how many times you see it.'

Paul turned his head. Cyclists slowed to see what was going on.

Lamérus said: 'You shouldn't have had to see him like that. But the memory fades, I know that from experience. After a while you'll remember him again the way he was.'

They smoked. Paul rolled his tongue around in his dry mouth and said: 'There was lots of blood.'

'Hmm,' the doctor murmured, deep in thought.

'Under the chair,' Paul said. 'He must have lost litres of it.'

'That's possible,' said Lamérus. 'If a person takes diluents, for example, which he didn't, at least not according to my records. The last time I saw him was three years ago, my nurse says. Whatever the case, all that's needed is a little hole, a bedsore, a little cut. Then they can run completely dry.'

'That much blood?'

'That much blood.'

'I thought ... That they killed him. That's what I thought.'

Lamérus nodded, his head at a slight angle. 'I signed the death certificate, and determined the probable cause. The rest is up to them.' He nodded towards the house.

'So what caused it, in your opinion?'

Lamérus suddenly looked him straight in the eye, as though catching sight of him for the first time. 'As far as I can tell ... his heart. Or else I'm sorely mistaken.'

'But what about all that blood?' Paul insisted. 'He was robbed a couple of weeks ago. They used a lot of force. He was scared as hell that they were going to come back. Now he's dead.'

'The heart is a sensitive instrument, it can do its work without stopping for eighty years or more, without missing a beat, but it can also stop unexpectedly after forty or fifty. Maybe it actually was the shock from the robbery that had that effect, who can say. I, for my part though, didn't see any external signs of a violent death.'

Paul tipped the cone of ash from his cigarette. For a long time, he had taken into account the possibility that Hedwig would put an end to it all. Men of that age, looking back on their lives and without the energy to backpedal and make something out of it, took that route more often than people of a different age group. That his heart might cut out on him while he was watching RTV East had never occurred to him.

'And suicide?' he asked, as the image of the hanging man in the attic flashed through his memory.

Lamérus crushed the cigarette underfoot and picked up his bag. 'No indications, not of pills or anything else either. That looks very different. Vomit. The body in a cramped position. No, nothing to indicate that.' The lines around the doctor's mouth seemed to express regret. 'A sudden death like this,' he said, 'has something unsatisfactory about it. There's no time for farewells, for a final word. But I … it seems to me that it all went naturally. Your friend seems to me to have died peacefully.'

At his car, Lamérus turned. 'Supposing that you want to talk about it, or that you have trouble sleeping or something, you know where to find me, don't you?'

'Thanks, doc,' Paul said.

He wasn't all that bad, he thought as he watched Lamérus turn the car round and drive off towards the village. Communicative and empathetic, not at all the grey soul he seemed when you visited him in his office.

The policemen came outside. One of them went round the house for a breath of fresh air. Dust puffed up around his shoes on the sandy path. The other wrote down Paul's particulars, as well as Hedwig's.

'Does Mr Geerdink have a partner?' he asked. 'Children?'

Paul shook his head.

'Next of kin?'

'He was an only child. He didn't have any friends. Except for me.'

'Nephews, nieces, cousins maybe?'

'Could be. Not that I know of.'

'We'll figure all that out,' the officer said. He was still for a moment, but then could no longer contain his curiosity. 'Mr. Geerdink,' he said, 'was he … Why was he alone, do you think?'

Paul shrugged reluctantly. 'Because that's the way it went,' he said.

Someday they would ask the same thing about him, and then no one would have an answer either.

'How long had he been lying there?' Paul asked.

The policeman frowned and said: 'No more than three days, that's what the doctor thought, too. But those were hot days, then it goes fast, something like that.'

'I visited him earlier in the week,' Paul said. 'He was very down. A couple of weeks back they beat him over the head and robbed him. And now he's dead.'

The policeman nodded. 'We've been informed about the robbery, yeah.'

'Is there any connection, you think?' Paul asked.

The man shook his head. 'Not likely.'

No one, Paul realised, neither the doctor nor the police, seemed to even consider the possibility of a crime or suicide. Death had snuck up on Hedwig in stockinged feet, the last thing he had heard were trifles on the regional radio station.

Around three that afternoon, coming from the direction of Kloosterzand, an opal-grey hearse pulled up at the door. A grey-uniformed man and woman climbed out, got quick bearings on who was who, and offered Paul their condolences for the loss of his 'loved one'. Their compassion was professional and convincing. Opening the liftback of the Mercedes, they unfolded the lower half of a rolling stretcher, with a plastic body bag on top. They pulled on gloves, put on surgical masks, and nodded gravely to the policemen, who showed them into the house. Paul sat in his car for the shade, the door open, his legs sticking out. His world had shrunk once more. The process went by fits and starts, with leaden irreversibility; the losses were fixed and final.

The group came out of the house a little later in procession, the stretcher between them, the body bag lashed down with tie-down straps. A little group of cyclists watched the stretcher slide smoothly onto the floorboards of the hearse. The electric liftback closed by itself with a discreet click.

A few moments later, the hearse zoomed round the curve in the road, the gaggle of cyclists scattered and divided itself over Verolmeweg and Bunderweg.

'Good luck, sir,' said the light-eyed policeman.

'I left Mr Geerdink's keyring on the table,' said the other. 'Will you lock up?'

Paul nodded. A wave of desolation washed over him.

'Would you like me to get them for you?'

'No, I'll make it,' he mumbled, turning away to keep from bursting into tears.

'Never mind, I'll get them,' the policeman said.

A few minutes later, they climbed into the cruiser. 'We'll be in touch,' the eldest of the two said. 'All kinds of things enter into something like this. In case there's anything, my name's Te Pas, Arnold Te Pas.'

'Thank you, officer,' Paul said. 'Also for …' His hand fluttered in the direction of the house.

'That's what we're here for.'

The slamming of car doors, the hand raised out of the window, followed by a silence so deep and lasting that it made him stagger. Under the cloudless sky, by full light of day, the tears ran down his face.

Thirtieth

On Monday there was a death notice in the *Tubantia* for Hedwig Johannes Geerdink, ending with the words:

> Relatives of the deceased are requested to contact *militariaweb@hotmail.com*.

That very same day, a response came from two brothers, second cousins of Hedwig on his mother's side. They had known about their cousin, one of them told him on the phone, but never met him.

The next day, a relative from his father's side reported in as well; Paul called the number listed at the bottom of her email. A voice, hoarse with age, told him that Hedwig's father and her own had been first cousins, she remembered that her mother had always referred to Hedwig as a *vrömde*, an oddball. She herself had left for distant parts with her husband when she was quite young; only when he retired at Shell had they returned to the Netherlands. She had never given Hedwig a second thought, not until a neighbour lady asked her if 'that Geerdink in the paper' was perhaps a relative.

On Wednesday morning, the heirs came to Paul's house. The female cousin was brought by a doe-eyed Iranian woman who had originally been her housekeeper; after the cousin's husband had died, she became a friend, who occasionally drove her places. The Iranian's almond skin stood out against the white of her dress.

The two men were in their sixties. They were corpulent and loud, which fit well with Paul's picture of the typical German businessman. One of them wore glasses with photochromic lenses.

Paul could not detect a trace of Hedwig in any of them.

He explained the situation. He had called a notary public, and this was the way it would go: if they, the second cousins, were in fact his heirs, the notary could at their request issue a certificate of succession. Paul said he was willing to act as authorised representative to round off Hedwig's affairs. He had been Hedwig's only friend, it was his duty to do so, but obviously only with their permission. If they preferred to arrange the liquidation of their cousin's shop and business obligations themselves, he was prepared to help them and give them advice. He had already sent mourning cards to Hedwig's regular customers. The funeral would be held on Monday, it was almost sure not to be particularly well attended.

He poured coffee for them, there was sugar, unsweetened coffee creamer, and sweetener on the table. The little plate of cinnamon Bastogne cookies remained untouched.

'Is there,' one of the brothers asked, 'actually anything to inherit?'

'Ah, the key question,' Paul said. The female cousin drew a bead on the man, like an angry little bird.

'As far as I know,' Paul said, 'there are no outstanding debts. The house is in bad condition, but the land is worth something, I'd say. I don't know whether Hedwig left a will, in any case he never talked about it to me.' He looked around the group. The Iranian woman's eyes were truly spectacular. 'Unfortunately for you, though,' he went on, 'Hedwig was the victim of a violent robbery a few weeks back.'

The brothers set their cups down on the saucers at the same moment. 'What do you mean?' one of them said.

'He said they took eighty thousand euros. They broke his dentures while he was still wearing them, and left him behind for dead.'

The relatives listened gravely as he told them about the robbery and the miserable state Hedwig had been in during his final weeks.

The old woman shook her head. 'How horrible,' she said. 'So terribly sad.'

Paul was about to tell them about that June evening at Shu Dynasty, and about how Steggink and the Russian's greed had followed hard on the heels of Hedwig's bluff, when one of the brothers, rattling the keys of his Audi A8, said: 'Well, shall we go and take a look?'

They can't wait, Paul thought. He climbed into the car with the two women and showed them the way to Hedwig's house.

At the door, the brothers pulled out their handkerchiefs and held them over their noses. The old woman sniffled and cried a bit when they entered the living room. Paul opened the curtains and let in the sunlight; they looked aghast at the blood on the carpet, the swaybacked easy chair, the general malaise of which the kitchen spoke. '*Gott im Himmel*,' one of the brothers said. Flies droned lazily around the room. Whenever one landed on a face or hand, they were hard to shoo off. They were a bit *sticky*. That these flies had had their fill of Hedwig was something everyone realised all too well. Paul felt the nausea rising up again. The old woman stopped for a moment before the portraits on the sideboard, but then moved on quickly out the door.

'A cleaning firm could straighten things up a bit,' Paul said once they were all outside. 'That's up to you.'

One of the brothers peered through the shop curtains and asked: 'Is there a key to this too?'

'You can get to the shop from the house as well,' Paul explained, 'but I have the key here.'

The shopkeeper's bell rang brightly when he opened the door.

The brothers nosed around, amazed to find that fate had made them the owners of an endless stock of fruit juice, syrup, cookies, canned vegetables, and tobacco, all of it scraped together in untidy stacks. Hedwig had always piled up everything into towers.

Paul felt in his chest a huge sense of loss when he looked around the grocery; however outdated, it had been the be all and end all of Hedwig's existence. This monument to stagnation had been his little window on the world.

'That this still exists …' the old woman murmured. She examined her cousin's handsome lettering. *'t Molenaartje cookies, now €1.89. Three cans of whipped cream for the price of two. Unox meat paste in the tin, seventy cents.*

Paul slid aside a few packages of detergent and sat down on the windowsill. Hedwig's mother used to stand here often, her arms crossed, watching for her husband to appear with the horse and wagon. When you cycled by, you were always startled by the way her eyes shot sparks at you from under the awning. His grandmother had stood in the very same spot; Hedwig himself had sold the wagon to a collector.

The woman took a jar down from the shelf and gazed at the pale frankfurter sausages under glass. She looked to be a few years older than Paul's own mother. On the day of Hedwig's funeral, his mother would turn seventy-five. In his mind she had never grown any older than she was on the day she left with the Russian. He himself was now already so much older than she had been then. If she were to go cycling by on Bunderweg today, at that same age, he would look at her as a *young woman*, like the Iranian woman standing outside there in her white dress and big sunglasses, as a movie star who'd wandered onto the wrong set. He turned his gaze away from her. The old woman was truly fascinated by the frankfurters.

'That all seems clear enough to me,' one of the brothers said. 'First the cleaners, and then the junk dealer. Whatever's left can go to the dump.'

The other brother nodded. The old woman put the jar of sausages back on the shelf.

'If that's the way you want to do it,' Paul said.

'Are there things of his,' the woman asked, 'that you'd like to have? As a memento?'

Paul shook his head. 'No, wait,' he said then. 'His camera. A Rollei. On holiday, he was the only one around who still took pictures with a roll of film.' And, a little later: 'If no one else wants it, I'd also like to have his mother's statue of the Virgin Mary.'

They dropped him at the house. The heirs all agreed that, pending the certificate of succession, Paul would start with clearing the house and selling the inventory.

He ate lunch later than usual, then left for the hospital. He took the new slippers with him. They had first been lost in the mail and then, after he had called a few times, were delivered only yesterday to an address in Mariënheem, a village thirty minutes down the road.

This was the first time he'd been to the hospital since he found Hedwig. At the start of the week he had called his father to tell him about his friend's death.

'Oh, but that's …' his father had said. He was silent for a moment, then asked how he had died.

'Tragic,' he said, and then: 'But maybe better this way than after a long illness.'

Stunned, Paul said: 'But he hadn't even turned *fifty* …'

He was right, his father said, but added: 'The boy had nothing, no one, Paul. Better this way then, maybe.'

Paul listened to him in silence. If you were suffering, then you were better off dead, that was the message his father was broadcasting from his hospital bed. Paul would never cease to be amazed by his father's lack of fellow feeling.

Stepping out of the lift on the fourth floor, he went by the desk first to ask how his father was doing.

'His leg is still a problem,' the male nurse in Scandinavian clogs told him, 'but he himself is right as rain. Your father was in the hospital swing of things as soon as he came in the front door.' The wound was a festering colony of streptococcus and staphylococcus bacteria, antibiotics alone hadn't helped; after a time, they had cut away part of the tissue. But Aloïs, the nurse said, had remained in good spirits the whole time.

Perhaps, Paul thought as he walked to Room 404, his father was glad to finally see someone other than his ageing son. In addition, potatoes were a staple of the hospital menu, he got as much gravy as a mushy eater could desire, and there was no one sitting across from him and waiting impatiently for him to finish. People were often better off in the hospital than at home. They received attention, the daily routine had a comforting effect, the meals were served at fixed times, there was a button beside the bed for emergencies.

'Your new slippers,' Paul said.

'Put them under the bed, I don't need them yet anyway.'

Paul tossed the old pair in the wastebasket.

'How are things at home?' his father asked.

'I mow the lawn every week, it looks like it grows while my back's turned. Apples are ripe. Almost. Lots of starlings.'

'Damned birds,' his father mumbled. He didn't ask about Hedwig. After the phone call a few days ago, he seemed to consider that subject closed. Wasn't it ridiculous and despicable, Paul thought, that a fifty-year-old man could still be aggrieved like a child?

'Monday's the funeral,' Paul said after a long silence. 'There's a lot going on the next few days. I'll try to stop by in between times, but I don't know if it'll work.'

'See how it goes,' his father said, flipping absentmindedly through the pile of newspapers Paul had brought for him. 'I'll get by.'

It was for good reason, Paul thought on the way home, that Genesis said a son should leave his father and mother and cleave to his own wife in order to become *one flesh*; the ties between parent and child had a limited shelf life. If a child never left its parental home, there was something wrong with it. The parents could never close their eyes to their failure. Aversion, sometimes turning to hatred, locked itself in place between them.

In the glove compartment was the Walther P38. He never went anywhere without it these days. He slept lightly and awoke with a start at the slightest thing.

Five more days till the funeral. The way things looked now, the house would be cleared out before there was even time to lay him in the ground. It would be as though Hedwig Geerdink had never existed.

On Thursday, Paul suddenly thought about the little box he'd seen under Hedwig's chair. A medicine box. White cardboard. But Hedwig, the doctor had said, wasn't on any medication. Still, there had been a medicine box there, he had seen it clear as day when he picked up the remote from the floor.

When he went back to the house with the heirs, though, he hadn't. Who could possibly be interested in a medicine box soaked in blood and necrotic fluid? He spent the rest of the morning mulling that one over.

At noontime he finally got officer Arnold Te Pas on the line; the policeman didn't remember seeing a box. They definitely hadn't thrown it away or taken it along with them. If it had been there at all, then it had to still be there.

'So how are you getting along now?' Te Pas asked, and Paul felt the swelling in his chest. After a brief silence he said: 'A few times every day, I think: Don't forget to say this or say that to Hedwig … I had always wondered whether, yeah, whether we were actually friends or only just fellow-sufferers. The way things are now … I have no doubts about that anymore. No doubts whatsoever. It's a ridiculous thing to wonder about, isn't it? We hung out together for forty years. Forty. That makes you friends.'

Without noticing it, he had walked out the door, he was holding forth on the lawn.

'That means you're friends, doesn't it?'

'Seems to me, yeah, after forty years,' Te Pas said. He was clearly letting Paul blow off steam.

'Even though I'd stopped listening to him years ago, you know. Death, nothing but death. How this one or that one had died, and that one's sister too, and that one's brother … Graves all the way out to the horizon, that was all he saw.' He took a deep breath, his gaze fixed on a flock of birds passing overhead. Big ones. Could they be cranes?

He'd read that there were cranes on the heath between Mariënveen and Kloosterzand.

'I miss that whining,' he went on. 'You'd have never thought that someday you would miss it.'

That afternoon, he crawled around Hedwig's house on hands and knees, without finding the medicine box. A few times he went outside for a deep breath of fresh air. When the people from the cleaning service showed up later, they were amazed to see him walking in and out of the house unprotected. They themselves wore white plastic overalls and gloves.

'A corpse can contain highly pathogenic bacteria, sir,' the boss of the operation lectured dully from behind his surgical mask, 'that can pose a risk for the living.'

Paul nodded forbearingly and said: 'Don't worry. I knew him. He was harmless.'

They packed the armchair in plastic foil and carried it to a small truck. Then they lugged the dining room table, the chairs, and the console to the living room, and cut the bloody patch out of the carpet. They rolled it up, wrapped it in foil, and carried it outside. A large, nebulous spot remained on the concrete. That, one of the men said, would have to be chipped out or sealed with a coating. Necrotic fluid was impossible to get out of concrete.

Paul wandered the house. He couldn't find his Luger anywhere, and that worried him. Somewhere, a loaded gun was lying around. In the bedroom he disconnected the old Hewlett-Packard and put it in the back of the car. He placed Hedwig's bookkeeping on the passenger seat, and while the men were spraying the house with a product that neutralised the smell, he searched fruitlessly for a will amid the papers. The most recent notice from the Rabobank, which Hedwig had apparently still been receiving in the mail, showed a current account balance of €6,089.45. There were no account numbers to indicate that Hedwig had kept separate track of his business and personal finances.

There were no savings, and Paul could find nothing about a retirement fund.

He sat staring out the front window. Hedwig was no millionaire, of course not. He'd been bluffing on a grand scale, that evening at Shu. Eighty thousand euros in an old sock, that was all the money he'd had. Until the rat came sniffing around.

Thirty-First

He chopped wood in the warmth of the early evening, the holster and his sports jacket hanging from a branch. He felt weak. It was remarkable, he thought, how quickly you grew accustomed to the threat of violence. He lived like a hare with its nose to the wind; shadow and menace were everywhere.

During his years of military service, he had crept through a cold, dark wood in Lower Saxony, black smudges on his face. In the display case in his office he still had a cardboard card showing a licence plate and a hammer and sickle, accompanied by the announcement:

> If you see a license plate like this one, you have sighted an SMLM-F vehicle.
>
> Report the sighting as quickly as possible to your COMMANDER, in accordance with the directions given on the back of this form.
>
> Time and place of sighting
>
> Colour and make of vehicle
>
> Licence number
>
> Number of occupants and their clothing (civilian clothes, uniform)
>
> Whether the vehicle was moving (and in which direction) or stationary
>
> Any information on activities of occupants (making notes, taking pictures, etc.)
>
> NAME, RANK AND COMPANY

IMPORTANT

Any delay in reporting will reduce the value of your sighting.

They had chuckled about it, the way the conscripts at Seedorf had chuckled about most everything. That was the only way to make it through the stupid, repetitive chores of national service. In the background there was always the fearful expectation that things could go wrong any moment; they were encircled by nuclear weapons with a combined payload of many thousands of megatons, training films had shown what remained of a body in the fireball of a nuclear explosion — the charred stump at the periphery, nothing but dust at the epicentre.

And cancer for those who survived. Cancer and deformities.

And the enemy was a Russian, then and now and always. There was nothing new under the sun.

Paul slammed the axe into the chopping block and left the woods.

He fried potatoes and defrosted a few blocks of spinach in a saucepan. This he ate with yesterday's leftover gravy, and a patty of ground beef.

He could, if he wanted to see other humans, go sometime soon to the Pretty Woman café in Kloosterzand, or Slomp's in Deurlo. Almost no one he knew ever came there. Blue as the mantle of the Holy Virgin was the evening sky outside the window; he avoided his reflection.

After dinner, he put Hedwig's PC on the desk in his office and plugged it in. While the coffee was running through the filter behind him, he pushed the start button. The fan in the housing began to purr, the monitor popped on. The edges of the keys, around the letters and punctuations marks, were a dirty brown. Hedwig had clearly never cleaned them since Paul had given him his old computer. The password was one he had created himself.

Hedwig had recently visited a site for shoes, the website of RTV East, a few news sites and wholesalers. He had led a thoroughly unremarkable digital life, there were no traces of general sexual interest or specific predilections.

Because it was Paul himself who'd taught him to work with Windows, a tedious and time-consuming process, he didn't think Hedwig would have been capable of wiping out his digital tracks. It had simply never occurred to him to visit sex sites.

He grazed through the Word files until he found a document called I WAS BORN IN MARIËNVEEN. He opened it. The name of the document was the same as the first line.

I was born in Mariënveen.

Family Geerdink, Pa, Ma, and I.

At home I was safe. Outside shy and unsafe.

The Lower School for the Retail Trade was far away, every Saturday back in the shop; happy.

I never abandoned the house, the family, the Church.

Once Pa and Ma were dead, I moved further and further away from the normal world.

I got older and made mistakes. The business kept going. A wonder.

I lacked support and moved further into loneliness.

I have not provided for the future, hence this abrupt end.

As far as I know, I have never treated anyone unfairly.

Paul wanted to read on, but couldn't. He wiped away the tears. What followed was a list of the names and phone numbers of those who were to be informed of his death. At the bottom of the document, Paul came across his own name.

Paul Krüzen and Ming Shu from Shu Dynasty. They are my heirs if there's anything left.

Paul can sell the shop inventory and the house. I have an account with the Rabobank with money in it. Paul knows everything about my computer, etc.

Otherwise important:

Henny Kreuwel, I had a loan with him, maybe I still owe him something (max. 1,000 euros). Important people in the village were

Baptist Weening, Ming from Shu Dynasty and Paul Krüzen, Mientje Fox, friend of my mother's, cuts my hair and drinks coffee here on Sundays.

Hedwig Geerdink, 6 July 2013

Paul closed his eyes. The letter was four years old.

What had stopped him back then, what had kept him from carrying through with it?

Paul dug around in his memory but couldn't remember anything about the summer of 2013. Only the spring, which had been extremely wet; part of the maize and potato crops had been lost. Farmers dug trenches in the fields to let the water run off. In December, he and Hedwig had gone to the Philippines on holiday for the third time, but of the summer he couldn't recall a thing.

The woman who cut Hedwig's hair, Mientje Fox, had died of lung cancer last year after a brief illness, even though she'd never touched a cigarette in her life. Her death, he remembered, had affected Hedwig deeply.

He and Ming as heirs, would that stand up in a court of law? Based on a four-year-old letter, written on a computer?

He reread it, again his eyes misted over at the words 'As far as I know, I have never treated anyone unfairly'.

'You never treated a soul unfairly at all, dipstick,' Paul said softly, 'not a soul.'

His premonition had been right: he could have found him hanging from the banister. Things had gone differently. He thought again about the medicine box, that he had clearly seen on the carpet, a ragged patter of pinkish fluid around the edges, but again his mental rooting around turned up nothing.

Eleven o'clock, total darkness outside now. He looked at the monitor of the surveillance cameras. Trees, the grass; the world without him. Branches moved in the wind.

The junk dealer, who advertised online with a 'total solution', came by the next morning. The man parked his Mercedes CLS right in front of the shop; he did absolutely nothing to disguise the fact that business was going swimmingly. 'What a glorious day,' he said, hoisting himself to his feet with a grip on the open car door. He took out a handkerchief and wiped his face. 'Lovely place you've got here.'

'Actually, my place is up that way.'

What the total solution meant, he said in reply to Paul's question, was that he would assess the value of the belongings and clear the house, 'After which the revenues from the sale of the belongings will be checked off directly against the costs of clearing.'

He took a giant-format iPad from the front seat and followed Paul into the house. After all this time, the stench was still unbearable, despite the cleaning and the ozone generator that had been running in the kitchen for the last twenty-four hours.

'Stop right there,' the man said when Paul made to show him the living room. 'I can't do anything with this stuff anymore. That smell … You never get that out again the whole live-long day. Not even the drop-off centre's going to want this stuff.'

Paul nodded. He led him through the little hallway to the shop. He opened the blinds to let some light in.

'Jesus-pleaseus,' the man said. 'The things you run into …'

He took jars and cans down off the shelves and examined the labels. Then he took pictures of the shop with the iPad, explaining as he did that he himself didn't do shop inventories, but that he had a colleague he could call in. 'I'll send him a couple of photos. But a lot of this stuff is past its shelf life, I'll tell you that right away.'

Outside, the man formulated his offer. 'I can clear the house, no problem, but that's going to cost you two thousand euros. Empty it out and take it away. That's what I can do.'

Paul looked at the man. He lacked the energy to argue with him. To be honest, he also had no idea whether there really was anything of value there. The house was worn out, the furnishings threadbare; Hedwig had left it behind like shedding an old skin, and in his mind's eye for a moment Paul saw his friend's white body, how he emerged naked and clammy from his old skin and floated up towards the light.

'So,' the man said. 'That's what I can do for you. But if you say …'

'Fine by me,' said Paul.

After the cleanout man had left, he combed the house again in search of the pistol. The flashlight in his phone shone even behind the canning jars on the shelves in the low cellar, filled with vegetables preserved back then by Mrs Geerdink, the labels long eaten by silverfish. He came out covered in cobwebs. He emptied kitchen cupboards and looked under shelves and drawers to see if the pistol hadn't been stuck there with duct tape. His apprehension grew — if Steggink and Ivan had come back, then they were armed now, no doubt about it. St Anthony, whom God has given the special power of restoring lost things, grant that I may find my Luger which has been lost …

He had played straight into Steggink's hands, and how! If they got hold of him now, it would be child's play to make it look like suicide, with his own gun … Of course, they would know it was his, how else would Hedwig have got hold of it? In double-quick time he pulled the Walther P38 from its holster and aimed it a random spot in front of him: acting fast, that was the crux of the matter now.

Then he went out to the car and gingerly placed Mother Mary in the passenger seat. Her hands, wrapped in the rosary, stuck out from under the seatbelt.

He locked the house and drove to the Happytaria.

Paul took a seat by the window, the better to keep an eye on the street. He read the *Tubantia* for the second time that day. Out of sheer desperation he even read the columns and the recipe of the day, some ridiculous thing with roasted duck and orange sauce.

'Xi, have you got a pen and paper for me?' he asked at one point.

'Are you going to write something pretty for us?' Xi asked.

'For the funeral, a little speech. Will you be there on Monday?'

The Chinese man shook his head, looking regretful. 'Snack bar's open on Monday, I can't.'

'And Wen, what about you?' Paul asked.

'Work too,' said Xi.

Wen smiled calmly. Paul tried to concentrate on his speech, but he'd been thrown off balance. He had sent them all a mourning card, Hedwig had been a regular customer, he couldn't understand how a few helpings of fries could take precedence over his funeral.

'And what about Baptist?' he asked. His voice sounded unpleasantly loud, he thought. 'Is he coming?'

They didn't know. Baptist hadn't been in yet today.

At the top of the blank sheet, Paul wrote FAREWELL TO HEDWIG. He looked at that for a while, then wrote underneath it

RITA
SUICIDE NOTE
CARDINAL SINS

Between catchwords and incomplete sentences, the paper was soon covered with writing. Sunk in thought, he ate a hamburger special with fried onions. A few minutes later he laid a ten-euro note on the counter. But while Wen was counting out his change, he changed his mind and ordered a soft ice cream for dessert.

Cone in hand, he crossed the street. Ducking into the alleyway where old Shu often stood smoking, he stuck his head through the bug curtain at the kitchen door. 'Anybody home!' he shouted, and stepped into the kitchen.

An insect lamp spread quiet, purple light. He heard the sound of slippers in the hallway. Old man Shu came into the kitchen, looking surprised.

'Ming,' Paul said. 'Is she around? I need to tell her something.' He licked at his ice cream, which was melting fast in the sweltering hot kitchen.

Father Shu disappeared. From somewhere in the house, Paul heard him shouting.

A few minutes later Ming appeared in the doorway, holding her phone.

'I came in the back way,' he said.

She looked worried.

'I've got something for you,' he said, pulling a folded sheet of typing paper from his back pocket and handing it to her.

She unfolded it, he watched her read. A few silver strands were woven through her pitch-black hair; she had become an old girl. Suddenly he hoped fervently that she would find a man at her next station who would disregard her bluish-black teeth and bony body, and that they would be happy together in their way. She read slowly, his ice cream was finished, all he held now was the cone.

Ming looked up. 'I don't get it,' she said.

'We're the heirs,' he said. 'I found this note in his computer.'

'Us? Heirs of Hedwig?'

'You and me,' he said, and realised how bizarre it was that Hedwig had singled out Ming of all people, a foreigner with whom he may not have been on extremely close terms, but with whom he had clearly felt an affinity. It was as though, with his bequest, he wanted to give Ming a place in Mariënveen, a strip of soil in which to take root. Half a house, half his possessions. Would that convince her to stay? Ming Collect-ing? He doubted it. She would use the proceeds to buy a flat in Arnhem and wile away her days there, in accordance with her wish to do nothing and want nothing.

She pointed to the date on the letter. 'Paul, come on, I don't understand!'

Even Hedwig's suicide note was past its expiration date, Paul thought, and sniffed amusedly. He explained that it was an old farewell letter; at the time, something had stopped Hedwig.

'But Paul,' she said in total confusion, 'I'm not Hedwig's *family*?!'

'He appreciated you, you know that. I'll have them figure out whether it will hold up, okay? I'll go to a notary.'

She nodded. 'Paul?' she asked then. 'Everybody says so much around here ... That he was murdered. That he did it himself. Because of that robbery and stuff. What are you supposed to believe?'

She lowered the sheet of paper. She cried a little. It was the first time he had seen a Chinese person cry. A few tears dripped from the corners of her eyes. She sniffed and wiped them away.

'That robbery,' Paul said, 'that part is true, and that he's dead, that's true, too. Everything in between is vague. But that Steggink has blood on his hands, that's all I know for sure. He and that Russian. There was no one around to stop them.'

She shook her head. 'You gotta be careful, Paul. Really, he's so angry, man. The police went to see him. He says he gonna kill you if he sees you. You need to go away for a while, that would be better, really. You know him. Come back when it's ...' She made a soothing motion with her hand.

'I'll watch what I do,' he said.

She looked at the letter again, her eyes skimmed the lines. 'I'm gonna make a copy, okay?'

Always the practical one, he thought. Staying on the safe side. She disappeared into the back of the restaurant and returned with two sheets of paper. She gave him his original back.

'Will I see you on Monday at the funeral?' he asked.

She tried to smile. 'I dunno yet,' she said. 'Monday's busy, always. A big wedding next week ... Maybe real quick.'

He had seen it with Baptist, with Xi and Wen and now with her: fear. Stay out of everything, keep smiling, be Switzerland.

'Could I use your bin?' he asked, holding out the empty cone in his left hand.

She stuck out her hand, he took it in his for a moment. It was limp, as though it had no bones; the edges of her nails were black with dirt. He let go. She took his cone and tossed it in the trashcan.

Thirty-Second

Monday 7 August, the day on which Hedwig's funeral and Paul's mother's birthday coincided; afternoon temperatures, according to the weatherman on the car radio, varied from 23 along the North Sea coast to 27 inland. There was a chance of thunderstorms in late afternoon, particularly in the central and eastern provinces. When the news was over, they played 'Summer in the City' by The Lovin' Spoonful for the umpteenth time.

The temperature in the walk-in cooler at the funeral home in Kloosterzand was just above freezing; in view of the body's condition, they hadn't been able to put Hedwig in one of the modern viewing rooms, where family members had round-the-clock access with an electronic key.

He was the only visitor. In the last few days, the manager said, there had only been an older lady, accompanied by a 'dark-skinned woman'.

The manager left him alone with the closed coffin and shut the door of the cooler behind him.

Paul had chosen a simple poplar coffin with a flat lid and eight rounded, nickel plate screws. It was difficult to imagine that that thing inside there, resting on a bed of unbleached cotton, was really his friend. His imagination, in fact, couldn't make its way through the wood.

In an hour's time, the coffin would be transferred to the Maria Church in Mariënveen.

These were his last moments alone with him. He felt cold in his best suit, his breath made clouds. No useful thoughts seemed to form, there was nothing he had to say to him. He placed his hand for a moment on the coffin lid, then left the cooler. The manager was nowhere in sight.

He stopped in at the snack bar in Kloosterzand for a portion of fries. A grotesquely obese young man, not a day older than twenty, was leaning his immense behind against the deep-fry installation. Motionless behind the counter, his arms folded across his chest, the boy watched Paul eat. The red carbuncles spotting his face simmered amid tufts of flaxen hair. In the adjacent cafe on the other side of the swinging door, the radio was playing. Sometimes a woman's voice rang out shrilly. The sun flamed at the window. Flies whined against the glass.

Paul hung his suitcoat over the back of his chair, his armpits and back wet with sweat. The pustules on the boy's face made him queasy. Why was he staring at him like that?

Paul left the plate half-finished and paid at the register. In hostile silence, the boy slid his change back over the glass countertop. Paul waited until he had withdrawn his hand, so he wouldn't have to touch it.

One bullet, straight through his fatty heart. He would explode like a whale.

When he reached the church at twelve-thirty, the coffin had already been wheeled in front of the altar. He found the priest in the sacristy, pulling a purple chasuble over his head.

On Friday, when Texeira visited him at home, they had talked about Hedwig. He had known him only superficially, the priest admitted; after he had started listening to church radio instead of attending services, he had sort of lost track of him.

'Water for me, please,' he had said when Paul offered him a cup of coffee. 'Coffee in the evening, then no more sleeping.'

In the course of these few years, his Dutch had improved by leaps and bounds. A staunch Catholic, he was nevertheless well-loved; his eyes behind the gold-rimmed spectacles were gentle. Paul let him read the farewell letter. After a few minutes, the priest shook his head and slid the paper back across the table. 'Terrible,' he said. 'And such a pity that we couldn't have done more for him. A person like Hedwig … I …' He took a cinnamon Bastogne from the plate, stared at it and said: 'I wish I could have shouted it in his ear, the comfort Jesus brings. Come unto Me, all you who labour and are heavy laden, for I shall give you rest.'

He was still young, Paul realised, he actually suffered under every soul that was lost. 'Well, anyway,' Paul said, 'he didn't do it in the end.'

'That's true,' the priest concurred, 'but he *wanted* to …' He took a sip of water. 'What are the things you will say about him; may I ask you that?'

'Sort of about … I'm not exactly sure yet. Maybe about the Blessed Rita, and a couple of the cardinal sins. I still have to come up with it all.'

'And about Hedwig, too?'

'Yeah, that too. Who he was. And about the difference between friendship and sympathy, I think …'

'You have …' The priest raised his left hand, searching for a word. 'You have a rather … abstract way of looking at life, I think?'

'Possibly,' Paul said.

'And the Blessed Rita! She is not so popular here, I think? At home, more.'

'No one likes to think of themselves as a hopeless case,' Paul said.

When the clergyman laughed, you could see a web of fine lines across his thin skin; he must have been close to forty.

Now, in the sacristy where Paul had sometimes come as a boy, Oswaldo Texeira poured two cups of coffee from the thermos jug. 'Be careful for stains,' he said to himself.

'Here, let me do it,' Paul said.

'Is okay, is okay.'

They ran through the programme together. After the communion, there was time for Paul to say something. He shouldn't stand too close to the microphone, or else it would squawk.

Paul walked into the church itself just as the service was about to start. None of the Chinese, no Baptist either. Even him. Eli, Eli.

Using the flame from the Easter candle, the priest lit the candles around the coffin, then stepped behind the altar. The noise of bodies in the pews when he asked all to rise. Paul heard the words he had used that night to ward off the evil spirits in the attic. *The Lord is my shepherd, I shall not want.* His lips followed the trail of words from the green pastures to the still waters ... *For Thou art with me, Thy rod and Thy staff they comfort me.*

Faith in God, he thought, and a Walther P38. He had left it in the glove compartment. How he longed for a rippling stream and a soft bank to rest upon; living in a state of violence had weakened him. Peace, he realised, began with exhaustion.

In a steady voice, the priest sang:

> If I say, Surely the darkness shall cover me; even the night shall be light about me. Yea, the darkness hideth not from thee; but the night shineth as the day: the darkness and the light are both alike to thee.
>
> For thou hast possessed my reins: thou hast covered me in my mother's womb. I will praise thee; for I am fearfully and wonderfully made: marvellous are thy works; and that my soul knoweth right well.

In his message, the priest made the link between Hedwig's life and the meek, those who mourn, the gentle in spirit, the merciful, and the pure of heart, who will inherit the kingdom of heaven.

Paul wanted to believe, he wanted to believe it all so badly, if only so that he, the born innocent over there in his coffin, would rise again in the hereafter.

He fished up some coins for the offertory and received the host in the palm of his hand; on his way back to the pew, he nodded to two old people who had once gone to Hedwig's grandparents for their shopping.

Then it was his turn. As he was unfolding his papers, he looked at the almost empty pews and said: 'I wanted to say a few things about Hedwig. About his life.' He looked down at his text but the words wouldn't focus. He lowered the paper and looked out at the church. 'I found a letter, in his computer. A suicide note from four years back. Apparently … yeah, he had a reason back then not to do it. Something. A straw to clutch at. He didn't have all that much to live for, Hedwig. Not much.' He nodded and rubbed his chin. 'That final straw broke. Everyone here has heard that he was robbed three weeks ago. His savings gone, and something even more important than that: his reason to keep on going.'

He pushed the stem of the microphone down a little lower. 'The Blessed Rita, I wanted to say, too, that she became our patron saint during a holiday to the Philippines. We went on holiday together at least once a year. Hedwig always got a terrible sunburn. His skin was thin and white.'

His gaze travelled along the pews, rested on Hedwig's second cousin and the Iranian woman. That the Iranian was there gave him courage. 'When Rita's your saint,' he went on, 'then you keep your head down. You don't want the hunter to see you, you remain sitting still right where you were, and you don't move.' He nodded at the coffin. 'And now he's lying there and they say it's a natural death. But of course it isn't. Hedwig is dead because he had no more reason to live. Two men in ski masks robbed him of that.'

Shrilly then, as though the silence had contradicted him: 'That's right, isn't it? That's why he's lying here now. Everybody knows who did it. I don't have to name names, because the names are known.

We sit around with them at the cafe and we drink a beer with them. We're afraid of them and act like we know nothing. We don't come to Hedwig's funeral because we don't want to be seen taking sides. And that way we see to it that Hedwig is really dead and buried.'

He looked at the paper and rubbed his eyes; the letters became legible again. 'Let me put it the way it says in Psalms,' he said, peering at the paper. 'I hate them with a perfect hatred, and I count them mine enemies.' And without looking up, he went on: 'Hedwig, I wanted to say, too, was no millionaire, of course not. That's what everyone thinks, but that's nonsense. He was bluffing when he said that, that evening at Shu. Early June sometime. He had put something away for a rainy day, the way we all do. I hope that that one sin, that stupid overconfidence of his, will be forgiven him. I hope that Father Texeira is right and that Hedwig will be comforted and filled with bliss, because if he's not allowed to enter the kingdom of heaven, who will?'

He lowered the paper and walked past the coffin to his seat, with the disturbing sense that he was weightless and stepping through a vacuum. He hoped he wasn't going to faint.

The priest rose to his feet, the machinery started moving again. He sprinkled the coffin with holy water, the chain on the incense burner clattered when he spread sweet-smelling smoke above the coffin. With that it was more or less finished — they said the Lord's Prayer and then the bearers carried the coffin out of the church. They traversed the church square in procession, traffic on Bunderweg stopped when they crossed to the graveyard. A farm contractor went barrelling down Dorpstraat, his thresher tore twigs and leaves off the lindens lining the street.

They passed the cast-iron fence that had been forged in Paul's grandfather's blacksmith shop, and followed the bearers along a white gravel path to the grave. Tall, round clouds were floating in the sky.

They placed the coffin on the crossbeams, the sexton held up a cross at the head of the grave. Paul looked around. The Iranian woman was a few metres away, she had given the old woman an arm. He nodded to the Hennies, who were standing amid the flowers on someone else's grave. The male cousins had not shown up.

The priest scattered sand on the coffin with the words 'dust thou art, to dust returnest', took one last, earnest look in the grave and left with the sexton.

One by one, those present tossed a spadeful of sand into the grave and left the cemetery. Their muted voices could be heard among the headstones; Paul was one of the last in line. He threw a handful of sand into the depths. 'Bye, buddy,' he mumbled to himself, 'take care.'

At the reception, there were even fewer people than in the church.

'Goodness,' the second-cousin said, 'you were quite vehement.'

'But only for those already in the know, right?' Paul said with a sad smile.

'You said something about a letter? A farewell letter?'

Paul pulled Hedwig's four-year-old testament from his inside pocket and handed it to her.

While the old woman was reading, he said to the Iranian: 'Had you ever been to a Dutch funeral before?'

Amiably, she replied: 'I've lived in Holland for twenty-two years already.'

'Oh,' Paul said. 'Then I guess this wasn't the first time, no.'

She said: 'It was very lovely. It was all so real, what you said. It came straight from the heart.'

'So in fact, what it says here ...' said the old woman.

He nodded.

'Well,' she said, 'that's quite something. What are we going to do now?'

'No idea,' Paul said. 'I haven't had time to work that out.'

The pearl pendants in her wrinkled earlobes swung with the nodding of her head. 'You're sure the letter is real?' she asked then.

'It was in the computer. Listen, it may not all be legally valid. Then that means nothing changes for you.'

An old farmer with a bristly head of hair stepped up to shake Paul's hand, as one of the only ones, and said loudly: 'My condolences. Well said.'

'Thank you,' Paul said.

'What's he saying?' the farmer shouted at his wife.

'He's deaf,' the woman said apologetically.

'Oh, aha,' Paul said.

The reception with coffee lasted no longer than half an hour. There was none of the relief and cheerfulness that sometimes arises after a funeral. By three-thirty, he was home again.

Thirty-Third

Evening came, and so did the thunder. But no rain fell. The storm was only brief, and drifted away to the east. Paul ate a mealy frozen pizza in the yard and rinsed it down with beer. The air was quiet and sticky, in the far distance you still heard the occasional crack of thunder.

All he had to do now was wait. Tonight or tomorrow night, it wouldn't take much longer. On the heels of one cardinal sin, the next was hard on its way; after envy and covetousness, it was now time for *ira* — the rage, the revenge. Paul's accusation from the pulpit would have reached his enemies just about now. Oxygen for the flames. Stegginkʼs behaviour was predictable; somewhere out of sight, he and Ivan were getting prepared.

Paul changed from his Sunday best into a pair of overalls. In the old piggery where he kept his tools and where the lawnmower was parked, he took the chainsaw down off the shelf and filled its tanks.

Saw in hand, he walked to the plot of woods between the house and the road, to the right of the drive, the stand of young oak that Aloïs had replanted after his father died. Ribbons of blossoming honeysuckle hung between the branches. Paul started the saw and gave it full throttle; the teeth bit hungrily into the wood of the first tree, moist sawdust sprayed from the cuts low on the trunk. The saw yowled hellishly in the early evening; he brought down the trees one by one, like his grandfather before him. The crowns spun above his head, hit the ground roaring and cracking. He wiped the sweat from his eyes with his sleeve and picked up the saw again. Within two hours, they were all on the ground.

Contentedly, he viewed the havoc he had wreaked. The foliage, the stumps. From his office window he could now see everything that came down the road from the bridge. A frontal attack was ruled out. It would have to come from the side, which was unfamiliar terrain to the enemy. The enemy would have to cross the brook and the woods behind the house, or the open field to the north; that placed him at an immediate disadvantage.

A small, pastel-coloured car came down Bunderweg. The driver braked in the curve, Paul ducked down amid the fallen trunks. The car came almost to a full stop in the curve, across from the sign KRÜZEN CUROSIA & MILITARIA, then turned right up the drive. Paul dropped to his stomach. The engine turned off, the door opened, he heard footsteps on the gravel. He took a handful of soil and rubbed it onto his face and forehead. Then he raised his head just above the trunk that hid him.

Ineke Wessels.

She stood in the driveway, hesitating. She walked up to the farmhouse and peered through the little windows of the old stables. She disappeared round the corner, he heard the heavy copper knocker pounding against the side door. A little later she came back, unsuccessful. She looked through his office window and then, leaning her forearm on the open door of her Renault Twingo, surveyed the yard — the house, the shed, the burgeoning linden that towered above the farmhouse. Climbing in, she turned the car round and pulled out onto the road. He pressed himself flat against the ground. It took her a long time to shift up into third.

The mist hung thin as gauze over the blue grass. It was as though the linden and the tall red beeches produced a darkness of their own.

He locked the house and withdrew to the shed. The sweat on his back dried up. The coffee machine gurgled, run-off hissed on the hotplate. He poured himself a cup and sat down at the desk. Blowing on the hot liquid in the Duralex glass, he thought about his mother, who had turned seventy-five today. An old woman, somewhere. In her womb he had been woven, but she had seen him as a flaw. Somehow, he had never got around to rejecting or hating her. He had always remained loyal to her. Her faithful little dog. *Meine Ehre heißt Treue.* As foreordained by his place in the zodiac, faithfulness was the anchor he dragged behind him through the mud.

He sat in the darkness, leaning back in his office chair. The display on the alarm installation was black as onyx, the pistol lay within arm's reach on the desk. It had a will of its own, it wanted to spread fire and mayhem. Everything around him was shadow, had become fluid and without form, only the weapon was hard and real.

Around midnight he got up and went into the dark shed. With a quiet tinkling, the fluorescent lights along the roof's ridge popped on and cast his treasure trove in a white glow. He rummaged around in a cardboard box of officer's shirts for as long as it took to find the smallest size. He took off the overalls and put on the shirt. It emitted a stale, mouldy smell. On stockinged feet he crossed the concrete floor to the tailor's dummy that wore an SS uniform, the wellspring of his collection. A showpiece. You didn't find them like this anymore. The jacket's worsted wool had stiffened, the buttons passed through the holes only with difficulty, but what could you expect? It had been made some seventy-five years ago in an Italian barrack by a tailor conscripted for labour with the Arbeidseinsatz, and after that had spent a time stretched across the lily-white frame of SS-Hauptscharführer Dieter Soltau. What had he thought about, that little Kraut? Did he have doubts? Did the unfathomable emptiness of the East across which he made his way put the fear into him? Or had the relentless ravings of the Ministry of Propaganda rendered him deaf to fear and defeatism?

He hopped into the uniform trousers, buttoned them up, and pulled on the jacket. The rough material scratched against his thighs.

The pistol slid smoothly in and out of the holster.

Tight and stiff as it had become, it was a uniform that banished all fear and doubt — the moment you donned the jodhpurs and sharply tailored jacket with its collar patches and epaulets, you became an Übermensch. The body was lifted erect, ready to trample everything it came across. It was too bad he couldn't wear it to the cafe anymore, even these days it would make the girls swoon.

The uniform, he realised, was the same age as his mother.

He had saved the boots, too. Boots like these went for a thousand euros a pair, the S&M crowd was crazy about them. And they were hard to put on. He had to stomp hard on the floor to get his heels into place.

He looked in the floor-length mirror — the Kraut against the Bolshevik, historical correctness had now been restored. In Feldgrau he would lie in wait for Ivan, the last thing the man saw would be the pistol of a Hauptscharführer pointed at his forehead. He would die like in one of his grandfather's nightmares.

The shed went dark again, he felt his way back to his office chair.

Boiled coffee dragged him through the motionless night; branches grated across the roof. The little red lamp on the coffee machine spread a grainy glow in the darkness.

Sometimes he dozed off, seeing images of the day gone by. Incense flowing out and dissipating above the coffin, the purple chasuble sliding round the priest's body. With her index finger, the Iranian caressed the inside of his wrist, her eyes filled with tears.

'Paul?!' Hedwig's voice suddenly rang out. 'Paul?!'

He woke with a start, too late to rush to his assistance. Their hands clutched at air in the transit from dream to wakefulness; the coffee left in the glass was cold and black.

Three o'clock had come and gone. He left the office and walked, stiff-legged, to the shed door. He unbolted it and stepped outside. The spotlight did not go on, it would only do that when he was two metres away from the building. He smelled the moist night-time air, the pungent tinge of cow manure spread across the fields. The night was silent, but if you held your ear to the big old oaks beside the shed you could hear the sap bubbling in their veins.

He tried to plumb the darkness on the far side of the drive, past the havoc he had wreaked there.

Ivan? Are you there?

Tired. Abysmally tired. The uniform was the only thing keeping him on his feet. The permanent hedgehog position had worn him out, hollowed him out, he was no more than an exoskeleton of worsted wool, leather, and buttons, reeling with sleep.

He took the pistol from the holster, cocked it, and stepped out of the darkness. When he reached the middle of the drive, the security lamps popped on. A flood of light encircled him with his own shadows. The LED lamps threw a blazing, immobile glare, four times 8,500 lumens, that pinned him at their centre like a flustered moth. The darkness had withdrawn behind the border of light, waited patiently to reassume its rightful place.

When he pointed the pistol at the darkness around him, his arm cast a long shadow. Come on, Ivan, put an end to this charade. Don't leave me alone — the hare wants to be shot where it was born. Let the darkness swallow me then, the light around me change to night.

Gravel crunched beneath his boots as he turned slowly on his axis.

Ivan?

Honeysuckle, and the warning cry of a redshank far away.